GW00630703

Also by Allan Prior

NOVELS

A Flame In The Air
The Joy Ride
The One-Eyed Monster
One Away
The Interrogators
The Operators
The Loving Cup
The Contract
Paradiso
Affair
Never Been Kissed In The Same Place
Twice
Theatre ('A Cast of Stars' in USA)
The Big March
Her Majesty's Hit Man
The Charmer
Fuhrer
The Old Man and Me

SOME TELEVISION PLAYS

Z Cars
Softly, Softly
The One-Eyed Monster
The Charmer
The Bookie Trilogy
A Perfect Hero
The Golden Mile Trilogy
Moonstrike
Romany Rye: George Borrow
The Charmer

SOME PLAYS FOR RADIO

Worker In The Dawn: a Portrait of George Gissing
Alias Baron Corvo: a Portrait of Frederick Rolfe
The Running Man: a Portrait of W. T. Stead
Nosey: a Portrait of the Duke of Wellington
Fuhrer: a Portrait of Adolf Hitler

STAGE

The West Pier (from a novel by Patrick Hamilton)

NON-FICTION

Script to Screen: The Story of
Five Television Plays: from Z cars to The Charmer

The Old Man and Me Again

Allan Prior

SINCLAIR-STEVENSON

First published in Great Britain in 1996
by Sinclair-Stevenson
an imprint of Reed Consumer Books Ltd
Michelin House, 81 Fulham Road, London SW3 6RB
and Auckland, Melbourne, Singapore and Toronto

A CIP catalogue record for this book is available
at the British Library

ISBN 1 85619 690 9

Phototypeset by Intype London Ltd
Printed and bound in Great Britain
by Clays Ltd, St Ives plc

Contents

The Green Card

The Old Man hadn't changed.

I had. But he hadn't.

The Woodrow hat was still on his head. His Northumberland Fusiliers tie was still neatly tied into the hard white collar; the dark hair had only a little grey in it. He looked the same. He was the same. I wasn't.

After all, I had been away at the War for over four years. I was a man, or I thought I was, twenty-three years of age, with a young wife and a small child I hardly knew. I had been in Belgium, France and Germany and had seen the ruins of Hitler's Berlin. I had a seen a lot of things nobody in Blackpool could imagine. Whole towns obliterated by bombers, smoking ruins, with women offering themselves for the price of a couple of cigarettes. Hungry children. Survivors of the Camps, pitifully thin, clogging the roads. German prisoners, trained by their years in the Hitler Youth to keep fit no matter what, bronzed and reasonably contented in captivity. A whole continent starving, typhoid raging, no man to be seen at all on the main streets of German cities, the Occupiers in uniform, smoking cigarettes and congratulating themselves that they were still alive.

The odds, I had to admit, were against it.

It had been a terrible war. Not, the Old Man said, as bad as the First War. But the Russians had lost eight out of every ten men in the Class of 1922. The British had lost maybe two in fifty. But two was a lot if you knew them personally.

Blackpool had never been bombed, so it looked the same. Rows and rows of boarding-houses, many still full of Civil Servants or RAF recruits. The Tower, unpainted for years. The Pleasure Beach, shuttered and still. The Golden Mile the same, waiting with an air of expectation for the first season since the War began, seven years before.

It all looked tired and shabby, like the rest of England.

A coat of fresh paint, said the Old Man, would change all that. He did not want to talk, any more than anybody else, about the War, the only subject the returning men knew anything about. He'd come back alive from the First War. He'd got on with it. His manner, as he sighed and smoked his Churchman's, implied that the only thing to do with the War was to put it behind you.

'The thing is,' he said, 'a place to live and a job. Simple as that.'

I was sitting in the flat he'd moved into, where Aunt Clara (known in the family as Tickle) had come to live with him after I'd gone into the RAF. It was too small, he explained, to offer me accommodation. The old house had been too big: Aunt Clara couldn't be bothered with dusting and cleaning the five bedrooms. It was a pity but there it was. He had even had to get rid of his beloved rabbits and mice and the large white rat he loved. No room for them.

Of course, there was a room for me, but, with steep stairs to climb, it was hardly the thing for a young mother and her child. The Old Man was not censorious, he had never been censorious of anything or anybody in his life, but most people (good Lancashire Nonconformists) were. You felt that getting married in wartime was a crime. Well, to them it was. Most of them had saved up for years to do it, during the Depression.

Blackpool had unseen wounds. The local Territorial Regiment had been taken almost intact at Singapore in 1942. Of the eight hundred men, only a third came back. I was soon to meet them. Their faces were yellow, their teeth gone; they looked like ill, bent old men in their new green demob hats and their new gabardine raincoats. I hardly recognised them, yet they were boys I had played cricket and football with, bank clerks and surveyor's clerks and men who worked for the Co-op. They walked slowly and painfully through the streets of the town, like yellow ghosts, and never spoke of their experiences, of the dreadful tortures and beatings inflicted on them by the Japanese. Oddly, they did not seem bitter and sometimes spoke almost understandingly of the Japs, saying that cruelty was part of their culture.

The rest of us felt ashamed of our own small hardships and greeted the men cheerfully in pubs and talked about anything but the Japs and wondered if our soldier friends would ever be the same as they used to be. I thought not. None of us were and we hadn't been tortured or beaten or starved. Some of us had been wounded and some were dead, but none of us had been through what they had been through. Yet we were different from what we had been. I was different. I felt different. I looked, however, much the same as everybody else. My demob suit, the only suit I had that fitted me (I'd grown out of everything else), was exactly like everybody else's. I wouldn't wear the demob shirts and I threw the porkpie hat away, like most other people. I was just bigger, stronger and more bolshy, as we said then. I wanted to see some changes in the way England was run, for my four years in uniform.

Like almost everybody else in the Forces, I had voted Labour. I was even writing articles for *Tribune.* I was determined to be a writer. I had won a Forces' competition with the first short story I wrote. I had been published already in a few of the Wartime Little Reviews. I had met men who wore woollen shirts and ties and had been to Oxford (though, often, not to the War) who also wrote things, usually for the BBC. I had enjoyed their company, on my last leaves, in London pubs and clubs. The fashion then was for writers to look bohemian. Hence the woolly ties and tweed jackets and long hair and the woolly conversations in pubs near the BBC.

Now, all that was over.

I was back in Blackpool, a young man, changed out of all recognition (or so I thought) and thoroughly out of sorts about it.

I longed for London, bright lights, artistic conversation, beautiful women and fame. If possible, very soon.

Instead, I was in Blackpool with a wife and child, talking to the Old Man – who had not changed at all.

'A writer?' he said. 'Well, I don't see why not.'

Everybody else saw why not.

Marthaann, my mother, who had in a small way done well out of the War (her shellfish shops were Off the Ration and she had accordingly prospered), was astonished. By letter from Newcastle she wrote saying how astonished she was.

The Old Man was still keeping what he called 'a nice distance' between them. Two hundred and fifty miles, to be precise. There was no divorce, nor would there ever be. Marthaann would have thought it shaming. And the Old Man didn't care.

The Old Man lived by his own rules.

Never be surprised by anything anybody does.

Just don't let it upset you.

He had been living like that all his life. It had its good points.

'Dickens died leaving a few bob,' he said. 'Also Rider Haggard and John Buchan and Henty, I should imagine.' These were his favourite writers but he had read none of them since he was a boy. 'J. B. Priestley seems to be doing well enough. If they can do it, why not you?' And he turned a page of the *Sporting Life*, which was down to four pages.

I waited for more, but there was no more.

'Meantime,' he said, finally deciding what he would back in the last race at Lingfield and glancing at the clock on the mantelpiece to confirm that there was still time to get a bet on, 'as I say, what you need is a job and somewhere to live.'

As ever, he spoke with the tongues of angels.

'I've left my wife and child with her parents in Kent but she can't stay there for ever,' I said. 'So, yes, the job is the first consideration.'

The Old Man pondered on my problem. It was a curious situation. He had a job and I hadn't one, which in itself was a sort of record. I had always had one since I was sixteen, while he, out of principle, hadn't, preferring to back slow horses for a living ever since he had come out of the Army in 1920. Now, astonishingly, he had a job in the Royal Air Force Headquarters, at the Lansdowne Hotel on Blackpool Promenade. He was an Administrative Clerk, whatever that was. His duties seemed light, for he always found time, it seemed, to play cards or billiards for money in his extended lunch hour, mostly at the Masonic Club, near the Winter Gardens. He won money at both these activities. It was the Dogs and the Horses that, as he put it, got him 'in a bit of trouble' from time to time. He was currently overbroke, he said. That is to say, not just broke but owing money.

I did not take that too seriously. It was a condition he was used to, and would have felt strange in any other.

I was reminded of Onkel Frank's story of the Old Man after

the First World War, 'walking the streets of Newcastle, puffing cigarettes, asking people if they could find *me* a job!'

Onkel Frank's eyes had almost popped out of his head when he told that story. He was apoplectic by temperament. But there was substance in it. The Old Man was ace, as they say nowadays, at finding jobs for other people.

Now, he ran true to form.

'So . . . a job?' The Old Man looked for his hat. It was Saturday and racing would start very soon. All this thinking and talking was valuable betting-time lost. 'Why not the Civil Service?'

I had never considered the Civil Service. If I had thought of it at all, I thought of people in pinstripes in Whitehall. I said as much.

'No, no,' said the Old Man. 'There are five thousand Civil Servants in the town. Some Ministries were evacuated here.' I nodded; I remembered. 'Lots of jobs for temporary clerks.'

'Now?' I said. 'The War's over. Won't they go back to London as soon as they can?'

'Would you,' asked the Old Man, 'if it was your choice? London's a mess, from all I hear. Never recovered from the Blitz. It'll take years to build the place up again. Shortages of all kinds. Food. Jobs. Housing.'

'Is Blackpool any better?'

The Old Man sighed. 'Blackpool has fresh sea air. It has never been bombed. These Civil Service people have been living by the seaside for four or five years. They are London suburban clerks, for the most part. It's been a permanent holiday for them. And. . .'

'Yes?' I said.

'Quite simply, Blackpool is the Black Market Capital of the North. If you have the money you can get anything here.'

'But we haven't the money,' I said, 'have we?'

'No,' said the Old Man regretfully, glancing at the clock again. 'But the opportunity is there, you see. There is, as ever, a few bob in the town.'

'With the same people getting rich,' I pointed out from my newly formed Socialist perspective.

'They always do,' said the Old Man. 'It's not a matter of class, as you probably think. It stems from a certain vulgar frame of mind. If you want money enough you can always get it, you know.'

'How?' I demanded. I had my eighty pounds gratuity from a grateful nation in a Post Office Savings Book. It was all I had in the world. I would have seriously liked to know the secret of how to get money, preferably a lot of it.

But the Old Man was saying, 'You'll need a Green Card.'

'What's that?'

'You need it to get any job.'

'Where do you get it?'

'At the Labour Exchange.'

'What do I do?'

'You go there and say you want a Green Card because you have a job at the Ministry of Ag and Fish.'

'But I've never heard of the Ministry of Ag and Fish.'

The Old Man closed his eyes at such innocence. 'I know a man there. I've spoken to him. There's a job for you. All you do is go to the Labour Exchange and ask them for a Green Card'.

'And that's all?'

'That's all.'

The Old Man looked at the clock. Racing had now started at Lingfield. He had to go if he was going to get a bet on.

'Good to see you back,' he said, as an afterthought, at the door. Then he was gone.

I sat and smoked a long slow Player's. Like everybody else in their twenties then, I smoked. I drank too, a bit. I didn't gamble. The Old Man had put me off that for life. The Old Man had survived the War with the aid of his sister, Tickle, who had been On the Halls and was now selling spectacles door to door. Nobody knew why anybody ever bought the spectacles, since the coming National Health Service was supposedly providing them free, but they did. 'That woman,' reported the Old Man, 'sold coal briquettes door to door in Newcastle before the War. If anybody can sell coal briquettes in Newcastle they can sell anything to anybody, anywhere!'

Aunt Clara had been married to the Scotch comic, Harold. She still was, since hardly anybody got divorced then. After their act had split up, and her house in Newcastle had been demolished by a land mine, she had moved in with the Old Man. She claimed it was temporary but, like the Civil Servants, seemed in no hurry to leave Blackpool.

For myself, I hated the sight of it.

It seemed familiar yet strange and a lot smaller, somehow.

But then, I suppose every soldier after every war feels much the same. The excitement and glamour had gone with the uniform and I now found myself staring at a boring job in a boring place.

However, first things first. I needed this job.

So I turned up at the Labour Exchange and asked for a Green Card. I was ushered by a clerk into a Presence, and offered a chair. I wasn't offered anything else.

'You want a Green Card, I hear?'

The Interrogator was forty, dark, a Londoner with glasses and the pallor of a man who has spent the last five years in an office, working very long hours.

'I believe I need one to get a job?'

'What job?'

'In the Ag and Fish.'

The Interrogator sat up. 'Do you know for sure you'll get a job there?'

'I'm told I will.'

'Who told you that?'

I couldn't say the Old Man had told me that so I said, 'I hear I can.'

The Interrogator looked at my file, which I'd filled out at the counter. It gave bare details of education and previous work. 'You don't need a job as a clerk. You're too bright for that.'

'Then what can you offer me?'

The Interrogator turned the pages of my file. 'There are jobs in Industry in the Midlands. You'd have to train for them and the pay wouldn't be much, but you'd come out as a draughtsman or something like that. Decent job. Beats the Ag and Fish.'

'It may,' I said, thinking hard. 'But I have a wife and child and need somewhere to bring them, here in Blackpool. I couldn't go and work in the Midlands, living in digs, my wife and kid still in Kent.'

The Interrogator said, 'That's my offer.'

'Is there such a thing as Direction of Labour still?' I asked him, in the manner I'd learned in the Air Force to make superiors feel small. It hadn't worked then and it didn't work now.

He turned the page with a slight smile. 'No. But I won't be giving you a Green Card. So, there it is.'

I took a deep breath and resolved not to lose my temper. Then I said, 'I suppose you've been sitting on your arse in this little funk-hole for four years, with your missus and kids just down the road?'

He went white, suddenly. He said nothing. He obviously thought I was going to hit him. Then I said, 'Shove your Green Card up your jacksy,' and walked out, slamming the door. The counter clerks watched me with disapproving eyes as I walked out into the street.

It occurred to me then that they'd seen something like it before. Often.

I had always had a bit of a temper. The War and my RAF ankle (which hurt every time I walked on it) had not improved it.

But I felt better for all that.

Of course, I didn't have the Green Card.

The Old Man received my report with a total lack of concern. 'You didn't hit him or anything?'

'I very nearly did.'

The Old Man merely nodded and said, 'The thing to do is, go back to the Labour Exchange tomorrow at twelve thirty-five, not a minute sooner, and ask for Mr Hooper. Say who you are, and he'll give you a Green Card.'

'Who is this Mr Hooper?'

'He's the Assistant Manager. Gets to the Dogs. Frank gives him a few tips. Fellow's hair went white during the War, with all the work, directing people to jobs and so on.'

Frank was Onkel Frank, the one-time handicapper, now retired. I hadn't seen him yet.

I went to the Labour Exchange and saw Mr Hooper, whose hair was indeed white, and he took a Green Card from under his blotter on the desk in his private office, gave it to me and shook my hand.

'Good luck, young fellow.'

'Thank you, Sir!' I said, moved.

When you have been shouted at and have shouted back at people for four whole years, you tend to forget your manners. Well, who wouldn't?

To celebrate, if that was the word, I looked up my best friend, Jack. He was still on two sticks from his war wounds, and I hardly recognised him as he limped into the vaults of the Dunes Hotel. Jack would not drink in a saloon bar, anywhere. He liked rough, knowing company and I suffered it. His mother, Sannah, had died while I was away. He and his father, Harold the Baker, lived alone in the largish family house, apart from lodgers in their front room. 'The fella works at St Dunstan's. He and his missus are all right, in their way, but they're Methodists and they disapprove of drink. Trust Stiffy to let the rooms to a couple who hate the Demon Drink!'

He laughed at the idea and so did I. At the same moment I noticed that Jack was drinking very fast and very hard. I called halt and asked, 'What's the rush? We've got all night.'

It was good to see him again. Once we had shared books and films. There was hardly a famous book he had not read or a famous film he hadn't seen.

Jack said, tapping his leg, 'They've given me pain-killers but I can't do with them. I just get pissed every night, then I can sleep.'

I said nothing. I just stared into my beer.

This was the best schoolboy cricketer I had ever seen. This was the boy they had said would play for Lancashire. There were no words.

'You've been home for three years, Jack', I said. 'What's it really like?'

He looked at me for a long moment. 'You'll find out.'

In a large room at the Min of Ag and Fish sat fifty-three young men. They were collating (a word new to me) figures – the number of acres under grain and grass in England and Wales. That is to say, they were adding them up without benefit of a calculator. Nobody had yet invented it, or the computer either. This work involved the Census Return Form (a very long document) mounted on wooden frames and counted by simple mental addition. This system had been in use for over fifty years. It still may be, for all I know. Fortunately, I wasn't doing it. I was allocated to a section dealing with correspondence with farmers, if any. For farmers will not answer letters beginning with the words 'The Minister has directed me to inform you . . .' Even the mandarins had found that didn't work. So they had devised small, self-folding forms on which the Correspondence Clerks (of whom I was one) wrote, in longhand, things like 'Do you still graze sheep on Castel Dynas Bran?' and received replies saying 'No, that is my brother'. Then you asked, 'Only you and your brother Thomas graze sheep on Castel Dynas Bran, then?' and lived to read the reply: 'Apart from Father and my Uncle Gwilym, and as to Pigs we haven't had a pig on the farm since Grandad died.'

The Welsh hill farmers thought and wrote in Welsh, a flowery and devious language well suited to a nation that had been occupied for five hundred years yet still had its culture. The Min of Ag and Fish was no match for it.

Sometimes a Welsh hill farmer would, in a moment of aberration, actually volunteer information. Once I went triumphantly to the Records Office with it.

To the Records Clerk, himself a Welshman, I said, 'Thomas Roberts of Penry has reclaimed ten acres of marshland and turned it into pasture. There are the details, to go in the Census!'

The Records Clerk surveyed me sadly. 'Can't do it, boyo.'

'Why not?'

'Because we have more land registered in Wales than there *is* in Wales!'

'What? Why?'

'Because when we started the Census in wartime nobody here realised that, in Wales, sheep belonging to several farmers graze on the same hillside.'

'Like Castel Dynas Bran?'

'Exactly. Every member of the family claimed for it. All six of them. So it was registered six times.'

'So any new land – actually *new* land – can't be put in the Census because we've got too much already?'

'That's it, boyo.'

'But we base our grants on having correct Census figures?'

'In theory, boyo.'

'What the hell are we all doing here?' I asked him.

But I knew the answer to that. The Labour Government was terrified of unemployment. It was the Black Spectre of the Thirties and would have unseated any Government who suffered it to happen. So everybody had a job, at low wages. Rather like Soviet Russia, where it was an offence not to turn up for work even when there was no work to do. Of course none of us knew that then. We thought Russia was a Socialist Paradise. But I ceased, after that, to take the job seriously.

I was not alone. The fifty-two other young men were all as bored as I was. They sat smoking furiously, adding up figures on the ancient wooden frames, all day long. At least I sparred with the cunning Welsh hill farmers, even if I lost every round.

Taffy was a Welshman and he'd never forgotten how.

The fifty-two other young men had been doing dangerous, impossible things for the last four, five or six years. They had flown Lancasters over the Ruhr; they had sailed in merchant ships across the Atlantic, suffering U-Boat attacks on the way; they had sailed in destroyers to Murmansk, been dive-bombed and torpedoed; they had fought in the burning sands of the African desert (no home leave for four years) or in the jungles of Burma. Now they sat in their demob suits and smoked. They looked older than thirty, more like forty, but their average age was twenty-five.

Now, burdened by wives, children and mothers-in-law, and imprisoned in this large room, they were presided over by a Chief Clerk, Tommy Boothroyd, a florid man in a check suit who drank a bit, and was liked for it. Everybody in the room would drink a bit if he had the money or the chance.

Sometimes, in the way of trade, Tommy had to show his authority, and this one day he did.

In the matter of Dicky Bird.

Dicky sat in the desk next to me and, when I told him I had been in the RAF, replied, 'I forgive you.'

Dicky had been a Navigation Officer on a merchant ship. He had crossed the Atlantic more times than enough, as people said then. When he had needed protection from Focke Wolf Condors of the *Luftwaffe* he had found the RAF absent. I explained that he'd been out of range of land-based aircraft like Spitfires or Hurricanes, but he would have none of it.

Dicky suffered terribly from his need and nostalgia for the Sea. He missed it like an arm. He'd been at sea since he was sixteen and now he was thirty-five (the oldest man in the room) and beached at a desk in the Ag and Fish.

'Why don't you go back?' I asked him.

'I promised the Missus I never would. She worried a lot during the War.'

'There's no War now.'

'No, but you see, I promised.'

To lessen his grief Dicky got drunk every night, which made it difficult for him to get up in the morning. He had somehow acquired a bone-shaker ladies' bicycle with no crossbar. On this machine he rode four miles to work each morning, head down into the stiff westerly winds of the region.

Once in the office, always later than anybody else (even me) by at least ten minutes, he opened a large brown-paper packet containing almost a loaf's worth of paste sandwiches, all of which he proceeded to eat at once, without the assistance of tea or any other liquid.

Tommy Boothroyd had finally to show his authority, such as it was. We ex-Servicemen had got ourselves a bad name discipline-wise (as they say now) owing to our habit of igniting balls of string and throwing them across the room at one another. Tommy had wisely ignored this as he had the blowing-up and batting around the room of french letters, now called condoms. Tommy had no doubt taken some flak, as we said then, from horrified superiors about this.

'Dicky, could you, as a personal favour to me, come in on time in the morning and please from now on have your breakfast before you get here?'

Dicky Bird went red in the face. He jumped to his feet, gripped Tommy Boothroyd by his breeches-arse, propelled him through the french windows of the office (which were open, it being summer) and deposited him on the grass lawn.

Dicky then took his last remaining Capstan Full Strength from his packet of twenty, lit it, inhaled deeply, watched by all, then smoothed out the packet and wrote on the unprinted section: *I resign, Yours faithfully, Dicky Bird.*

He addressed the company on his way out. 'Bugger the wife, the Civil Service and all you silly sods. I'm going back to sea!'

We cheered him to the echo.

The Old Man heard this tale without surprise. 'Don't blame the fellow. Must have been hell after the ship.'

'I felt like leaving myself. There must be something better, yes?'

'Well, you could,' said the Old Man, 'but I suppose now you've got a job the next thing is somewhere to live?' The Old Man has this knack of answering a question with a question.

I said, 'I've knocked on fifty doors asking people if they can let me have rooms, offering half my wages. The moment I say that I have a wife and child they slam the door in my face!'

The Old Man nodded. He knew all that.

Houses were going at three thousand pounds for a semi-detached. No Ex-Serviceman could afford that. The only hope was a Council house, which the Labour Government was sluggish in building. As my friend Jack said, 'In wartime, everything was possible. In the Peace, bugger-all moves!'

'Of course, if Winston had got in,' I said, 'we'd have got some help from the Yanks. With Attlee in, not a hope.' All the same, we supported him, an unlikely schoolmasterish figure with a pipe. He stood for decency and fair shares, we thought. We liked that, having talked about it for so long, on airfields and in barrack-rooms.

Still, he wasn't building any houses, was he?

I said as much to the Old Man. 'If we wait for Attlee, we'll wait for ever.'

He yawned, bored by all this domestic business. He had left it all behind in his own life, many years before. 'The thing is, I've got you some rooms. It's fifty-bob-a-week rent, I'm afraid, but there it is!'

'You have? Where?'

'With your friend Jack. I saw his father, Harold, at the Dogs and arranged it. He liked the idea of the fifty bob.'

'But he'd got people in those rooms!'

'Not now. They were only paying a pound-a-week rent.'

'Where will they go?'

The Old Man looked pained. 'How do I know? You move in with your wife and the child next Monday. What more do you want?'

A lot. But I didn't say so.

Some Very Responsible People Are on the Favourite

The Old Man was in the Nine Hole.

Again.

To be in the Nine Hole is to be overbroke – that is, to owe money with no possibility of getting it, and an insistent creditor in the offing.

'The thing is,' he explained, glass of whisky in hand and only a moderate irritation in his manner, 'I've been elected Treasurer of this damn Union at my office. Been doing the job twelve months.'

We were sitting in the flat. Smout, his cat, now ten years old, lay along his thigh.

'They must have been mad,' I said, under my breath, but the Old Man slung me a deaf 'un – that is, affected not to hear. He never heard remarks he did not want to hear.

'How much is owing?' I asked, loudly.

'It comes to two hundred.'

'Pounds?'

'Of course pounds.'

Two hundred pounds then was about two thousand now and a lot harder to get.

'In fact,' I said, 'you've spent all the members' subscriptions and now it's cashing-up time?'

'No need to put it quite like that.'

'Is that the case or isn't it?' I did not have the patience with the Old Man I used to have as a boy. I was now a bit brutal, in some ways. After all, I'd been in a War. Of course, it didn't last. His uncaring charm always worked wonders for him. However, I had the presence of mind to say, 'If you're thinking about my Air Force gratuity, it's long gone.'

'All of it?'

'All of it.'

The Old Man sighed and I felt guilty. Then I felt irritated again. 'You must have known this is how it would end when you took the Treasurer's job on.'

'Not necessarily,' said the Old Man. 'I just seem to have had a very poor season.'

To all gamblers the year divides neatly into two seasons: the Flat and the Jumps. If you have a bad season on the Flat you look for the steeplechasers to rescue you. Or vice versa. That way there is always hope, even for the biggest Guesser in the Game. The Old Man was not a Guesser (by definition a mug punter who pisses his money away on the Flat *and* over the Jumps) but he might as well have been. He regularly ignored the advice of his brother, Onkel Frank, a trained and reliable handicapper (with all a handicapper's irritability), and of his brother, Edwards the Bookmaker, who sometimes knew when a horse was trying. All you can ever know, unless the Fix is in, is that a horse is trying to win. That is, everybody in the stable, from the owner to the youngest stable-boy, is *on* it.

Such a horse is likely to be the Favourite.

The Old Man was always looking for one to beat it. I said, innocently, 'None of Onkel Frank's tips winning, then?'

'Damn few, this year. There's no form for him to go by. No racing to speak of for five years. Nobody knows what the horses can do. All new, you see. Nobody's getting rich, except the Bookies.'

'Then you'll have to see Edwards and beg it from him. You have no choice.'

'No, I don't suppose so.' The Old Man sipped his whisky. 'So the gratuity has all gone?'

'On nappies, baby-powder, cots, bedclothes, linen, all that. Wives and babies take all the money.'

The Old Man sighed at the waste.

I added, for good measure. 'At the end of the week I've hardly enough money to buy a packet of Players.'

The Old Man ignored that and stood up abruptly, shaking the startled Smout to the floor, where he landed neatly, bemused. The Old Man picked up his hat and made for the door.

I called after him, 'What happens now? Do they vet the accounts or what?'

'Worse,' said the Old Man. 'Dick Firwood's coming up, in person.'

'Dick Firwood?'

'Secretary of the Union. Big man. Only one leg.'

'Well, what happens if you tell him the truth?'

Said the Old Man, 'A believable story, that is what we require.'

'Why not tell him you lost it at the Dogs?'

The Old Man seemed to consider this seriously for a moment. 'He'd never wear that. He'd be bound to take steps.'

'Which would end in the County Court?'

If there was any institution the Old Man respected above all others it was the County Court. For a simple reason. They had the power to send you to jail.

'Hardly.' The Old Man straightened his regimental tie. 'But it would cost me the job.'

'As Treasurer?'

'No. The job. In the Air Ministry office. They wouldn't like it. They're pretty narrow-minded about such things.'

'I'm surprised you stay in that job anyway.'

'Nice people. Gentlemen. And I don't do a lot. Feel at home there, y'see?'

I saw. The Air Force officers who worked on the Headquarters staff were his own kind. Simple-minded, generous and fair, and, most importantly, gentlemen who held the King's Commission, as he once had. Unlike most of the citizens of Blackpool, who, as the Old Man said, hardly knew how to hold a knife and fork.

'You'll have to talk to Edwards,' I concluded.

'Yes, I know.' The Old Man put on his hat and went out.

I strolled along to the Waterloo Hotel to meet my friend Jack.

Although we lived in the same house now, we met mostly out of it. There was nothing to detain Jack at home except his father, Harold the Baker, who was in the house even less than Jack was. They exchanged no more than twenty words in the course of a normal day, as Mr Ashworth got up at six o'clock to tend his bakehouse fire and Jack was working, as every ex-serviceman in the town seemed to be, in the Civil Service. Jack had recently been made a Permanent Officer, on account of his war wounds.

These, as usual, were hurting him.

Ordering a pint for himself and a gill for me, he said, 'How's the Old Man?'

He liked the Old Man. They had a lot in common. They both regarded life as something to be enjoyed without thought for the morrow.

'He's in the Nine Hole,' I said.

'What's that?'

'Broke.'

'He'll not be for long. He never is.' Jack swallowed his pint like medicine, which in a way it was. 'I tell you, I wish I had his nerve. I went to a few card schools with him while you were away. He sends it in, you know.'

To send it in is to gamble wildly but with cool nerve. The Old Man had always had that.

'He sends it in,' I said. 'A pity more of it doesn't come back.'

Just then I espied through the pub door the Old Man going into the Vicarage on the opposite side of the street. I pointed this out to Jack.

'What's he going in there for?' I asked.

'No idea,' said Jack.

I had never seen the Old Man go anywhere near any place of worship. He wasn't too keen on weddings (disliking the unfounded optimism and noise), and funerals he never went to, on the premise that his own would be soon enough.

The Old Man emerged from the Vicarage and came straight across to the pub. He was surprised to see us but bought us both a drink, paying with a pound note from what looked like a roll of six or more.

'What were you doing across at the Vicarage?'

The Old Man looked surprised but not disconcerted. 'Oh, you saw that?'

'Yes.'

'Well, the Vicar likes a bet. Good health!' And he raised his whisky-and-water to his lips.

Jack and I exchanged glances.

'You collect his bets?'

'Of course I do. Why not?'

'Does he ever back a winner?'

'The next time will be the first.'

And he smiled, showing the wonderful teeth he broke brazil nuts with as a Christmas trick. Standing there in his dark suit, no longer new, stiff white collar, brightly polished shoes and Woodrow hat, he looked, at a glance, twenty years younger than he was. Jack and I looked, temporarily, ten years older than we were.

I said, 'This is the Vicar's money you're spending, then?'

'He'll never miss it.' The Old Man drank up his whisky.

'You've stuck it?'

To stick a bet is not to pass it on. In this case, to his brother Edwards.

'The point is, the Vicar never backs a winner,' was the Old Man's explanation.

I thought of saying: 'It's only a matter of time,' but I knew that would be useless.

'Must go,' the Old Man said. 'Sit down, Jack, I would – give the legs a rest.'

Then he was gone, stepping briskly into the autumn sunlight.

Jack said, 'He's one on his own. There's nobody like him.' His voice held a certain admiration.

'No,' I said.

Then we went to watch Stanley Matthews at Bloomfield Road and forgot the war wounds, money, jobs or disappointments for a couple of hours.

It was all we could do, watch. We were both only twenty-three and would never play football again. But plenty were worse off, as they used to say.

A week later the Old Man was still a hundred short of the two hundred pounds. Half of what he needed had been 'extracted' (his word) from his brother Edwards, the Gentleman Bookmaker.

It had been sent to the Old Man in the form of a Telegram Money Order from Doncaster Racecourse. It was for one hundred pounds only and there was no appeal, for the Old Man didn't know where Edwards had gone after the end of that meeting.

'Was he Making a Book there?' I asked.

'No,' said the Old Man. 'He's given that up. He only Makes a Book at the Dogs now. That and his SP office.'

SP means Starting Price.

'Who's looking after his office?'

'The Ogre. No use asking her where he is.'

The Ogre was Edwards's ex-showgirl wife, Dorothy. Edwards had taught her the Business. She had been a great beauty, but the strain of being married to Edwards (her heart's desire) came with attendant ills: difficult punters arguing about bets they'd never made; runners late with their clock-bags; the constant worry of whether to 'lay off' to the London bookies such as Ladbrokes and, if so, how much – all that had turned her into an irritable and snappish virago. It did not bother Edwards, now sixty-five, because he had been doing it all his life, and a hundred lost or a hundred won was pretty much the same to him. She thought of it all as real money. Which it isn't; it's money in play.

Now, puzzlingly, Edwards was adrift from his office and on the Race-tracks but plainly not Making a Book. And in some secrecy, for even the Old Man didn't know where he was.

Normally, Edwards was never far from the telephone and the tape-machines in the office in his house in South Shore.

'Not like him?' I hazarded.

'No, it isn't. So it has to be something hot, something he has a money interest in, something he can't control from his office, so he's left the Ogre to hold the fort while he does it, whatever it is.'

Once again, I was astonished at the Old Man's acumen. Once again, from nothing, he had produced a workable scenario. It was a great talent and I never ceased to wonder at it.

'Isn't it worth going to see Aunt Dorothy and telling her you're still a hundred short?'

'It would be the act of a madman to do that. She'd be furious at Edwards for sending me the hundred in the first place.'

I said, trying to think like the Old Man and, as always, failing, 'But why didn't he sent two hundred instead of one, if he was going to send anything at all?'

'Because,' said the Old Man, 'he needs his money for something else, something big.'

'Like what?'

'I can't tell you that. I'm not clairvoyant.'

'Damn near.'

'What?'

'Nothing. What do you do now?'

'Dick Firwood turns up on Monday. The hundred's no good. I need the two or nothing.'

'What, then?'

'Well, I'm going to Haydock Park this afternoon, I don't know about you.'

I said, alarmed, 'You're not going there to try to play the hundred up into two hundred, are you?'

Said the Old Man, 'What choice have I got?'

I started to outline the choices but realised that he was right. A hundred pounds short was the same as two hundred pounds short. Disaster.

'Is Onkel Frank going with you?'

'Certainly he is. He's been through the Card and he has a few fancies for me.'

'Does he know you're carrying a hundred pounds?'

The Old Man looked pityingly at me. 'Of course he doesn't. He thinks I have to get a few bob together. Perhaps fifty. Don't disabuse him.'

'All right,' I said, 'but I'm coming along. I'll pick up Jack at the Waterloo.'

'I thought you disliked the whole business of gambling?' said the Old Man.

'I do, but I think you need somebody to hold your hand at Haydock Park.'

Said the Old Man, mildly, 'Nobody's held my hand since my old nurse did it fifty-odd years ago.'

The Old Man had had a nurse all those years ago. He had been, as he said when he joined the Fusiliers in 1916, the Son of a Gentleman. He had been in need of that nurse, I thought, or somebody like her, ever since. Now, it was me.

We met Onkel Frank at the Bus Station. He was wearing a hat and coat, despite the warm day, and was early, having walked the three miles from his house in Marton. When I expressed surprise, he snapped, 'It's only a furlong or two.'

Like all handicappers, he thought in furlongs. Nowadays, as with miles and yards, nobody except racing people use the term.

Onkel Frank fixed his black and piercing eyes on the Old Man, who, as ever, was uncomfortable under his scrutiny. Onkel Frank was the middle brother, the cleverest brother, of the three. His skill at figures was phenomenal, he listened by now to nobody but Beethoven and he had read all the philosophers, ancient and modern. He was a Freethinker and Darwinist.

When I mentioned his remarkable intellect to the Old Man, he replied, 'Then why is he always broke, or near enough?'

'Because he's honest?'

'Honest be damned, the man's insane.'

The Old Man, I knew, was referring to the scandalous act,

recently performed at the Dogs, when Onkel Frank had picked up a roll of banknotes from the ground and given them to the man who had dropped them – a Bookie – before the Old Man had had a chance to put his foot on them, drop a newspaper on them, stoop and pick newspaper and banknotes up and pocket them: the correct and proper thing to do.

I'd seen him do this with stray tenners and fivers outside race-meetings, where people, having lost money, are inclined to throw away their racecards in anger and sometimes, in their misery and upset, throw away fivers and tenners with the cards.

But the Old Man had been too late. Onkel Frank had handed the roll of banknotes to the Bookie, who had looked shocked and surprised, as well he might.

He had rewarded Onkel Frank with a tenner.

'A tenner,' the Old Man had said, in despair. 'There *was* two hundred pounds in that roll. The man is, without doubt, certifiable.'

'Now, Frank,' he said, with an attempt at bonhomie because he needed Onkel Frank's goodwill, 'been through the Card, then?'

'Of course I've been through the Card. I have one for you in every race. If you back it.'

The Old Man was famous for disregarding Onkel Frank's tips, which were carefully worked out in the small hours, with the aid of very strong black tea and, if funds allowed, whisky. Onkel Frank had been, in his time, probably the best handicapper of dogs in the country. Now, he had semi-retired, but could not resist the lure of the Handicap Books and the midnight oil. He rarely had a bet. His satisfaction was all in the prediction.

The Old Man cared nothing for prediction. For him the thrill was in the uncertainty.

Today, I suspected, that would not do.

As I saw it, if the Old Man was to play up the hundred into two hundred he had to back Onkel Frank's chosen horses (often two in one race) for small amounts, and hope to accumulate, in the small sums won, the extra hundred pounds. This, as Onkel Frank explained to him, sitting on the lurching bus, was the only chance he had of winning. Any plunging would spell disaster. It was as well Onkel Frank didn't know that the Old Man's job and peace of mind depended on his predictions. He thought the Old Man simply owed his normal amount of money (say, fifty pounds) to somebody who was pressing for payment and that it was, as they say now, no big deal if he didn't get it.

'It may mean backing a few animals for a place,' said Onkel Frank, presenting the marked Card to the Old Man. It was embellished with C for Cop (Win) and B for Blow (Lose) and W for (possible) Winner or D for Danger, that is, the horse that might beat it.

The Old Man took the card politely, the money burning in his pocket.

Jack, sitting with me behind them, lit one cigarette from the end of another, propping his sticks on the seat in front. He grimaced in pain as he moved but said nothing. He never did.

I said, 'The Old Man's hoping for a good result this afternoon.'

'He always is,' said Jack.

'He's going to have to back Onkel Frank's tips.'

'He'll never do it. He never does.'

'He will. He has to.'

'They're not sure to win, anyway.'

'Just the same, it's the only chance he has.'

'To do what?'

I lowered my voice. 'Get two hundred quid!'

'What?'

'Not a word.'

'How much has he got now?'

'A hundred.'

'Never!'

'He has. He's going to play it up.'

Jack laughed admiringly. In the world of gambling the Old Man was macho, as they say nowadays. All gamblers admire risk-takers, especially when they lose the lot. It is how you bear yourself then that counts and the Old Man never showed that it mattered. Because it didn't. Usually.

Today was different. Today he had to win. I felt more uneasy than ever as the bus trundled through the green lanes towards the Race-track.

Jack said, 'Have the Old Man and Frank always been together?'

'Apart from the War.' I meant the First War.

'What about when the Old Man was married to Marthaann?'

'Frank moved in, the first day.'

'So, they've been together all their lives?'

'More or less.'

'But they can't stand each other!'

'Just the same.'

Jack laughed again, delighted at the idea, as the bus turned into the Race-track car park.

It was a full house at Haydock that day. Bookies were cheerful that punters were coming racing again, after a lay-off of five years, and punters were as gullible as ever, looking for One to beat the Favourite.

Punters are dreamers, and the Old Man was the biggest dreamer of them all.

But today he was a reformed figure. As Onkel Frank directed and dictated his bets, he put on one small wager after another, as instructed, always disguising from Onkel Frank the real amount staked. Soon he was winning twenty, then thirty, then forty pounds, as Onkel Frank's sagacious selections came in: either a win or a place, but almost always short-priced, because in the main they were favourites.

'A favourite isn't a favourite by chance,' said Onkel Frank. After a while he began to have a small bet himself and after five races he was twenty pounds in front.

As for the Old Man, he was now within thirty pounds of the two hundred.

I could not believe it.

Nor could Jack, who had given up, having plunged heavily on the first few races with what cash he had, with the result that he was now sitting in the Bar, nursing his pint of bitter and his legs.

For that reason he was not present to see the historic meeting of the three Brothers. Edwards came walking casually onto the track, one of a crowd of affluent and shady-looking people, ten minutes before the Big Race of the afternoon. He was dressed, as ever, in a very expensive Crombie coat, a silk scarf, Lobb's shoes and a Savile Row suit. A new Woodrow hat was atop his brilliantined head and he smiled gently at those people who knew him, who were many.

Edwards was a popular and golden figure. One-time Amateur Snooker Champion and a friend in his time of all the great racing and sporting figures of the era. Jack Johnson, Carpentier, Steve Donaghue, owners, trainers, jockeys, stewards: there was almost nobody in the Game he hadn't met or had a drink with. He bore his popularity easily and greeted the Old Man and Onkel Frank without surprise, shaking hands with them with two fingers and somehow managing to press a flimsy (five-pound) note into their respective hands as he did so. They showed no sign of gratitude, this being expected of him.

'How are you doing?' he asked Onkel Frank.

'At the moment,' said Onkel Frank, 'I am going Through the Card.'

Edwards looked impressed. 'Every winner?'

'Every winner or a place.'

'Well,' said Edwards after a pause, as all around him Bookies shouted and punters pressed forward to get their bets on, 'I don't know what you have for the Big Race but . . .' He paused again and lowered his voice. 'Some Very Responsible People are On the Favourite.'

He passed on briskly to join the group, who were waiting for him, and made his way up into the stands, presenting me with a pound note and a mild nod as he did so.

He did not seem to take the money from his pocket. It just seemed to appear by magic in his hand. Of course, he'd had years of practice, working where public gambling was illegal.

'What now?' asked the Old Man.

Onkel Frank said, 'I have the Favourite as the Danger. I don't see it beating my selection.'

'Your selection be damned!' hissed the Old Man. 'You heard what Edwards said?'

'I heard him.'

'Well, then?'

'I still think my selection will win it. Grand Day. I stick by it.'

The Old Man closed his eyes for a moment. 'He said "Some Very Responsible People are On the Favourite". You saw the people with him. Two were professional gamblers. Two were Bookies. One was an Owner. One was a jockey. They are all On the Favourite. It's wanted.' The Old Man paused and his eye brightened. He had seen the light. 'It's why Edwards hasn't been home for two weeks! He's been with these people, putting money on this animal very quietly for them, up and down the country, spreading it about so the Big Bookies have no suspicions. But enough money, just the same, to make it Favourite.'

'Then it's a false Favourite: the money has dictated the odds,' said Onkel Frank stonily.

The Old Man said, very slowly, 'It has, at some level, to be a Fix.'

'Possibly,' said Onkel Frank.

'No possible doubt about it,' said the Old Man, and put every banknote in his pocket, all one hundred and seventy pounds' worth, on the Favourite.

Onkel Frank's selection beat it by a short head.

The Old Man's face was imperturbable as the result was confirmed. A curious calm seemed to have settled on him despite his frenzied calls of 'Come on, You Beauty!' to the Favourite as it led for most of the way.

'That's how it goes when your luck's out,' he told me, tearing up his betting-cards.

Said Onkel Frank, 'That's how it goes when you don't *think*.'

He was unsurprised at the Old Man's action, having seen him do something like it many times before – since, in fact, they were schoolboys and the Old Man had been arrested by the police for under-age and illegal gambling on the sand hills of Newbiggin, at the age of fourteen.

'By God,' said Jack, on hearing the news as we travelled home on the bus, 'You have to hand it to the Old Man. He knows how to send it in.'

'Madness,' I said, but he wasn't listening.

'Did you see Edwards again?' Jack asked.

'We saw him afterwards and he shook hands with them both again and gave them a fiver each.'

'Did the Old Man tell Edwards he'd put them off the winner?' asked Jack.

'What would have been the point?'

'Thirty pounds short of the two hundred, that's all,' said Jack. 'And the Old Man had a go! Bloody wonderful, is that.'

The Old Man, on the Monday night, put on a new white starched collar and his regimental tie. He brushed his oldish suit and polished his black shoes very brightly. He had applied Yardley's Lavender Brilliantine to his hair and a twenty-packet of Churchman's was in his pocket.

Also in his pocket was five shillings, all he had in the world.

'You meet this Dick Firwood tonight?'

The Old Man nodded. He seemed calm. I could not imagine why.

'What are you going to do?'

The Old Man put on his Woodrow hat, not as new as the one Edwards wore but recently cleaned. 'Throw myself on his mercy. What else can I do?'

'He'll never wear it. Two hundred pounds short of the subscriptions money!'

'Just the same.'

And he nodded and went out, the hat at a rakish angle.

As I saw it, everything depended on how Dick Firwood reacted. There was no way the Old Man could stay in the job if a report had to be made. And how could that not be? The irony was that for once in his life the Old Man had a job he loved. The camaraderie of the young RAF Officers in the offices took him back to his youth in the Trenches. It was a place of male banter and ready humour and a certain code of honour and behaviour.

I wondered what he would do when he lost the job. When, not if. So I waited up for him. Aunt Clara was a late retirer (a habit formed during her years on the Music Hall, born of the need to unwind after a performance) but at one-thirty she gave up and went to bed.

The house and the night went quiet. There were very few cars in the streets then. I read Ernest Hemingway but my mind wasn't on it.

The Old Man came in at two o'clock, by taxi. He was smoking a cigar and a bottle of Sparkling Pomade was in his hand.

I couldn't wait. 'What happened?'

'Dick Firwood,' said the Old Man, 'is without a shadow of a doubt a White Man.'

'Yes, but – '

'Not only did he give me the best dinner the Imperial Hotel could put in front of us, he talked like a gentleman the whole evening.'

'What about the missing subs money?'

'Never mentioned.'

'What?'

'I tried to, but gave up. Every time I tried to tell him, he talked about the War. Lost his leg there, First War. You know that?'

'No, but – why?'

'Why?' The Old Man pondered.

'Why didn't he mention the missing subs money?'

The Old Man poured the Sparkling Pomade into teacups for us both. 'Because he didn't want any kind of financial enquiry into the Books?' he hazarded. 'Because he was At It himself, possibly?'

'Was he?'

The Old Man shrugged. It was all behind him now. 'Who knows?'

I sat down and sipped my Pomade, which was really a kind of cider.

The Old Man raised his glass, shook his head and said, in a wondering voice, 'What a day we would have had at Haydock Park if we hadn't met Edwards! We would have Gone Through the Card! Won hundreds!'

He sipped the Pomade.'*Wouldn't* we?'

'Yes,' I said.

Best Man

Mr Ashworth the Baker turned up at his son Jack's Wedding Reception at the Co-op Hall, Burnley, without a tie. He had attended the Ceremony but sat at the back of the Church so as not to meet any of his many, many relatives.

Now, he had no choice.

His brother Albert, to whom he had not spoken for at least fifteen years (Mr Ashworth spoke to nobody at all if he could avoid it), now stood in front of him in the foyer. Albert's hat was firmly planted on his head and he was dressed in his best black suit. He was a small bantam cock of a man.

Mr Ashworth looked startled to see him, but he recovered well. Putting a hand to his tie-less pink collar, he tugged at in an aggrieved manner. Mr Ashworth wore a blue union shirt in honour of the occasion, with a bright brass stud. He had shaved a day early, this being a Saturday. His weekly shave with a cut-throat razor was performed by ritual on a Sunday morning. He wore the black suit which at that time was *de rigueur* for weddings, funerals and christenings in the North of England.

'Nah then, Albert,' he said non-committally, in a greeting that amounted, as his son Jack remarked, to a courtly bow in other circles.

His brother Albert did not respond, at first.

Behind them, a great but subdued roar came from the Hall as guests and bridesmaids and bride and groom jostled into their seats at the long trestle-tables, which were already laid with white linen cloths and shining cutlery. It was the old working class at play and they were enjoying themselves.

As Best Man, I should have been in the Hall by now but I had decided to stay in the foyer and guide to their seats, quietly and unfussily, those guests who had drink-taken. There was another reason for my hanging back: Jack had said in an aside, 'Look after the old fella and for God's sake get him a tie!'

Mr Ashworth may have been drink-taken but he showed nothing. He never did.

Thinking his brother had not heard him in the noise and clangour of dishes and plates and voices, he very reluctantly spoke again. 'Nah then, Albert, how arta?'

His brother took a deep but combative breath. 'Wheer's that Hundred Quid?' he asked, in a clear and carrying voice.

'Nay,' cried Mr Ashworth.

This answer did not satisfy his brother, who refused to shake the now outstretched hand but continued to stare, without mercy.

'Nay,' sighed Mr Ashworth, dropping his hand to his side.

Albert spoke again, with great conviction. 'There's a Right Way and a Wrong Way to go about things, Harold. You know that as well as I do.'

'Nay,' said Mr Ashworth again, in something approaching defeat.

The two men stood there absolutely still for what seemed a long time. I took Mr Ashworth by the arm and said, 'We'd better get in. You're on the Top Table.'

'Right, lad,' said Mr Ashworth, warmly. He had never ever

spoken so warmly to me before. He hastily followed me into the Hall, avoiding Albert's stony eye.

His brother's words followed us as we went. 'Top Table be buggered! Inside Walton Jail more like!'

Even Mr Ashworth felt some explanation was called for after that. As I found him his seat (and a few glances were exchanged at his lack of a necktie) he said, 'He's allus been like that, has Albert.'

I waited for more but there was no more. 'You've forgotten your tie,' I said. 'I think I can get you one somewhere.' Where? I wondered.

'I'm not called on to speak or owt, am I?' said Mr Ashworth, who was not, for once, covered (anyway as far as I could see) by his usual film of flour. He ran his own bakery and seemed to spend most of his life in it. People did, then.

'No,' I said. 'Vicar. Father of Bride. Me. That's all.' I had it off, as they used to say, by heart. Or so I thought.

Mr Ashworth surveyed the company at the Top Table without evident pleasure. Several of his relatives smiled and waved from other tables but he did not acknowledge them.

'I might find a shop open that has a tie,' I said. I saw Jack's quizzical eyes on me as he sat down next to his bride, Elsie, a humorous and common-sensical girl. The general consensus was that she would have to be, with Jack.

'Nay,' said Mr Ashworth and produced a tie from his left-hand trouser pocket. It was crumpled and had a bright-yellow diamond pattern. I recognised it as a Tootal I'd bought for one-and-ninepence before the War. I had loaned it to Jack almost ten years before. Mr Ashworth knotted it round his neck, watched by all. He did not seem embarrassed. So nobody else was. I saw Jack choking into his pint, which he had obtained early, before the promised but dreaded Pomade for the toasts. I avoided his eye. I had enough on my plate. I'd never been Best Man before.

The Old Man's reaction to the news of Jack's wedding and the invitation to attend had brought on a reminiscent mood. 'My own Father had a wonderful wedding, by all accounts. In Norfolk. Married a rich farmer's daughter. A Bryant. Well, nearly everybody in Norfolk is called Bryant. Described himself as a "Gentleman" on the Marriage Certificate. Well, I suppose he was. He'd made a small fortune at sea with the P. & O. They were married by the Rural Dean.'

'Sounds like a lot of archaic Victorian fuss,' I said. I disapproved of archaic Victorian fuss on principle, like everybody my age.

'Oh, I don't know,' said the Old Man, tolerantly. 'People like ritual, prayers and hymns and all that. No harm in it.'

I pointed out that none of the Brothers, including himself, had got married in a Church.

Edwards, the eldest of the Brothers, had married the Ogre Dorothy, a dancer in George Edwards's Company, at the age of sixty, to her forty, after a particularly bad season, in a Register Office. She had money saved, which came in useful.

Onkel Frank had married Florrie, a widow, aged twenty-seven, when he was fifty. Asked why, he had looked nonplussed and then responded testily, 'I had had a particularly good season, you understand me?'

That, too, had been in a Register Office.

The Old Man had married my mother, the redoubtable Marthaann, in a Register Office when she was sixteen. His words on that (when criticised years later) were, 'Well, I married the bloody woman, didn't I?'

Even the Old Man's Sister, Clara, had run away with a Scotch Comic and married him at Gretna Green. They had toured as Comic and Girl for years but had now parted – on Fighting Terms, as the old song had it.

'Nobody in this family seems to want the occasion solemnised,' I said. 'In any religious way.'

'Possibly,' said the Old Man, 'because they don't expect it to last.'

His own marriage to Marthaann had lasted until she inherited her Father's fish-shops. The Old Man had refused to join her in the enterprise, pleading aversion to the smell of the stock.

They had never divorced but had lived two hundred miles apart for years. 'Just a nice distance,' reflected the Old Man.

'Are you coming to Jack's wedding or not?' I asked him.

The Old Man picked up his hat. 'Can't do it.' He meant the Dogs were running that afternoon. He added, 'Besides, the general optimism at weddings is a bit too much for me. Usually unfounded, y'see? All that kissing and crying, too much. But enjoy yourself, if you can. Best Man can be quite a job.'

As they used to say, he had never spoken a truer word.

The day had been long and it was nowhere near over. The Old Man had, of course, been telling me in his oblique way that the office of Best Man had to be taken seriously, that there was an order and tradition to these things. I didn't believe in any of that, being twenty-four years old, and I had simply dressed in my usual tweed suit and woollen tie and shirt (the dress of any artistic young man of the time) and got on the bus for Burnley, along with my young wife, Edith, to whom I was not to speak for the rest of the day. She was with the women and I was with the men. That, I discovered, was how it was done at weddings.

The tweed suit was my first mistake but I hadn't discovered that when I met Jack, as arranged, at the door of the Church. To my surprise, it was a very large black-stone building in the mock Gothic style. It was, in fact, a Swedenborgian Church, named after the philosopher. I wondered at the somewhat eccentric choice. Everybody attending the Wedding would be Methodist or Baptist, certainly Low Church.

'The Service won't be difficult, will it?' I asked Jack.

'Buggered if I know,' he said.

'Then why did you pick this Church? Burnley's full of Bethels and Chapels.'

'It's also got the highest suicide rate in the County,' said Jack. He was full of information like that. As Duke Gutterson, a clerk in his Civil Service office, had said to him, 'Jack, you know a hell of a lot about a hell of a lot of things and none of it's any bloody good to you.'

'True, is that,' Jack had replied, cheerfully.

The same Duke Gutterson was famous for his unceasing string of dirty stories. I asked him why he never talked about music, which was his first love. He had played dance music for years, on the great ocean liners before the War, and had adopted the name Duke after the great Ellington.

Duke had looked around the room packed with ex-servicemen smoking and picking their noses. 'I'm not talking about music to them as knows bugger-all about it,' he said.

Jack knew something about music as he knew something about almost everything, so he qualified. Now, all he could say was, 'Swedenborg's a philosopher and I fancy being married by a philosopher.'

'But he isn't here in person. He's been dead for ever.'

It was then I realised Jack had drink-taken, possibly a lot of it. I reproved him.

'It's the legs and the standing we'll have to do,' he said. 'I'm going to be standing up for hours.'

I said, 'How much have you had?'

'A pint or two.'

'Then,' I said, 'I'd better lead on.'

The Vicar, if he was a Vicar, a tall, thin man, received us in the Vestry. We were, of course, late.

Asked Jack, 'What's ten minutes? We're talking about a lifetime here.'

'I hope you appreciate that, my son,' said the Vicar, frostily, smelling Jack's breath.

As Jack said later, a gill smells as bad as six pints half an hour after you've drunk it.

As the Vicar fussed with documents Jack asked, 'Is Percy here?'

'He doesn't care for religious occasions.'

'Nor do I,' said Jack. 'It's a lot of rubbish is all this, when you think about it.'

The Vicar – as we were all to call him – looked startled at this and motioned me to one side, as Jack slid slowly into a wooden seat and rubbed his legs. He was perfectly relaxed back-stage in a Church, having once been, surprisingly, a choirboy. He had been thrown out of the Choir at St Mary's in Blackpool by the Choir Master, Mr Martin, a man who owing to a throat wound sustained in the First War, spoke in a whisper and yet sang in a clear tenor voice.

When I say thrown out, I mean by main force. Down the steps with a box of the ears.

I was outside and saw it happen. 'He'd no need to do that,' I protested.

Jack replied, 'He means nowt. He just takes it all too seriously and it's a load of rubbish, isn't it?'

Now, the Vicar was saying, 'As Best Man and the Bride-groom's Friend, I have to ask you a serious question.' He lowered his voice. 'Is this young man in a proper frame of mind for such a solemn occasion as this?'

I said, 'Certainly he is. He loves her. And she loves him.'

'That is not what I'm talking about,' said the Vicar. 'This is a formal religious service.'

'How formal?' I asked. Well, it seemed a quick way to change the subject.

'Are you not familiar with our wedding service?' he asked severely.

'I'm afraid I'm not.'

He looked upset. He had every right to be.

I said, 'I expect it's Low Church, isn't it?'

I thought: Swedish means Calvinistic, Low Church, Non-Ritual, doesn't it?

Apparently not.

The Vicar looked at my unpressed tweed suit in quiet despair. He turned round to see Jack fumbling absently in his pockets for his cigarettes and matches. 'I think I might have to prompt you.'

I nodded. 'Most grateful.'

It occurred to me that he was beginning to realise the depths of ignorance he was facing in Jack and myself, who held the fashionable view, then usual amongst young people, that Darwin had buried religion ten feet under the ground.

'Let us proceed,' said the Vicar, clutching at straws. 'We must do the best we can.'

Jack sighed and put his cigarettes and matches back into his pocket.

The rest of the proceedings passed in a blur. I remember speaking lines from the Good Book which seemed subtly different from those I knew. I stumbled a few times. It was all – the responses and the rest – different from anything I had experienced before, certainly from anything in the Wesleyan chapels to which Marthaann had sent me as a child.

Jack spoke confidently and only slightly wrongly whenever it was his turn to speak.

The Bride spoke impeccably and seemed serene. She appeared to know what was coming, to be familiar with the Form of Service. Had she had a rehearsal? I felt foolish but kept going, conscious of the censorious eyes of the Methodists and Baptists in the serried ranks behind, who probably understood even less than I did.

Jack's sister Mary and his Brother-in-law Cedric, both firm churchgoers, represented Jack's family. The Bride's father and mother were pleasant and modest people but Jack's new Brother-in-law, a local butcher and plainly a veteran of many weddings, funerals and christenings, was frank, in the North Country fashion, about my performance.

'They couldn't hear you at the back.'

I replied, loftily, 'Are you a Swedenborgian? If so, you would have known what to do! I didn't.'

He considered this. 'You could have spoken up, just the same.'

'I didn't want to speak up because I didn't understand what I was saying.'

The Brother-in-law pursed his lips and consulted his pocket watch. It was of gold and was engraved. He was dressed in a tight, striped suit and wore a porkpie hat. He was older than I was, maybe by fifteen years. He put the watch back in his pocket. 'Have you ever been Best Man before?'

'No,' I said. 'And I don't care if I never am again.'

'That's a funny attitude to take.'

I realised that this man didn't work in a Butcher's shop. He *owned* one.

We were having the photographs taken outside the church by now. There was a keen wind.

I said, 'Look, tell me what's needed and I'll do it.'

He shook his head in sorrow. 'A good Best Man does his homework properly before ever he sets foot in the church.'

'How would I do that? I live fifty miles away.'

'Just the same.'

I suddenly realised he was lumping me with Jack. That is, as a drinker, a smoker, a gambling man: somebody who would be admitted to his family with many reservations.

'What's next, anyway?' I asked.

He looked incredulous. 'You mean you haven't got a list?'

'A list? Of what?'

'Of what your duties are. As Best Man.'

At that moment the Photographer called us to order. The women smiled and the men put their cigarettes out and looked serious. Everybody had a flower buttonhole, except of course Mr Ashworth, who had refused to wear one.

'I feel a right soft nelly – an', besides, they make me sneeze.'

If Mr Ashworth was anywhere in the group I didn't see him. Yet he must have been because when the developed photographs were passed around, a week or two later, there he was, a mysterious figure at the end of a row, like somebody who had wandered into the ceremony by accident.

Without his tie, of course.

Now, sitting at the Top Table in the Co-op Hall, he was waiting, as we all were, for the food and drink. I sat down in the wrong chair and had to be directed by the Brother-in-law to the right one. I sat down in that and looked around, relieved. At least I could get a drink and something to eat now. I was exhausted from the tribulations of the Church ceremony. I hadn't eaten since eight that morning and it was now about one o'clock (In those days, being young, I was hungry most of the time).

'Grace!' A voice rang in my ear. It was the Brother-in-law.

'What?'

'Say the Grace!'

I looked around, wildly. Everybody at the tables, probably a hundred people in all, seemed to be looking directly at me.

The Brother-in-law hissed, in a voice that must have carried to the very rafters of the Co-op hall, 'Ask him to say Grace!'

'Who?' I hissed back.

It didn't help that we were four seats apart and this conversation was being conducted behind as many people's backs.

I looked to Jack for help but he was, as they would say today, pissing himself.

'The Vicar, ask the Vicar to say Grace!'

'I'm not sure he is a Vicar. Is he?'

'Then just give his name!'

'I don't know his name.'

'Call yourself a Best Man!'

'What *is* his bloody name, then?'

The Brother-in-law told me.

As I stood up, Mr Ashworth said, 'You're making a bit of a balls-up of it today, young fellow.'

'If you're not careful,' I said, 'I'll call on you to speak.'

'Nay!'

I stood up and asked the Vicar to say Grace.

'About time. Grub's getting cold,' said Mr Ashworth, in a loud voice. There was a titter from the Bridesmaids, who had taken Mr Ashworth to their hearts. Coming from Burnley, they recognised the type. They all had at least one relative like him.

The Vicar said Grace.

It lasted a long time.

'Where's grub?' asked Mr Ashworth, audibly.

'Hush, Father, you're showing us up,' said Jack's sister Mary in a loud whisper, across the Top Table.

The food arrived just on cue and everybody ate with appetite.

The men drank beer and the women, in the Nonconformist fashion, soft drinks, orangeade or lemonade. Women did not drink in public very much in those days. Although the War had changed the habits of some of the younger women, it was still thought unwomanly to be tipsy.

The men drank as much as they liked and were tolerated in this by the women. It was thought to be manly to drink a bit too much on an occasion like this. Many of the women were better off than they had ever been in their lives because their men were now in regular work. It was a Labour town, Burnley. The Mayor of nearby Nelson (Mr Ashworth's birthplace) had once ordered the Town Band to play 'Mucking About The Garden' instead of the National Anthem. It had caused a national scandal. Nelson was also known as Little Russia.

We were all Socialists then.

Except, that is, for Mr Ashworth and the Old Man, who were Conservatives; the Old Man only when he had money. Mr Ashworth, on the other hand, had never voted anything but Tory in his life. This gave him an excuse to argue stubbornly and with a profound lack of logic that silenced his opponents, in the Working Men's Clubs, where few Tories were to be found. He did it for the pleasure of being cussed and unpopular.

He liked it that way. It was at one with his boast that he'd never worked for another man. It wasn't quite true but we all pretended it was.

Now, he had cleared his plate first, wiping it clean with a slice of bread, and was asking for a second helping of chicken and mushy peas, an unheard-of thing at a wedding. He got it, too.

The Bridesmaids tittered and Mr Ashworth winked at them.

When the meal was over, I got to my feet and was about to call on the Father of the Bride to say a few words, when the Brother-in-law's voice hissed, 'The Royal Toast!'

'What?'

'Propose the Royal Toast!'

'I don't know it.'

'It's always done!'

'Not to this lot. They don't believe in Royalty. They all vote Labour.'

Said the Brother-in-law, heavily, '*I* don't! Propose the Royal Toast and have done!'

I stood up and said, 'I now call on the Father of the Bride to say a few words.'

Mr Ashworth's comment was, 'It'll have to be a few an' all!'

He had refused Pomade and was drinking his favourite tipple, Rum-and-hot-water. How he had persuaded the waitresses to get it for him was a mystery never solved.

The Father of the Bride acquitted himself unexpectedly well, with many sly jokes, some verging on the *risqué*, and sat down to applause and laughter.

The Brother-in-law hissed again. 'All wrong, was that!'

'Sorry?'

'You didn't vet any of the speeches, did you?'

'No. Should I have?'

'And what about the champagne?'

'Is there any?'

'No, it's more Pomade.'

'Where?'

'It's already opened *waiting* to be poured! You're ten minutes *late* with it!'

I stood up and shouted, 'Ladies and Gentlemen, please fill your glasses and drink to the Bride and Groom!'

A despairing voice said, 'That's not how it's done!'

I ignored the Brother-in-law's prompting and called the speakers in no particular order and proposed new toasts on every possible occasion and somehow managed to get most people tipsy. So much so that the Pomade ran out. That way, I thought, they wouldn't notice my Balls-up, as Mr Ashworth called it.

'I will say this for thee,' said Mr Ashworth: 'tha' calls more toasts than any three. They've run out of stuff to drink.'

They had, but reserves were brought up. The Brother-in-law was not best pleased but I was past caring. I was enjoying myself and was by now seeing everything through an alcoholic haze.

Finally, we all stood outside the Co-op Hall in the thin wind and watched the Bride and Groom, to cheers from all present, step into the ancient hired Daimler.

Mr Ashworth should by now have been very drunk, but he showed nothing. He had long ago taken off the hated tie.

His brother Albert stood close to him but they did not, as they used to say, break silence.

Mary and the Bridesmaids and my wife and the other women wept or dabbed their eyes. The men stood stolid with beer and cheered and made what would now be called sexist remarks.

Jack swayed into the car, which was festooned with ribbons. Confetti flew and stuck to everything, because the rain had started.

Burnley, Jack said, had the second highest rainfall in the country. The confetti was home-made, as was just about everything else, there still being shortages in Attlee's England.

'Good luck!' I whispered.

Jack closed one eye. He said, 'I'll be the only Bridegroom in history going on honeymoon with Aftershave on the face and on the feet!'

Jack's feet perspired. They never had before his wounds.

I shook his hand and slammed the door and the ancient Daimler drew away slowly, like a hearse.

The Brother-in-law was at my side. His face was indignant. 'You should never have done that!'

'What?'

'Shut that door.'

'What door?'

'That car door!'

'For God's sake, why not?'

'Because it wasn't your job. It was *her* job!' He indicated a crone-like old woman, possibly a gypsy, who had appeared from nowhere.

'Why?'

'Because it has to be a Strange Old Woman who shuts the bridal carriage door!'

'Why?'

'The Brother-in-law's patience gave out at last. 'How the hell do I know why? It just does, that's all.'

'Balls!' I said.

'Language!' he said.

I never did find out why Mr Ashworth owed a hundred pounds to his brother or if he ever repaid it. As the Old Man once said, 'There are some things only known to God and some not even to Him!'

The Orators

The Old Man had heard Lloyd George speak.

He had heard F. E. Smith.

He head heard Ramsay MacDonald.

He had heard Winston Churchill. Everybody in the Forties had, all too often. Every other Tory politician of the day spoke in a parody of Churchill.

Now the Old Man wished to hear Nye Bevan, who was coming to Blackpool for the Labour Party Conference.

Bevan was our hero, Jack's and mine; in fact he was hero to just about everybody else we knew. He had a stutter and a lisp and was a Welshman, but all these impediments were forgiven him, because he was the Scourge of the Tories (whom he had castigated as 'lower than vermin') and fell out, often, with Attlee, Bevin and Morrison, who represented the old Labour Union Bosses and the massed ranks of The Movement. To young men like us they seemed to belong to another age.

Bevan was a young (well, not so young) Turk, and we liked that. We all of us met in the Grand Hotel Billiard-room, haunt of the Old Man and Onkel Frank, on the Friday night before the Labour Party Conference. None of us was a member of the Party because that involved boring things like knocking on doors and attending party-meetings and listening to boring old farts (as they would say today) sounding off about Ca-pit-al-ism and the evils of Tory rule. Always ending with Votes of Thanks and Any Other Business.

We didn't want any of that.

The local Labour Party smacked of Trade Unionists calling for Points of Order and Shop Stewards with glasses, who hadn't served in the War, asking if the leaflets had been distributed.

We didn't want that, either.

We wanted Revolution. As Jack said, 'Up with them that's Down, and Down with them that's Up!' Of course, we hadn't the foggiest idea how to bring it about. Nobody did. So we talked.

Jack and I had read (or anyway I had) *Das Kapital* and the *Manifesto.* We also perused *The New Statesman and Nation* and *Tribune.* I had to read *Tribune* because I was writing for it by now. Not long, politically correct articles as today but End-pieces about the pay and conditions of the workers in Boarding-houses (Bad) and about living on a Council Estate (Good) and how Racing needed Betting shops where an ordinary working-man could get a bet on without being in danger of arrest. In those days, the Street Betting Act was still in force. This *Tribune* piece was perhaps the only one the Old Man read with interest, offering the comment, 'No possibility of ending it with this Government. They're all Methodists and spoilsports generally. Like Stafford Cripps.'

As I defended him, the lean and ascetic visage of Cripps came to mind, and I laughed. As Orwell had already said (or was anyway soon to say) the Labour Party was indeed full of 'Back-stairs creepers and Methodist cocoa-boozers'! Well, it was but it had a leavening of Oxford dons and semi-dons too, and these were the people whose articles we read in the *Statesman*; Crossman and Crosland and the rest. Later, it occurred to me that these Wykehamists could just as easily have been Tories. They certainly spoke like Tories, in, to us, a fluting and affected way. But all highly-educated people in England spoke like that in those days. Except Nye.

Nye had started life down the Pits.

Nye spoke in a Welsh lilt and it didn't matter.

And Nye would be addressing the *Tribune* meeting the following Tuesday at the Co-op Hall, opposite the Winter Gardens.

We were all agreed that we would be there. No doubt about it. This 'Fringe' meeting (as they are known today) had a leavening of other, safer, politicians, but Nye was the star turn.

The Old Man, now playing snooker for money, as usual, enquired what time the meeting started and then gave attention to business – that is to say, startling his opponent by clearing all the colours (which he needed to win), in a rapid staccato of cue and ball, the balls dropping gently into the pockets or smashed down hard, if that is what the shot required.

Onkel Frank appeared, behatted and dutifully glaring of eye. He had read more politics than any or indeed all of us, and had recently reproved a student who had dared to argue politics with him on the strength of having bought Onkel Frank a pint of what the Old Man called 'Brackish Mild', the cheapest and most general beer on sale in Blackpool at that time. The student had foolishly taken Onkel Frank's silence as he talked half-baked Socialism to be a mark of respect. Onkel Frank was simply drinking his pint.

'So, if the Workers have to take to the barricades like they did in the French Revolution, then that's what it's got to be, eh, Frank? We have to get behind Uncle Joe Stalin, don't you agree?'

The student, who was about twenty and dressed in an old sports coat and glasses, gazed long into Onkel Frank's brooding face. He thought that Onkel Frank was giving his idea thought. He was not to know that Onkel Frank had substituted Stalin for Hitler now that Hitler was dead. He was now watching Stalin as he had once watched Hitler, as a Man To Be Reckoned With, as if he was a bent but redoubtable jockey.

'What d'you think, Frank?' asked the student.

Said Onkel Frank briskly, finishing his free pint, 'Come back and talk to me of politics when you have some hair on your cock.'

Then he sat down and the delighted Jack, ever on the look-out for outrageous behaviour, bought Onkel Frank a whisky. With Onkel Frank there was never any shortage of outrageous behaviour. The thing was, Onkel Frank didn't know it was outrageous. He simply could not listen to waffle or woolly reasoning of any kind. To him, everything was logical. It was a piece with his profession, handicapping, with its rules and logic and mathematics with just a hint of imagination and inspiration thrown in.

Onkel Frank was almost the only person in Blackpool, anyway amongst the Labour supporters, who did not see Uncle Joe Stalin as a saviour. 'Already the man has a military base in Berlin!' he instructed us. 'The Red Army is soon going to be in place for an attack on the West.'

When Jack and I remonstrated with him, he contemptuously snarled, 'Read *Das Kapital*! Read Lenin's Letters! It's all *there*!'

Said Jack, 'Listen, Frank, we've just had a bloody great War. So have the Russians. Why should they want another when all that will happen is we'll drop a bloody great Atom Bomb on them?'

'If we have the guts to do it,' said Onkel Frank.

'Well, of course we do,' I said, 'and Joe Stalin won't want his grandchildren burned alive any more than Eisenhower will!'

'The difference,' said Onkel Frank, 'is that Stalin means it, as Adolf Hitler meant it and Eisenhower doesn't.'

'I still can't see it, Frank,' said Jack.

'No, I know that,' said Onkel Frank, 'which alters nothing.'

Onkel Frank, on politics, had the firmness of expression of his previous political opponent, Adolf Hitler.

For us, now, he had a problem.

Sipping his whisky, which was a large one (nobody in their right mind would even consider giving him a small shot of anything), he said, 'You young fellows think you're smart? Well, do you or don't you?'

I had half an idea what was coming so I edged towards the billiard-table, where the Old Man had started a new frame, with the same opponent. This tall and gangling young man, known to the Old Man, for some reason, as 'The Looby', was thirsting for revenge.

When I asked the Old Man where the name 'Looby' came from, he replied, 'Read Shakespeare.' And potted a long and difficult Red.

The Old Man and Onkel Frank had received a Victorian education and had read a lot of Shakespeare and Dickens. They had little French, but enough, and, as my friend Jack said, they possessed an astonishing command of the English language. All this included their elder brother Edwards, the Bookie. None of them had gone on to what nowadays would be thought to be Higher Education. They simply went to Victorian Boys' Academies, until they were in their late teens. Small classes and constant reading (their father read Dickens to the entire family by candlelight each evening) had obviously given them a command of language that was often, certainly in Onkel Frank's case, leavened with the pungent argot of the Race-track. As it was now.

'If you young fellows are half as clever as you ought to be, you will follow what I'm saying without difficulty. In short, you'll know your arse from your elbow, mathematically speaking.' Onkel Frank glared enquiringly into the faces of Jack (apprehensive), Allan Coop, my actor friend (wondering which role to adopt), and Norman, ex-Navy and now, like everybody else, employed in the Civil Service, who was always himself. He was much later to be the Curator of a Museum and a talented painter but none of us knew that yet.

Onkel Frank's black eyes under the hat (he almost never took it off) first fell on Jack, his natural prey. Jack's grasp of mathematics was tenuous at the best of times. He had good reason to be apprehensive.

'Jackie,' said Onkel Frank, not unkindly, 'I am going to put to you the record of two horses that are running tomorrow, Saturday, at Sandown Park.'

'I'm not with you, Frank. If – '

Onkel Frank's basilisk eye was raised from a long foolscap page that was black with calculations. 'It is a perfectly simple exercise. Come over here and sit by me and I'll take you through it. It won't take an intelligent man longer than two or three minutes.'

Miserably, Jack sat next to Onkel Frank at the small marble-topped table. The fact that games on the billiard-tables were in full swing, with players cueing and walking around, did not bother Onkel Frank in any way. He had spent his life in such places. So had the Old Man. A billiard-room was home to them.

Onkel Frank laid out two sheets of foolscap. One represented the record of Gilded Cage. The other represented the record of Blue Boy.

Onkel Frank took Jack rapidly through the records of the two horses' last outings and average speeds on 'slow' and 'heavy' going over the distance involved; then, with the aid of much calculation, he predicted the odds both horses would probably start at (they did!) and wound up his preparation by asking Jack the simple question: 'Which one is the Favourite?'

It was obvious to all that he had lost Jack some time before. Bravely, Jack put a confident finger on the foolscap sheet marked GILDED CAGE. 'It has to be this one, Frank.'

There was an awful silence, finally broken by Onkel Frank putting his eyes close to Jack's and booming the word 'Bullshit!' Jack was as stone as Onkel Frank added, with enormous scorn, 'Grade Two!'

Jack was a Grade Two clerk in the Civil Service, owing to his Ex-Service status. Onkel Frank, despite his erudition and mathematical ability, was Grade Three.

Said Jack, hastily, 'I'll get you a pint, Frank.'

Onkel Frank accepted it with ill grace.

Next was Allan Coop, who had elected to adopt a cavalier attitude, as this was basically a discussion about money. Like all of us, he was contemptuous of money, since he didn't have any and neither did we.

Onkel Frank ran through the figures. At the end, he said to Allan Coop, 'Which *One*?'

Allan Coop smoked a large pipe even then and was, like myself, already a father. He had an amazing array of clothes, the tools of the actor's trade. There being no steady work for young actors after the War, he too was in the Civil Service. He had not appeared in any Service Concert Party during the War, as many other performers did. He had spent the entire War in the mud and shit of an RAF Squadron.

Now, he looked dandified, not to say debonair. His response was in keeping with this. 'Whatever you say, Frank.'

The reply enraged Onkel Frank more than Jack's failure to follow him. This was not giving proper attention.

'It's not what *I* say,' hissed Onkel Frank, the brim of his hat touching Allan Coop's. 'It's what the *figures* say!'

Allan Coop made a hasty retreat, to talk to a friend at the bar. He did not offer to buy Onkel Frank a drink. I didn't blame him.

Onkel Frank's eye fell now on Norman.

Norman was a private man, and was to remain one all his life. He had been a Royal Marine Commando at eighteen years of age and had lived to drive in a convoy commanded by an ancient Admiral (the Navy often had what they called Pay-and-pension Officers) into Trieste. They had been warned by New Zealand gunners that there were some very unfriendly Panzers ahead, and were advised to turn back, since they were only fifty *matelots* with small-arms and ammo, and were sitting ducks in the Navy trucks with canvas sides.

'The Royal Navy never turns back,' said the Ancient Admiral.

Fortunately, the unfriendly Panzers had gone in the night and the Naval convoy liberated the City and got the best billets. Norman recounted these and other stories through his pipe, which remained clenched around the stem as he spoke. He was the youngest of us, only twenty-one now, and looked the oldest. He was the only young Tory we knew.

Onkel Frank went through his two cards with Norman, pausing only when Norman interjected: 'Onkel Frank, I'm not familiar with the phrase Five-To-Two Each of Two.'

Onkel Frank was taken aback. 'How old are you, Norman?'

Said Norman, patiently, 'I'm twenty-one, Onkel Frank.'

'Serious!' said Onkel Frank.

In the end, Norman had to choose. 'It is this one, Blue Boy, isn't it?' he asked gently.

Onkel Frank exploded. 'Of course it is! Any bloody fool can see that!'

But he went to the bar and bought Norman a large rum to go with his pint of brackish mild.

'He didn't ask for a rum,' I said.

'The man,' said Onkel Frank, 'is a *sailor*.'

Norman drank the rum imperturbably.

Onkel Frank then took off his jacket to engage in a Snooker double with Walter Boothroyd, a man of awful temper, who was well known for starting fights at Bloomfield Road Football Ground with anybody who disagreed with him – including on one occasion a black American soldier who could have known too little about the game even to discuss it. Walter it was who had gone to the Station Hotel at Euston with his partner on the Pleasure Beach, Freddy Douthwaite. As Freddy reported, 'Walter did no more than put his false teeth in the water-jug, and when the Head Waiter came up and asked us if we were enjoying our food Walter said to him, "Bugger off, Jack. I don't like nobody standing atop of me when I'm eating me bloody dinner!" '

Added Freddy Douthwaite, 'I'm not going on holiday wi' Walter again. He's got a few bob now, we both have, and we can enjoy uzselves if we want, at posh places like that. But never no more wi' Walter.'

That seemed to be about the state of play between Walter and Onkel Frank as well. Walter had started by running in-off and Onkel Frank had begun by missing the ball altogether, attempting a very thin cut. The two of them were explaining vehemently to each other the reason for these awful gaffes. Neither blamed the other, both knowing what a terrible temper the other had.

From the agonised expression on the Old Man's face it was obvious to me that, for want of a bet on something, he had backed Onkel Frank and Walter to beat the Looby and his father-in-law, the redoubtable Hooky Walker.

They didn't, and as the Old Man paid up, I strolled to the bar to greet Peter, the last member of our group. Peter was tall and thin and wolfish; he had an awful pallor but was extremely fit and well. Already holding a gill, he was looking around the company in case some young women might be present. None were.

The billiard-room was attended by wives of long standing, with large handbags and large gin-and-limes. Occasionally a despised and properly ashamed mistress of one of the players, in every case a married man of means, would sit nervously apart. These ladies ran to bright lipstick and silk stockings and were rarely talked to or acknowledged by anybody. It was as if they were not there.

'Hello, Peter,' I said.

'How are you, mate? Getting much?'

It was his usual greeting to all manner of men, accompanied by a leering wink and the delighted wolfish grin. A son of Plymouth Brethren parents (killed in the Blitz), Peter had experienced a very Sin-orientated upbringing, with the result that he found Sin very attractive.

'I'm all right, Peter. Glad to see you.'

Peter looked round, winking openly at one of the mistresses, who smiled, turned pink and looked away. Peter, cheered by this, said, 'I see the lads are all here.'

By that he meant the others – Jack and Allan Coop and Norman. He knew them only vaguely, as he disliked the sole company of men, preferring young women with whom he could exchange banter of a sexual kind. A Southerner, he had come North early in the War, having been, as he put it, 'thrown off flying in the RAF'. He had made a name for himself at the Vickers factory – where I had first met him – by dint of his phenomenal memory. He was reputed to know the serial number of every component of a Wellington bomber by heart and was thought by many to be a conceited young sod, in consequence. Much good this achievement was to do him anyway: like everybody else, he had lost the job, at which he was quite simply better than anybody else, when the War ended.

Now, he had applied for a Mature Student Grant to a University. At the Board he had been told that, far from being considered for the Grant, he had been directed to a job filling shells at the ammunition factory at Chorley, some fifteen miles away. This was thought to be the worst job in the County, bar none. Most of the operatives who worked there, men and women, had bright yellow faces, brought on, it was said, by the dangerous explosives they handled. And the pay was nowt special, they reported.

They complained no further. But Peter did.

Fixing the local Jobsworths and an Advisory Government Official who constituted the Committee, with his bird-like eye, Peter asked, 'Gentlemen, I don't know if you have recently read the Act?'

'Of course we have,' said the Chairman. No 'Chair' then. People would have thought you meant something to sit on.

'Then you will know,' said Peter, 'that the Act contains the word "suitable" as in "the person in question shall be directed to *suitable* employment".' He had then bestowed upon them his wolfish grin. 'Anybody who thinks that filling shells is suitable employment for me, recently Assistant Manager of a Department in a large aircraft factory, has got to be in severe need of a pair of spectacles.'

The Chairman, Peter reported, hadn't liked his tone or his attitude, but the Advisory Government Official had whispered in his ear and Peter had eventually been excused. Then he had applied for a grant to study Politics and Economics at the London

School of Economics. They had taken him, no doubt in a state of shock, since he never modified anything he said to anybody, come what may. He would not be called for study for many months, as there was a waiting list.

Meantime, he was On The Chairs. Translated, that meant he was employed, on a temporary basis, to give out tickets to the trippers when they paid their sixpences for occupancy of the deck-chairs on the Sands.

This was thought to be the last resort of those on casual labour, but Peter welcomed it. His workmates were men of like kidney, whose habits, as the Chicago Police say of their charges, were 'Irregular'. In Chicago, you are only allowed one alternative. The other is 'Regular'.

Peter was soon burned black by the sun and relished the opportunity for banter with the mill-girls, who gave as good as they got. When I asked his wife, the daughter of an ex-Labour Lord Mayor of Wigan, why she put up with Peter, she said, 'He makes me laugh!'

His most recent gambit had been to charge a passing Mill-worker sixpence because his dog had, as they said then, cocked his leg up on a parked deck-chair.

'That'll be sixpence to you, mate!' Peter had declared, ringing up an official ticket on his machine, as the blazing sun beat down on them all.

The becapped Mill-worker asked hotly, 'What the bloody hell for?'

'You dog's put that chair out of action for an hour. It'll take that long for it to dry.'

'You're not charging me for that!'

'*I'm* not. Town Council is!'

It developed into a splendid row, to Peter's po-faced delight, with his workmates called on to declare solemnly that such a charge was definitely Town Hall policy and many irate holiday-makers taking the Mill-worker's side. A hundred people were shouting at each other in the end.

This continued until a local policeman strode idly by. Then they all stopped arguing and went about their business. People did that in those days.

To Peter, the policeman said – with a long look at his awful, stained mac, which had but a single button on it, just one at the top, and flapped around him like a cape – 'Watch it, *you*!'

Peter had relished that. It had also given him a chance to use his affected Lancashire accent, which was terrible.

Now, sipping his gill of bitter, he retreated to the Vaults, with me in tow.

A local prostitute, so old and revered that most people didn't know she was one, sat on a stool reading a newspaper. Said Peter, with one of his massive winks, 'Hello, Doris. How's trade?'

'Oh, hello, Peter,' she said, and went on reading and sipping her gin-and-lime. She wore a wig and must have been fifty.

Cheered by the scandalised glares of the locals, who resented anybody they didn't know coming into the bar, Peter sat down and winked and said 'Evening!' to several people he did not know.

At least he didn't ask them if they were Getting Much.

'To the matter in hand,' he said. 'Have you got any tickets for the *Tribune* meeting?'

Peter was Labour. But on a severely practical level. Politics had no emotional content for him. He just thought Labour had marginally better politics. Logic was his thing.

He was, much later, to occupy the top job in the country as a statistician. But none of us knew that then.

'No tickets going, except to delegates to the Conference,' I said. 'We'll get in at the door, no danger.'

'You sure?'

'As sure as I can be.'

'You write for *Tribune*, so you should be all right.'

'Well, I should be.'

Peter drank up his beer and made for the door.

'Come and have a drink with the lads,' I said.

But I knew he wouldn't. Too many women were waiting, ready to laugh, in too many bars.

After Peter had gone, Jack said, 'When I was at the Labour Exchange last week Peter trudged in, in that bloody mac, spraying sand all over the place. I was talking to the Manager about Trade Union business and Peter shouted, 'Hello mate. Getting Much?'

'What did you say?' I asked.

' "Not Much but Regular!" What else could I say?'

'What did the Manager say?'

'He said, "I rather think we're prosecuting that man!" '

We all laughed. We laughed easily in those days.

It was the evening of the *Tribune* Meeting.

The Old Man looked up from his chair next to the fire. Smout was on his knee and the Old Man was eating a bowl of what we in the family called 'Tickle Broth'. The dish was a relic of Aunt Clara's days on the Music Hall with her husband Harold the Scotch Comic and contained a sheep's head as the basic ingredient.

The Old Man liked it because it was an informal dish and did not take too long to eat. The cold flesh of the sheep's head was reserved for the next day and was delicious with home-made bread and Black Market butter.

The butter was obtained by the Old Man from Andy and Tony, the Greeks, who owned a café. They also supplied us with lard, which was in short supply and essential to Aunt Clara, for her baking. The Old Man had put down on the table a large slab of lard, about the size of a brick, ten minutes before. It had covered the *Evening Gazette*, which bore the headlines WE ARE SHORT OF THE ESSENTIAL FATS, SIR BEN.

The Old Man had mouthed these words as he slammed down the lard. I was expected to laugh and did. Sir Ben Smith was Labour Food Minister and wore, to the delight of all, a black Anthony Eden hat two sizes too big for him. He resembled Eden in no other way, being fat and far more at home in a cap.

'How much did you pay for that lard?' demanded Aunt Clara with a laugh. She still wore her tammy and scarf.

'Tickle, it would shock you if I told you,' said the Old Man, accepting his soup and pouring a saucerful for the starving Smout, who was kept not too well fed, in case it interfered with his mousing instincts.

Smout had no mousing instincts. He bit, exclusively, other cats and sometimes small dogs.

'You can say what you like about Smout,' said the Old Man, proudly, 'but he fights his weight.'

Smout was small for a Tom. No cat of any size had yet mastered him, despite his age and size. Since his fighting diet consisted entirely of butcher's lights and milk it wasn't surprising.

'Are you coming to the Meeting or not?' I asked the Old Man. 'We're congregating at the Co-op Hall ten minutes before Kick-off.'

'Who else is on the bill?' he asked.

'Dalton, I think, and one or two others. Maybe Wilson, I don't know.'

'Plenty of time yet,' said the Old Man, not bothering to look at the clock. Racing was over for the day so it didn't matter what time it was. Also, he must have been holding a certain amount of folding or he wouldn't have bought the lard at whatever extortionate price it was. Now the War was over the Old Man didn't mind trading in the Black Market. During the War he had regarded it as unpatriotic.

'Well, I'll see you there, then,' I said.

'Bit of business I have to do first,' said the Old Man.

Decoded, that meant he had more winnings to come, yet to be collected.

'Will Onkel Frank be there?' I asked.

'He will, but I doubt he'll hear much.'

Onkel Frank was what the Old Man described as 'corned beef' – that is to say, slightly deaf. He was irritated, however, if you shouted, as deaf people are.

'Has he heard Nye Bevan?'

'No. But he's heard Lloyd George. Another Welshman,' said the Old Man.

'What was he like?'

'Heard him on the Town Moor at Newcastle. Before the First War. Your grandfather Isaac Henderson carried a barrel there so he could stand on it and see the great man.'

'Was he a great man?'

'Got the Working Man Sick Money, had to be.'

'And F. E. Smith?'

'Got nobody anything, except Partition with the Irish. Told Collins when he signed it, "That's the end of my political career." Said Collins, "That's my death warrant." Right in both cases.'

'And Ramsay Mac?'

'Wonderful doddering old Doric. Rambling Ramsay, they called him. Some say they should dig up his body and throw it into the sea,' said the Old Man. He meant extreme Socialists who thought Ramsay Mac a turncoat.

'Only mad people, surely?'

'All political people are mad. Have to be, couldn't take it seriously otherwise.'

'Then why go to hear Bevan?'

'Because I like a thing done well. Churchill did it well. Nobody will ever do it better but he had the material.'

'So you're not interested in the content?'

'There is no content. Or, put another way, the content is the same.'

'No, it isn't,' I said hotly. 'It's an entirely different content now. Labour is in power!'

'Haven't noticed it much,' said the Old Man with an air of boredom.

The Old Man might have been bored by politics but Harry Playford wasn't. Harry Playford lived for politics; ate, slept and dreamt them. Harry Playford was my Father-in-law.

When I got out of the RAF I went to Sheerness, on the Isle of Sheppey in Kent, where my wife Edith and our baby were staying with her family. Now, often described as 'The Land that Time Forgot' (because of the Nineties Recession), the Isle of Sheppey was then a bustling seaport, with a huge Naval Dockyard, and Sheerness was full of pubs and the sailors who drank in them. The men who worked in the Dockyard were known as Dockyard Mateys and amongst them Harry Playford walked tall, being their Trade Union Representative as well as six foot two in height – remarkable stature then, but not now. Harry also sat on many Co-op and Municipal boards but refused to become a Justice of the Peace or to serve in any position where he might have to adjudicate on, say, a case where an employee of the Dockyard has been found, at the Dock Gates, to be carrying out a roll of felting, wrapped around him, like a cummerbund, or an array of brass fittings secreted in his satchel. No workman had a car then.

Said Harry Playford, 'I couldn't do that: sit in judgement on such a man. I've brought many a useful thing out of the Dockyard meself but never anything that wasn't going to be thrown away or burned.' He was talking of oaken writing bureaux or suchlike items. 'The Royal Navy,' said Harry, 'is very prodigal with the country's money.'

As an ex-army man (a Sergeant at Gallipoli in the First War), Harry Playford did not take too warmly to the Upper-class manners of the Naval officers (always called Pigs by the ratings) with whom he had to negotiate to reach agreement on working conditions and promotions and, sometimes, pay.

'But I give a man his rank. If he holds the King's Commission, then I address him as Sir. I put every request to him, whoever he is, in an unofficial way first of all, to see if there's a chance of doing it that don't involve committees.' He took a deep drag on his pipe, which never went out. 'I can't abide committees: all people do is talk. I can't abide talk when it's not backed up with action.'

We were striding, as he said this, to a meeting at Sheerness Pavilion, to decide, he told me, what should be done with the money from the Sheppey Ex-Servicemen's Welfare Fund, collected by the townspeople for the sailors, soldiers and airmen who had fought in the War and 'might need a little help afterwards in civilian life'. Well, I thought, I qualified for that. But so did a thousand others, and since I didn't come from Sheerness, didn't even like Sheerness and didn't care how soon I got out of Sheerness, it was of purely academic interest to me. Harry had pressed me to go with him and I had agreed, having nothing else better to do. He had also hinted that I might be interested in a job as a clerk in Sheerness Dockyard. I told him I was interested not at all.

Harry received this silently, as if he hadn't heard it. He didn't need to tell me I had a wife and child to think about. So he didn't. But I knew that anyway.

I was finding that when you are married, just out of a War, and have no money at all, it cuts down your options quite a bit. I was not the only one, of course, to whom that applied.

It applied to everyone.

''Mornin', 'Arry', said the Police Sergeant at the corner of Sheerness High Street.

'Reg,' said Harry Playford.

We walked on, in step and at a brisk pace, Harry Playford nodding but not replying to the ''Mornin', 'Arry' that greeted him from the Dockyard Mateys and others who, like us, were making their way this sunny Sunday morning to the glass-domed Pavilion on Sheerness Promenade.

Sheerness was nothing like Blackpool, my home town, which I hadn't seen yet, because I'd been in Germany and Belgium and France since I'd last been on leave in Blackpool. I'd also, since then, married a girl I had met in the RAF. Edith Playford was a 'plotter' – that is, she worked on the table in the Operations Rooms of Fighter Command, plotting the height, position and direction of aircraft, enemy and friendly, taking her information through an ear-piece, which was One Way Only. No repeats. You got it first time or you were taken off the table. Few were, because they were well known as Bright Girls and were designated as being on 'Special Duties'. Many of the girls were middle class and thought to be snobbish. Edith Playford was not snobbish. It was not possible to be snobbish and to be Harry Playford's daughter: the contradiction would have been too great. She was out of the RAF as anybody pregnant was, inside a week of being diagnosed as such. Those kind of things were done without fuss in those days. Two weeks' pay and your War Gratuity was the form.

Now, she was at home with the healthy, noisy, frightening and seemingly wildly expensive Mike, whom I had not seen until he was almost a year old. Far from being In At The Birth, I was hardly conscious of it happening at all. Many men serving abroad found three or four-year-olds waiting for them when they got home at last from the Far East or India.

Edith's mother (also Edith) had greeted this twenty-year-old's enthusiasm for her daughter by remarking only, 'I can see what you see in him!' Just that. No more. No less. As my new mother-in-law had been Sittingbourne's Queen of the May three years running (on her fifteenth, sixteenth and seventeenth birthdays) I had to treat her with respect. Great looks – which she certainly had, but which she ignored, as was proper – are always treated with respect wherever they are to be found, and in whatever company, anywhere in the world.

I was On Probation in Sheerness, as the Old Man pointed out to me, in an aside, much later.

The wife of Harry Playford, like the daughter of Harry Playford, had to be a bit special, as they say nowadays, because Harry Playford was a bit special himself. A born leader of men, wounded at Gallipoli (where he met a brother serving with the Australians he hadn't seen for fifteen years, shook hands, and never saw again), Harry could and should have been a Labour Party Member of Parliament in the years after the Armistice of 1918. That he wasn't was due entirely to his modesty (he felt he wasn't educated enough) and to his affection for his beautiful wife, who didn't want to leave Sheppey, where all her sisters and cousins lived, for life in London or wherever Harry Playford could obtain a seat. A man who would not give ground an inch on a principle he believed in, he gave way on that and he shouldn't have, not for *anybody*, even a beautiful wife.

But he loved her and that was that.

Anyway, he was certainly a Big Fish in a decent-sized pond at Sheerness.

But the Faversham Division had never returned a Labour MP, because the rural farm-workers wouldn't vote Labour either through fear or conviction. 'I've canvassed them on a motor bike,' reported Harry, 'and I've had to get back on it a bit quick when the farm bailiffs let the dogs loose on me.'

'What about the farm-workers?' I asked, laughing at the idea.

Harry shook his head but not in despair. He never despaired. 'They don't know which side their bread's buttered. They're terrified of losing their cottages and their jobs.' He understood that but he was not sentimental, viewing the ordinary working-man, as exemplified by the Dockyard Matey, as being a weak and feckless creature, who is easily seduced by a pint or two of free beer or a cheerful word from a cunning Tory candidate with a title, be it only Captain. 'They're all for a quiet life,' he reported, 'but they don't get one from me!'

That much was plain to see from the way the Mateys greeted him with their chorus of respectful but noisy ''Mornin' 'Arry's. We were still getting this salutation as we turned into the glass-domed Pavilion, to find it chock-full of men (no women at all present) sitting in vast rows, smoking and talking.

On the platform – where, Harry told me, he had refused to sit, on the grounds that 'you can't speak your mind from a platform, you have to agree with the other people up there, don't you?' – sat some local Big Wigs; doctors and dentists and solicitors, keepers and adjudicators, so it soon appeared, of the Sheerness Ex-Servicemen's Welfare Fund. One of them, a portly, well-dressed man of sixty, a local doctor, held up his hand for silence and got it.

'Gentlemen,' he said, in a voice very different from the Kentish of the Dockyard Mateys and wildly different from that of Harry Playford, who had been born in the Lambeth Cut, 'Gentlemen, we're all here to talk about what we should do with the monies collected for the Ex-Servicemen's Welfare Fund. You have in your hands details of the disbursement as to the expenses of running the fund and so on. If you have looked at them I know you will agree that our advisers have done a very good job of getting the funds in order. Now, we are open to suggestions, obviously in broad outline only at this stage.' The Chairman paused. 'What this meeting is about is, as it were, testing the water, to see what most people feel we should *do* with this money. Later, we can sit down in committee and talk details of how to implement the feeling of this meeting.' He coughed. 'Anybody is allowed to speak. I would only ask for brevity – say, two or three minutes to each speaker, certainly no more than five?'

The Dockyard Mateys coughed in agreeable assent. They liked being called gentlemen by a gentleman.

'Excellent,' responded the Chairman. 'Who would like to start the ball rolling? Please introduce yourself when you stand up to speak.'

I felt Harry Playford stir next to me, but too late.

A thin man in a cap, half-way down the tiered seats, was on his feet. Cupping his Woodbine courteously into the palm of his hand, he introduced himself as 'Alfred Smith, Sir, Able Seaman Royal Navy, 1914 to 1919, Sir!'

'Gawd Blimey,' breathed Harry Playford, not too silently, in exasperation.

Continued the ex-Tar, 'Served in HMS *Indomitable*, HMS *Indefatigable*, HMS *Intrepid*, HMS – '

'Garn, we've 'eard yer,' said Harry Playford, in a clear voice that carried across the entire Pavilion.

The Tar was not put out. 'Sir, what I think we need, Sir, is a better Statue to the Fallen than what we 'ave, Sir. It's a disgrace, the one what we 'ave, and I think – I know a lotta my mates think also – that we should build us a new War Memorial, twice the size of what we 'ave, with the Names of the Fallen in this last War on it as well. It'd need to be twice the size to get everybody's name on what's died.'

There was a stir of assent to this simple sentiment throughout the Pavilion.

The Chairman stood up, briskly. 'Thank you, Mr Smith. I can sense you have support for that motion. May I ask anybody else who has *other* ideas to speak?'

There was silence. The Chairman gazed around the hall. 'You, Sir?'

A thickset, red-faced man in a nautical cap stood up. To Harry Playford's disgust, he saluted, Naval fashion, and came to attention.

'Gawd blimey,' breathed Harry, 'he was only in the Coast Guard!'

Said the Coast Guard, 'Sir, what we need, I reckon, and I reckon plenty of people in this Pavilion agrees with me, is a bigger British Legion Hall.'

There was a favourable stir at this.

Heartened, the Coast Guard went on. 'Sir, it's too small, the British Legion Hall is, and the Legion ain't got no funds to spare to enlarge it and I reckon as 'ow some of the money from the Ex-Servicemen's Fund could go to that. I mean, they'll be using it, same as we older blokes will, won't they?'

The Coast Guard sat down to some applause, on account of brevity and substance.

The Chairman stood up, and nodded approvingly. 'I think I can say that the Committee will respond to that sentiment, yes indeed.' He paused. 'Anyone else?'

One after the other, five speakers stood up and backed either the bigger British Legion Hall or the bigger Memorial to the Fallen, or both.

That took half an hour, by which time every man in the Pavilion knew that the pubs were open in Sheerness High Street. Even the Chairman glanced at his watch, with, I thought, some relief that things had gone so well, seemingly.

At that moment Harry Playford stood up.

He did not introduce himself. He did not need to.

An audible gasp, part exasperation, part resignation, went through the Pavilion. Many of the Dockyard Mateys lit cigarettes against the coming discourse, which, I realised, they knew from long experience would include facts ignored or unpleasant to face or have to do with some neglected aspect of duty.

Well, they rarely heard anything else from Harry Playford, who, after all, represented them and got them better conditions of work and rises in pay on a local level and all that. They just didn't wish to hear about it now, when the pubs had just opened.

But, as the Americans say, they sat still for it. Harry Playford was Harry Playford and that was that. They drew in tobacco smoke and gave him a grudging silence.

Said Harry, magnificently unaware of any of that, 'I've 'eard the speakers ask for a bigger War Memorial. Why? They never look at the one they've got now. It's never been cleaned, that I know of, all during the War. That's what the good citizens of this town think about the War Memorial.'

There was a loud collective sigh from the Dockyard Mateys.

‘As to the British Legion Club,’ said Harry remorselessly, ‘all it is now is a drinking place for them as has nothing better to do with their time. All a bigger club would do is give some people more room to spread themselves when they put up their medals and tell each other ’ow they Won The War.’

The Dockyard Mateys, who plainly approved of such behaviour, sighed again. This was bad manners from ’Arry but that was ’Arry.

‘What we should do with the money so generously given by the citizens of Sheppey Island, whether they were men, women or children, whether they were evacuees or visitors or workers and residents of this place, is to give it to the people it was intended for. The men and women who put on a uniform and went out and Won The War for us and suffered, a lot of them, a good deal of ’ardship in doing it!’ Harry Playford paused. There was an absolute, resigned silence in the Pavilion now. ‘Like my own son-in-law, who’s a-sitting next to me at this moment, as you’ll see from his uniform an RAF man, who’s coming out of the Service this very week and who, like millions of others, has a wife and child, no house to put them, and No Job!’

There was a long, pregnant silence at this, as the five hundred eyes of the Dockyard Mateys turned towards me, to have a good look at Harry Playford’s Son-in-law, who was Out of a Job.

Said Harry, with enormous finality, ‘He is the sort of young man we ought to be helping, in finding him a house and a job! He and others like him don’t want no new Memorial to the Fallen or a bigger British Legion Hall.’ Harry looked down at me. ‘A job and a house is what he wants! I vote the money – all of it – should go to him and those like him for that purpose!’

The Dockyard Mateys, looking long and anxiously at the Son-in-law of Harry Playford, who for all they knew would neither work nor want, did not clap or show sympathy of any kind.

Undeterred, Harry commanded the meeting. 'I so move, Mr Chairman!'

The Chairman started to his feet, his head inclined in defeat, to an old and experienced campaigner.

'Naturally, Mr Playford. It is so noted. The Committee will discuss all that has been said here today.'

'One in the eye for the Tories,' whispered Harry, sitting down imperturbably. 'Way of keeping them in their place. They've got to be made to remember we have a Labour Government, am I right?'

I understood now why Harry Playford had been so keen for me to come to the meeting.

'Yes, Harry,' I said.

At least he was right about one thing. Labour in Sheerness, as in Blackpool, ruled.

Jack was waiting at the outside of the Co-op Hall. So was Norman. So were Peter and Allan Coop and Eric, an actor and producer at the local Players' theatre, several members of which were to end up in my proposed novel, but I didn't know that yet. There were twenty journalists waiting too, all identified by their hats and scarves and the notebooks in their pockets and the cigarettes in their mouths. They looked angry.

'What's to do?' I asked Jack.

'You might well ask. They're letting nobody in.'

'Nobody?'

'They're full up. Not a seat left.'

'What about these newspaper fellows?'

'They're barred. They're all from Tory papers and they're not wanted because they'll write hostile copy.'

I said, 'Let me have a go!'

I looked at the Custodian at the door. He was tall and thin and had a *Tribune* badge in his lapel. Several familiar faces, known only from newspaper photographs and the British Movietone News since there was no television yet, pushed past the Custodian, importantly showing their tickets. They ran to short haircuts, shiny blue suits and alcohol. There was a distinct whiff of it in the air.

I said to Jack, 'You should have got a ticket, the Trade Union work you do.'

'Too far down the totem pole.'

He had thrown his stick away since he got married and now walked in a curious lurching gait. I said, 'Sit on that step. I'll see what I can do.'

He didn't sit on the step.

I walked up to the Custodian and said, 'There's five of us here, staunch Labour Party Men. How about it?'

'Have you got a ticket?'

'No, but – '

'Nobody allowed in without a ticket.'

Several prosperous, bustling well-known men pushed by. It was getting late. We could hear the buzz of the crowd in the hall.

I said to the Custodian, 'Well, what about me? I write for *Tribune*!'

'Have you got a ticket?'

'No, but I write for *Tribune* and this is a *Tribune* Meeting, isn't it?'

'Listen, lad, I don't make the rules. We're full up and you can't come in without a ticket. Now step back and let people in.'

I fell back, abashed.

Said Jack, 'No good?'

'No. The man's a cretin.'

'Whatever he is,' said Jack, 'he's no Socialist.'

The others – Norman and Peter and Allan Coop – elected to go to a pub for a drink. Several journalists decided to try a way in by a lift at the rear of the building. They were guided by a local newspaperman. They got locked in the lift and had to be rescued by the Fire Brigade, but not for many hours, as nobody knew they were there.

'I suppose we might as well go for a drink ourselves,' I said, desperately.

There was nobody else waiting now.

The Hall was full. We could hear the words of the early speakers and bursts of applause coming from inside.

'So near and yet so bloody far,' said Jack. Then he pointed.

The Old Man and Onkel Frank were walking towards us casually and in no seeming hurry. We watched them as they approached, walking in step steadily, as they had done all their lives.

'No room,' said Jack. 'Full up.'

'*What*?'

Onkel Frank paused to hear Jack repeat that.

The Old Man walked on, never breaking step, Woodrow hat on his head, hard white collar and regimental tie gleaming, and spoke a few casual words to the Custodian.

'What is the problem?' demanded Onkel Frank, again.

He looked up as the Old Man gestured us forward. We began to speak but he motioned us in, and once inside we were guided swiftly by an usher to the very front row of the vast Co-op Hall. We sat down, as the booming Hugh Dalton – a huge man, a huge voice – was telling the delegates, in a public-school voice, of the iniquities of Toryism.

We sat down not more than twenty feet from him. Onkel Frank lit a cigarette and cupped his hand to his ear. He didn't take off his hat. The Old Man did and listened politely. He seemed perfectly at ease.

Whispered Jack, 'This has to be the only time in recorded history that a man has bribed his way into a Socialist Meeting!'

Said the Old Man, 'Not a bribe really. More a gesture.'

We looked at each other, laughed, and waited for Nye.

Pig in the Middle

The Old Man smelled the Pig as soon as ever he walked into Fenton's Scrap-yard.

What was odd about it was that the Pig was surrounded by tons of scrap metal (old car-bodies, prams, rusty tramlines, tin cans), a huge mountain of it. Yet a Pig, the Old Man said, it undoubtedly was.

Pigs were On the Ration.

Or, more correctly, pork was. Meat of every kind was On the Ration. So small was the allowance per person that even those lucky enough to have three or four Ration Books had hardly enough meat for a roast dinner on a Sunday. The ordinary citizen had very little chance of getting any extra protein. In the country, there was a rabbit or two going; in the town a buyer had to be sure he bought the rabbit with the fur still on it or it might turn out to be a cat. Cats were disappearing off the streets at an alarming rate.

'That is a Pig,' said the Old Man, 'that Fenton has in that Scrap-yard of his, or I'm a Dutchman.'

'Did you see it?' I asked.

'I smelled it, that was enough.'

'How could you be sure it was a Pig?'

'Because it smelled like every Pig I ever smelled when I was a boy on the old farm.'

In the remote days of the Old Man's childhood almost everybody had a few relatives still working on the land. The link with our agricultural roots had not yet been entirely broken. 'The farm women,' recalled the Old Man, 'used to shout at me, "Master Percy, stop chasing those chickens or you won't get any supper beer!" I was six.'

There were photographs of my great-grandfather Bryant in the family album. He had a long white beard and it was said his pony stopped without bidding at every public house between the Railway Station at King's Lynn and the farm. In those days, people still talked of horses and ponies as if they were people and always called them by name. Motor cars are no longer even called 'She', as for a while they were. All sorts of animals, not just the racing variety, figured large in the Old Man's life, always had, from the linnets and canaries and white mice and tame rabbits he'd kept as a boy to now, Fenton's Pig.

Of course, the Pig was an animal doomed for slaughter. On the family farm, insisted the Old Man, nothing was left of a Pig when the slaughtering process was completed, except the whistle the Pig makes when it dies.

'The Pig, like the Elephant, will die in water if it can,' said the Old Man. 'Hence the mystery of the Elephants' Graveyard, a pool in Africa where thousands of elephants' tusks and bones, a fortune in Ivory, were once rumoured to exist.'

I said it all sounded like something from the Old Man's favourite volume of light reading: *Fifty Famous Fights of Fact and Fiction*, by Lieutenant-Colonel Graham Seaton-Hutchison. The opening story, I recall, was 'How Umslopogaas Held the Stair', by Rider Haggard, possibly the finest short action story ever written.

'Nobody reads Rider Haggard now,' said the Old Man. 'He went with the great days of Empire.' He sighed. 'Two World Wars and we end up giving it away.' In that, he found agreement with Onkel Frank, who said that the Americans would get all our markets. And, also, that Uncle Joe Stalin was waiting in the wings.

'Did you tell Fenton you smelled the Pig?'

'Not yet. I'm thinking how to put it to him.'

'Isn't it illegal, keeping a Pig?'

'Certainly it is, what of it?'

'Well, won't Fenton get into trouble if he's found out?'

The Old Man looked irritated. He hated those kind of facts being pointed out to him. He had run his entire life in firm contravention of all social rules, which he considered were the work of busybodies – clergymen, politicians and suchlike – who had nothing better to do than interfere with the law-abiding citizen.

In that, he was a total Victorian and had a freedom of mind and spirit now totally lost. He really believed it was nobody's business what he did and none of his business what they did. Like Lord Rosebery, whose horses he had often backed for sentimental reasons, he didn't care what people did so long as they didn't do it in the street and frighten the horses.

'Of course Fenton's breaking the law. But who cares about that so long as nobody shops him?'

'What will he do with the Pig?' I asked.

'He'll have to butcher it at some point, obviously.'

'Well, will you ask him for some meat from it, or what?'

The Old Man looked hurt. I had obviously read his mind. 'Not a word to Tickle about this. You know how she is about anything to do with her belly.'

Tickle was my Aunt Clara, who looked after the Old Man.

She spent much of her day (when not selling her spectacles) finding Off-the-Ration food: offal, sausages, sheep's heads – anything to make up an interesting and varied diet. She was almost sixty now but still possessed of great energy. Said the Old Man, 'She needs the food to keep her going. She is a force of nature, as most women are.'

Said Onkel Frank, 'There's nothing wrong with that woman that an apple a day and a walk along the length of Blackpool Promenade would not cure.'

Blackpool Promenade is seven miles long.

The Old Man got to his feet and opened a cupboard in the kitchen. It contained a bag of butcher's lights (for Smout), various potatoes and carrots, and some rather mouldy bran that he had left over from his (now deceased) rabbits. The lights (actually the lungs of a cow) he cut up with a kitchen knife. The bran he spooned over them. He stirred up the noxious mixture in an iron bucket. Over the bucket he placed a newspaper, to disguise its contents.

I carried it all the way along Waterloo Road to Fenton's Scrap-yard. The Old Man had never been known to carry anything in the street apart from a newspaper, or possibly a cane when he was in the army.

Fenton, a small ferrety man wearing two waistcoats but no jacket, greeted us in traditional fashion. 'Nah then, Percy.'

'Hello, Mr Fenton.'

The Old Man never called the Blackpudlian working class by their first names. It was, from him, a mark of respect. 'A fellow is entitled to his rank.' In reality, it was to put a distance between them.

Fenton barely nodded to me. 'Working?' he asked.

'Civil Service,' I replied.

He sucked a hollow tooth non-committally. 'They tell me

they pay pounds-ten to fellas for turning up in their Sunday suits to do bugger all.'

'That,' I said, 'is about the size of it.'

Fenton nodded, satisfied. He had, in a long life of desperate unceasing work, found no need for reading and writing, although he doubtless could do it because everybody could, then. Times-tables, simple spelling, writing a good hand: even Fenton could do that. He'd been taught it under strap and rod in the Council School. Nowadays he'd rank almost as an intellectual, as the Old Man might have said.

'What's in the bucket?' asked Fenton.

Around him loomed the vast pile of scrap, towering ten, twenty, thirty feet in the air. It never seemed to grow any bigger or any smaller. It gave off a rusty, rotten smell.

I drew my breath in deeply, and held it. I could detect no scent of Pig.

'This bucket is by way of a present,' said the Old Man.

'A present?' Fenton looked suddenly watchful. He was plainly a man who had never, ever, been given a present at Christmas and who, if he had, would have sold it. This was the Old Man's evaluation of him, not mine.

'For the Pig,' said the Old Man.

There was, as they used to say, a Pregnant Pause.

'The Pig?' echoed Fenton, at last.

'Smelled it yesterday,' said the Old Man. 'I thought you might be a bit short of the right food for it.'

It was a statement, not a question.

Fenton stood still a very long moment. Then he sighed, took the bucket from my hand and proceeded along a duck-board walkway into the heart of the Scrap Yard.

We seemed to walk for miles behind him. What we were doing was walking in circles, each one narrower than the last.

All round us towered the great heap of menacing scrap. Somewhere one of Fenton's men sang as he smashed up metal with a coal-hammer, but we never saw him. Perhaps he was the only other person in the Scrap Yard. Fenton did not believe in carrying surplus labour. For one thing, they might see the Pig and talk about it, as the Old Man said later.

First, we saw the chickens. They were in coops, well kept and clean, in contrast to Fenton's own hands and clothes, which were ingrained with the grime of years; but that is the way of men who look after animals. The animals come first.

'Rhode Island Reds?' said the Old Man, admiringly.

'Can't keep a Cock,' said Fenton.

The Old Man nodded. 'Give the game away.'

Rabbits came next, silent in their hutches, duly inspected by the Old Man. Finally we ducked under a bridge of solid metal, then through an old car door, set in what seemed like a solid wall of scrap, and there it was.

The Pig.

The animal gleamed pink in the filtered light from the lattice of scrap about it. It grunted and moved sleekly towards us.

'That's some Pig,' said the Old Man.

'It is,' admitted Fenton, mashing up our offering into the Pig's bucket, which already contained a mess of potato peelings and crusts of bread soaked in water. The Pig attacked the new bucketful with relish, grunting and swallowing as if it hadn't many days to live.

Which it hadn't, for Fenton said, 'I'll have to butcher it soon, Percy.'

'Can you do that here?' asked the Old Man.

Fenton shook his head. 'I have a farmer out Preesall way set up to do it for me. I need a proper job doing.'

The Pig finished eating the food. It looked up for more. It seemed an intelligent, knowing beast.

Asked the Old Man, 'How will you get the Pig to Preesall? It's ten miles away.'

'I'm thinking on it,' said Fenton, who was obviously saying no more than he had to.

The Old Man persisted. 'When were you thinking of transporting the animal?'

Fenton pondered. 'In a week or ten days. He's ready, you can see that. And if *you* smelled him, so might somebody else. So he has to go, soon, he has that.'

The Old Man nodded. Despite his love of animals he did not seem upset, as I realised I was rather, at the idea of butchering the Pig. Obviously his years on the old family farm had inured him to such things. Nowadays, everybody is squeamish about killing anything. Not then.

We walked out of the vast cemetery of Fenton's Scrap Yard, the Old Man looking very thoughtful. I could not think why.

While the Pig fattened up for Christmas (the second since the War) other disasters hit the long-suffering population.

Snow, for a start.

The Winter of 1946–7 was said to be the coldest since the frosts of the early years of the century, when the Thames froze over. At Blackpool, in 1946, even the sea froze. And everybody froze with it, in offices, shops and in the streets. Every pavement was a skating-rink that winter. There were shortages of food, but nobody could remember there being anything else. First the Depression, then the War. The populace was used to a permanent, nagging hunger.

Now, there was no coal.

Even Aunt Clara could not coax an extra bag from the surly

coalmen perched on the seats on their horse-drawn wagons. 'There's rationing, Missus, haven't you heard?' was their sarcastic reply to her pleas.

We suffered from the cold in our rooms with Jack and his father Harold. Our house-fires consisted mainly of coke or dross (coal-dust) eked out with what few lumps of genuine coal we had. In a blizzard of snow, the Old Man visited old Davies, the nearby Coalman, with whom he was not 'registered' (everybody had to 'register' for everything in Attlee's England), and obtained from him a bag of dross at more than the going rate. He then picked up, with Jack's assistance and under the cover of the blinding snow, the biggest lump of coal in the yard and man-handled it with main force on to the bogey we had borrowed from Davies.

'It's half a week's ration, is that!' said Jack.

We made that block of coal last for a week.

When it ran out, it was back to the coke and dross again. The house, being large, was impossible to heat. The living-rooms were cold and the bedrooms icy. The mornings, with little hot water, were hard to face. Jack and I found ourselves so late one morning that we elected not to go to work at all but to ring in 'sick', and stayed home.

We sat around the fire, shivering and smoking and talking politics and books, when suddenly we saw a blur of activity in the back garden.

It was Mr Ashworth and he had an axe raised high above his head. As always, he was in two waistcoats and his stockinged-feet, despite the frozen snow that covered the grass.

'Stiffy! Don't,' shouted Jack, on the wrong side of the window to do anything about it.

For down came the axe on Jack's mother's oak writing-bureau.

Jack ran out into the garden.

Too late.

The bureau had been the pride of his mother's eye and had been left to her by an ancient aunt. Now, Sannah's heirloom was a mass of splintered wood, the highly polished top separated from the smooth-running drawers by the savage blows of Mr Ashworth's axe.

'Nay, Stiffy,' shouted Jack, in despair.

'I can't do wi' bein' cold, can I heck!' cried Mr Ashworth as he proceeded to throw the wood from the bureau on to the fire. We were glad of the heat but, aware of its provenance, we watched it burn in silence.

Mr Ashworth had no such reservations. He made himself a broth of tripe and meat gravy, which he ate with a spoon because it did away with washing-up.

'He can do more things with a spoon,' said Jack, 'than anybody who's ever lived.'

The fire cheered us all up in the end – especially the baby, who cooed and chuckled at the flames.

In the general shortage of everything the Old Man was a source of plenty.

He 'ran into' (his phrase for a meeting of any sort) an ex-boxer of some local repute, who offered him several dozen tins of meat. 'Corned beef', he reported, was what the tins contained. He had taken a single tin on 'appro' and opened it with some ceremony.

It seemed to be all right. We sniffed at it and nobody could fault the smell. Aunt Clara was all for eating it there and then, but something deterred the Old Man from that.

'The label's new – look at it!' said Aunt Clara.

'So it is,' said the Old Man, pushing away the slavering Smout, who had already scented the meat and was being driven frantic by it, as he was, declared the Old Man, the hungriest cat in Blackpool.

Smout clung on to the Old Man's trousers so persistently that finally, to placate him, the Old Man tossed a slice of the corned beef into his saucer.

Smout ate it in one swallow and looked up for more.

Said Aunt Clara, 'Get away, Cat! Are you never full?'

The Old Man thought a bit. 'It's probably all right. I'll take it along to Andy the Greek and see what he thinks.'

Decoded, that meant the Old Man was acting as a go-between for the ex-boxer with a hundred more tins to shift and Andy the Greek, who owned a café. That way, there was a commission in it for him. Andy the Greek had told him he was interested and the Old Man said he would procure the very best price for him.

The Old Man returned that night to find Smout asleep in front of the fire, an unheard-of thing, since Smout was a nocturnal creature and spent the nights, however cold, in search of sex and skirmishes on the icy roofs of the flat and the adjoining shops.

When the Old Man attempted to rouse him, Smout merely grunted and turned over.

The Old Man went white and ground his teeth. He was the only man I ever met who ground his teeth when awake. Smout was more to him than just a cat. He was now ten years old and had had a hard life. The Old Man felt an affinity with him.

'Go to the Vet's,' he said to me. 'Now!'

'What? It's miles away!'

'Run there!'

'The Vet'll be in bed!'

'Wake him up, then! Tell him the cat's swallowed poison and

we need an emetic that works at once!' He fumbled in his waistcoat pocket and produced a half-crown. 'Tell him it's for me and give him this half-crown. Run!'

I left the Old Man sitting in his basket-chair staring at the motionless Smout. If there was not a tear in his eye, then I was mistaken.

The Vet was not in bed but he was in his dressing-gown against the cold and held a glass of whisky-and-hot-water in his hand when he answered the door.

He was in no mood to come out but, at the mention of the Old Man's name, beckoned me inside his Surgery. He gave me a small phial of dark-brown fluid. 'Here, take this. Give the cat all of it. I'll be five minutes behind you.'

'Right!' I said, and ran back fast to the flat. Aunt Clara had still not returned from her whist drive, but she often stayed late with her cronies after closing-time, drinking a glass of Guinness or six, at one of the bars frequented by Professionals from the Pantomimes. She was always at home amongst performers, having been one herself for so long.

Smout did not want to take the medicine. He woke from his stupor, fighting. He was the fiercest Tom in South Shore. He bit and scratched and we were at full exertion.

'I'll hold him,' said the Old Man. 'When I have him fast, you open his mouth and pour the medicine in, all of it!'

It was easier said than done. Smout struggled and squirmed in the Old Man's arms. But finally the Old Man (still wearing his hat) had Smout pinioned hard against his chest and unable to move.

'Open his mouth and pour the stuff in!' said the Old Man.

I did it, somehow.

Nothing happened for a full minute. The cat stared at me

and I stared back at the cat. Then its eyes rolled in its head.

'He's going to die,' I whispered.

'Not him,' said the Old Man. 'It'll take more than this to kill Smout.'

Still the cat did not move.

'It's all right,' I said, sweating. It was hot work. I put the empty phial down on the table.

The Old Man relaxed his hold on the cat.

It was a mistake.

Smout, with a moan, shot clean out of the Old Man's arms, up into the air, and landed four-square on the floor. He did not stop there, but sprang on to the table and in one swift movement dived through the window, which the Old Man had opened to let in some restorative fresh air, and was lost to sight on the icy tiles of the houses.

'What was that for?' I asked, awed at the sheer speed of it all.

'Gone to be sick,' said the Old Man.

The Vet said the same, when he arrived in time to join the Old Man in a large whisky-and-hot-water. He did not request any further payment and sat companionably with the Old Man, talking about the First War, in which they had both served. He was, as the Old Man said later, fond of a bet but had, like the Vicar, to be discreet about it and was, the Old Man reported, a poor judge of a horse.

About Smout, however, he was right.

The cat returned two days later, thin but hungry, and ate bread and milk, lovingly prepared by the Old Man.

As for the ex-boxer, a week or two later he was sent to jail for selling condemned corned beef. Everybody, including the Old Man, who was usually totally on the side of the underdog, considered this outcome no less than just.

The sentence was a year, every day to be served. There wasn't a lot of probation around in those days and no counselling whatsoever.

After much thought the Old Man found a way of transporting Fenton's Pig to Preesall. He sought out the services of Harry Budd, who had a car and some dodgy petrol to run it, and who was, as the Old Man said, Game.

The Pig was dressed up as a human being, in a hat and scarf and gloves, and put on the back seat of the car. He was, of course, already dead.

The farmer out at Preesall jointed the Pig and the Old Man got an enormous leg of pork as a reward for his efforts.

Jack, Mr Ashworth, the Old Man, Aunt Clara and my young wife Edith and the baby all shared in the succulent dinner that Christmas. None of us had eaten so much meat at a sitting since before the War, if ever. It was washed down with beer for the men and Port or Guinness for the ladies. Nobody, save the Old Man in his Army days, had ever drunk wine. If offered, nobody would have said, as they used to say, a Thank You for it.

Replete, we all sat back and admitted it had been as good a Christmas Dinner as any of us could remember.

'It must've been a hell of a Pig, must yon,' said Mr Ashworth. 'It must've been a big 'un, wi' a leg like that on it.'

'It was certainly a fine Pig,' said the Old Man, feeding a morsel of it to Smout, who was hungrier the more you gave him, as Aunt Clara said.

All remarked once again what a fine Pig it had been. But I kept seeing it pink, sleek and alive in its pen in Fenton's Scrap-yard. It had been a fine Pig, alive. But *dead*?

Nobody was a Vegetarian then, except, as Orwell said, some lower-middle-class eccentric members of the Labour Party living in Welwyn Garden City who ran to shorts, pacifism, fruit juice and nuts and yoga.

So, when pressed, I ate a little more.

We all did.

Especially Smout.

Enter the BBC

I walked out of the Min of Ag and Fish.

To write a novel.

Well, wouldn't anybody?

Apparently not.

My mother, Marthaann, arrived in Blackpool seemingly within the hour but certainly inside twenty-four of them. By accident, of course, crocodile bag in hand (containing, as always, at least two hundred pounds in cash) and staying at a Guest-house on the South Prom. She had plenty to say on the subject.

Summarised, it was: 'You've no idea who'll pay you for this book when you've finished it? I never heard of such a thing!'

'No, Mother. I agree it's not quite like buying six boxes of prawns this morning knowing you'll sell them by tomorrow night. But it's similar, in that you aren't sure, are you, that you're going to sell the prawns?'

Marthaann looked perplexed at this sophistry, as well she might.

'Of course I know I'm going to sell the prawns. I wouldn't buy them otherwise, would I?'

'All your experience tells you you'll sell the prawns?'

'Of course it does.'

'That's the way I feel about writing a book.'

'You're sure somebody will buy it?'

'Absolutely.' I wasn't, but I wasn't going to tell her that.

'I know where I am with the prawns. I know exactly how many boxes I can sell. Always. I don't see how you can know that about a book.'

Marthaann had been making judgements about shellfish ever since she had taken over the Prawn Shops of her father, Isaac Henderson, in the Twenties. Every morning at seven o'clock she went to the Fish Quay at North Shields and bought stock for her shops. Just the right amount of prawns, crabs, lobsters and oysters. She never sold mussels, considering them scavengers. I do not eat them to this day. There was precious little refrigeration in the Forties, and Marthaann's stock of shellfish was kept fresh in salt and ice, as fishmongers had been keeping it for two hundred years. Of course, it went off, sooner or later. The trick was to sell it before it did.

Marthaann had done well out of the War, since there had been no rationing of shellfish, there being so little of it available. The North Sea had been full of warships and floating mines for five years. Only a few inshore fishermen ventured out. Lobster-pots don't need to be far out from shore, so they had done best. Now, the War was well over, supplies of shellfish were more plentiful and everything Marthaann could get she could sell. Accordingly, she was surely now in what Mr Ashworth would describe as 'Two Banks'. In other words, 'Made-up'. If she was, she wasn't saying so.

'I suppose, young fellow, you're looking to me to help you with this mad idea?'

'No, not really.' I was, of course.

'You'd do well to remember you have a wife and family now. You've got responsibilities to them.'

'I've also got some responsibility to myself.'

'That sounds like your Father talking.'

It was, except the Old Man had not put it in those words. He had merely remarked that, after all, Dickens had done well enough out of the writing life, and resumed his perusal of the racing pages.

'I don't suppose,' said Marthaann, 'that your Father has offered any money to get you started?' She sounded as if I was opening a fish shop.

'No,' I said. 'I haven't asked him for any.'

'Just as well, because he wouldn't be in a position to help anybody. Never could. Never has. Never will.'

Well, it was no good denying that, so I went over to the attack. 'I believe you've lent Ted three thousand pounds?'

'Who told you that?'

'Everybody in the family knows it, Mother.'

Marthaann looked scandalised. 'That's private business.'

'No, it isn't, it's family business.'

'I don't see what you're complaining about.' Marthaann took an even firmer grip on the crocodile bag. 'My arrangement with your brother has nothing to do with anybody but ourselves.'

'Three thousand pounds is a lot of money, Mother.'

'Ted has a proper business. He had to raise the money to get old Mr Withers' furniture shops. Mr Withers only left him a weekend to get it.'

I knew that was true. I also knew that old Mr Withers, Ted's father-in-law, had so much money tucked away under the floorboards that, as Onkel Frank said, he didn't know what he was worth. Mr Withers did not trust banks. Or authorities. Or Sons-in-law who couldn't raise three thousand pounds over a weekend.

Hence Ted's reluctant approach to Marthaann. It had to be

reluctant because, as the Old Man said, nobody in his right mind would put himself in hock to Marthaann. 'In all the years I lived with her, I never asked her for a penny-piece,' he told me, in tones of pride. 'Despite the fact that old Isaac Henderson was one of the richest men in Newcastle.'

Onkel Frank told a different story. He said the Old Man went to Masonic dinners with Isaac with only one thing in mind: the procurement of racing monies. In that, he failed signally, for Isaac (who had discovered women and drink by then) had still retained his Methodist horror of gambling. 'Percy,' said Onkel Frank, 'mostly drew a blank.'

According to the Old Man's version, far from wanting anything from Isaac he had accompanied him to the Masonic dinners in the guise of a minder. This, he said, was because Isaac, a very large, very strong man, would, when in drink (of which plenty flowed on such occasions), become what the Old Man described as 'obstreperous, and noisy with it', especially when not referred to by his full Masonic rank.

'Isaac,' reported the Old Man, 'was a bit out of his depth. 'For example, he told Lord Euston, a member of one of his London lodges, a succession of dirty stories that his Lordship patently did not wish to know.'

'Were you there?'

'Certainly I was.'

'Where was that?'

'I forget which lodge it was. Isaac was in seventeen of them. London ones were full of titled people.'

'Why did Isaac bother with such people or they with him?'

Said the Old Man, 'The Masons don't work that way. If you're in, you're in. Ever thought of joining?'

I didn't know much about the Freemasons, but I knew I

didn't approve. They seemed to have very little to do with Socialism, to which I was committed, or thought I was.

'No, it's a lot of archaic old rubbish. It wants sweeping away like the Church of England, the Royal Family and the House of Lords,' I declared.

Sighed the Old Man, 'They've all been there a long time. Don't see Attlee getting rid of them. Went to a public school himself.'

There being nothing to say to that, I didn't say anything.

'The thing is,' added the Old Man, 'no point in falling out with your Mother. She could still be useful, you never know.'

I knew he meant money.

'Of course,' he added cryptically, 'everything in this world comes at a price.'

Now, sitting in the guest-house on the South Prom, having tea and thin bread-and-jam, I knew exactly what he meant. Marthaann might lend money but her interest would come not in cash but in interference and bossiness. However, she was normally in Newcastle looking after her shops and Newcastle was two hundred miles away. I reckoned it was worth a try.

While I was eating my bread-and-jam (no cakes available yet) and ruminating, Marthaann was ready with a keen, knife-like thrust.

'What does Edith think about all this?'

'What *should* she think?'

'That you have a good job and you're giving it up.'

'It isn't a good job and I hate it.'

'Plenty of people don't like work. But you have to work to live, you know, young fellow.'

'Writing a novel's hard work.' I didn't know how hard it really was because I hadn't started yet but it seemed the obvious thing to say.

Marthaann however, was undeterred. 'Hasn't Edith tried to talk you out of it?'

'No, she hasn't.'

'Hasn't she said anything at all?'

'No. She lets me get on with it.'

'More fool her.'

'No. I might get lucky.'

Marthaann fell silent a long moment. She had tried attack and it hadn't worked. All she had left was defence. 'I have the shops but I haven't any money to waste.'

'I'd pay you back.'

A long silence greeted that. War had not only been declared, it had begun. 'Ted's paying me back inside a year.'

'Well then, so will I.' As they say now, 'promises, promises.'

'He's in a position to do it. Everybody's short of furniture. His business will do well.' She paused. 'He'd give you a job looking after his books, you know.'

'I know he would.'

'But you don't want it?'

'I'm going to *write* a book, Mother.'

'No matter what anybody says?'

'No matter what anybody says.'

'Well, then I don't know, I don't really.'

'Three hundred pounds would do it,' I said. Seeing her expression, I hastily added, 'Or even two.'

Marthaann looked around the lounge of the guest-house. Large overstuffed sofas from before the War dominated the room. She drank the last of her tea. Obviously, she hadn't taken anything I said seriously. 'I couldn't go to more than a hundred,' she said.

'Done,' I said, as her crocodile bag closed with a final loud click.

Everybody said, 'Don't do it.'

Except the Old Man, who asked, 'How much?'

'Nothing fixed up yet with Marthaann.'

'Ah,' he said, disbelievingly.

'Sheer lunacy,' said Onkel Frank. 'The Odds are all against it.'

The hundred pounds wasn't enough. Even I could see that. At five pounds a week (the least we could live on) it wouldn't last long enough to complete the novel. Plainly, I had to think of some other form of income, on a free-lance basis. Accordingly, I rang Sir Harold, the editor of the local newspaper, and offered to write him a weekly column on Radio programmes. I had already written a couple of radio documentaries for the BBC. To my surprise Sir Harold said, 'Write me a sample, then I'll see.'

I did that and then telephoned him and he said, 'The prevailing winds in this office are dead against it, but I am the man who says yes or no and I say yes. Copy, three thousand words, by Wednesday noon; payment three guineas per piece. Goodbye.'

I put the telephone down, dazed. I was to write that column for a long time, never once having it edited or changed. Sir Harold, a staunch Tory, remained a lifelong friend and benefactor. He'd come home from the First War, he later told me, and knew what it was like.

Good as that was, I needed more.

Enter the BBC.

They had actually entered almost a year before, in the form of a letter from a man who had edited a small literary Wartime magazine and remembered I lived in Blackpool. This was important because he was now a Features Producer for the BBC at Manchester and wanted to do a Radio Programme on Blackpool.

He had got the job through being at Manchester Grammar

School (very important in Manchester) and then Oxford. He had attended the job interview in his uniform, having just got off the troopship at Liverpool. We were the same sort, and together we roamed Blackpool Promenade, gazing at the Tower, the Piers and the Golden Mile, which had just reopened for business, wondering what to put into the sixty minutes of radio-time the BBC had allocated to us.

Norman was a bigger Socialist than I was, if anything, so we got plenty of 'colour' interviews with trippers in caps, and their busty womenfolk burned red by the sun of the first real holiday they'd had since the War. Together we traipsed the arcades, the Oyster Bars, the Tower Ballroom (where the Quickstep still held sway) and the crowded pubs and cafés. All this, to me, was everyday, but Norman was entranced. He saw the place, seven miles of Golden Sand, as a working-class fairyland. But he didn't have to live there.

And I had a shock for him.

We went to see Adam.

It was Epstein's *Adam*, the statue that had caused a scandal when first shown in exhibitions in London and elsewhere. It had been roundly condemned in the national press as obscene and not fit for the eyes of the fair sex. Which made it a natural for the Golden Mile at Blackpool.

And there it was. Or rather it wasn't, because Norman insisted on seeing it like one of the trippers. We queued up, paid our shilling (which went against the grain for me, as no local ever paid a penny to a stallholder, on principle) and filed along a tented cubicle, fringed – in case we were bored with the waiting – by shrunken heads from the Amazon. As the mock-standard Voice on the loudspeaker told us, the heads were perfect but very small indeed. It did not explain the process of shrinking but that was all right, since nobody seemed curious about it, except me.

The Voice also warned us, 'Ladies and Gentlemen, we trust you will not be shocked when you see Adam! *Gentlemen*, we hope that no feelings of envy will pass through your breast when you view Adam in all his Masculine Glory!'

'Nay,' said the becapped men in wonder, as Adam suddenly loomed large above us.

The shrunken heads from the Amazon were no more. Now, we stood before Adam at marble testicle height. He was bathed in a pool of bright light and his muscles and his carnal-equipment were a wonder to the eye.

Said the loudspeaker voice: '. . . And *Ladies*, we hope that when *you* see Adam you will not be disappointed in the Man You Know Today!'

The mill-girls shrieked with laughter. Norman grimaced. I knew then that Adam would never get into our Programme. After all, we were working for the BBC. And the BBC stood next to God.

After 'Why Blackpool?' went out (on the North Regional Home Service) I suddenly became a known figure in Blackpool, which was then, as it is now, an extremely publicity-conscious town. People I hardly knew called out in pubs, 'How's the writing going?' These enquiries I acknowledged with a smile or a nod, which seemed to suffice. The Old Man basked in whatever reflected glory there was, saying to all who spoke to him about it, 'Well, the thing is, he has the gift, you see.' Adding, in a wondering voice, 'The lad never has a bet, you know.'

The BBC entered my life again, after I had written a couple of chapters of the novel – I felt totally free, for the first time in my life, that summer – and the book was, I thought, going well, as far as I could tell.

I went across to Manchester on the bus to talk to Norman about an idea for a programme, only to find he had been 'posted' to London. The old BBC was a club and used military words such as 'posted' and 'leave'. There were (and probably still are) yearly assessments of producers and other staff, and a certain probity was expected of all who worked for the Corp (as it was then called) either on a free-lance or permanent basis.

The Front Door of the BBC building in Piccadilly, Manchester, was presided over by a uniformed commissionaire with an Alamein Star. He used to say that he and I, alone of the hundreds of people who passed through the portals each day, spoke with a proper Northern accent. He approved of that. Everybody else had a standard voice, or more probably an affected Standard voice, as used by all temporary-commissioned ranks in the War. Nothing sounds worse to a Northern ear than that, but people did it because they didn't want to seem common. It was called Talking Far Back and was generally considered foolish beyond belief. These days a Northern accent is considered an advantage, pointing to an enviably proletarian background. Not then.

Anyway, Northern accent and all, I presented myself to a Features Producer, Joe Burroughs, a saturnine, decent man, who was intrigued to learn that I was writing a novel and had chucked up a job to do it. He was a London producer, temporarily marooned in Manchester and filled with longing for the George public house and the company of such as Dylan Thomas and Julian MacLaren Ross to be found there. As far as I could see, on my visits to London, everybody did more talking and drinking than writing. To Joe's surprise, I said I disapproved of that. I thought writers should write if they had anything to write about and not dissipate their talents in such frivolity. Joe looked rather shocked at this show of North Country Methodism and said, hastily, 'I wonder, do you know anything about Gypsies?'

'Not a thing,' I said.

'Just the man to do a programme on them.'

'Am I?'

'I think so.' He didn't sound too sure. I waited. There was more. Said Joe, regretfully, 'I can't commission anything until you put something on a few pages for me.'

'How would I do that?'

Joe reached for some newspaper clippings. 'Go and see this fellow Ted Arkle. He's an expert on the Gypsies, apparently. Had the job of rounding them up for the Army during the War. Don't know if he's still at it. Anyway, why not arrange to meet him and see what you can make of it, what?'

'Yes,' I said. 'Fine.'

'By the way, what's the novel about?'

'A crowd of people coming back to a Northern town after the War.'

He looked relieved. Most BBC producers in those days had a novel 'in work'. Only one or two ever finished them. Plainly, whatever Joe's was about I hadn't infringed on it. It's odd to think that in those days everybody, anyway every educated person, wanted to write a novel. It had been the most preferred and prestigious literary form for three hundred years. Rather like a TV play now.

I didn't tell Joe the book was also about broadcasting, of which I knew just about enough to spread it thin. Nobody, not even the dozens of BBC producers with novels in work, had written anything about broadcasting. It was under their noses but they just didn't see it, as people don't.

To me the Radio was, quite simply, wildly exciting. For one thing, it reached millions of people. For another, it got one into the company of actors and, even more exciting, glamorous actresses, and the feeling of belonging to something. As a novelist you don't get any of that, and I was beginning to realise that it could become a hermit's life, if you let it. Allied to which, hermits never see anything except pictures inside their own heads, and like Ernest Hemingway I was against writers who Made Mysteries in The Head, considering such people not serious.

I went In Search of the Gypsies. That was to be the title.

First, I found Ted Arkle. He was the only heterosexual man I ever met who wore lipstick during the day. Actors wear it at night, but that's different. Ted was astride a large and ancient AJS motor bike, with a blonde young lady, in glasses, showing a lot of leg under a silk dress, on the pillion seat behind him.

Ted, who ran to a large sombrero-type hat, a long, very old leather coat and boots (and the lipstick), said, by way of introduction, 'This is my secretary, if you want to believe it.'

I managed a wink at the young lady, who didn't smile back.

Ted pointed to the side-car. 'You get in there, Young Literary Cove, and I'll find us some Gypsies.'

I got in and we roared off into the soft green lanes of Cheshire, finishing up, a couple of hours later, on the banks of the Wyre in a Romany encampment, where the men sat and smoked and whittled clothes-pegs and talked horses. The women worked apart, cooking on open fires and looking after the children and putting the washing on the hedges to dry. In Romany society the women do most of the work. The men like drinking, arguing, fighting and going to see Westerns, so they can price the horses on view. They don't read newspapers because they can't read and these Gypsies knew nothing about their European brothers and sisters who had perished in the Camps.

'Don't tell 'em anything about that,' Ted advised me. 'They

don't understand it. And don't give them any money or cigarettes or they'll think you're a mug. Just keep your eyes and ears open and don't write anything down. They don't like that.'

I took his advice but I did do some drawings for the children, who loved fast caricatures, as all children do. Ted took some photographs of me, sitting on a bucket, entertaining the barefoot kids, and the *Radio Times* caption-writer headed it, 'The author of tonight's programme makes notes at a Gypsy Encampment.' Well, he wasn't to know.

Ted's breathlessness, he told me, was due to being gassed in the First War. Like all old veterans he was sympathetic to me, a veteran of a more recent war. He put at my disposal all his notes and directed me to the Gypsy Lore Society, with whom he seemed to have an on-off relationship. These earnest and studious people were initially suspicious, but as soon as I said the magic words 'BBC' all doors opened. They did, then. The BBC had been the Voice of the Nation during the War. It stood for everything English, including the BBC Voice. Not Scots or Welsh or Irish, perhaps. Not the Workers, certainly. Quite simply, for the England of the Royal Navy, the Guards, the Eton Boating Song and Crumpets for Tea.

I disapproved of most of that (everybody I knew did) but it was a comfortable club then, and in the words of Evelyn Waugh's Captain Grimes, in another connection, 'They may kick you out but they never let you down!' I was to be grateful for that, sooner than I expected.

Ted Arkle took me around and about amongst the Gypsies, devoting several separate days to it, and I wrote my outline and got it commissioned. I couldn't believe I was being paid at a guinea a minute for my script, but the same rate applied to everybody – Priestley or Rattigan or me. The BBC was obviously even-handed about underpaying people.

Not that I felt underpaid, then. That was later.

Anyway, I wrote the script and Joe seemed to be impressed because he asked me to add another fifteen minutes to it, and I did. I asked what kind of money Ted Arkle could expect for assisting me, but Joe said he'd arrange that when the time came.

Ted Arkle seemed to think the time had already come but I told him what Joe had told me and with that he seemed to be almost satisfied. I had not yet learned the first lesson of writing and producing. Nobody, ever, is satisfied with their fee.

Ted Arkle was no exception.

A month passed. Moodily showing me the neatly folded khaki uniform and tin hat and gas mask of a Gypsy recruit he had helped to Go On The Trot, Ted explained: 'This lad couldn't stand the discipline. He'd have spent all his time in the Glasshouse.'

In those days military prisons were terrible places. Nobody had any rights there. Nobody ever went back a second time. The reason: men had to be happy to go back to the Front Line after that experience.

I said, 'I don't know why a Gypsy would ever join up.'

Ted Arkle, smearing lipstick on his blue lips (an effect, he said, of the Gas), said, 'Money. Gippos like the feeling of a few bob in their hand.' He lit a Capstan, which was forbidden him. 'Look, has Joe said anything more about money for my contribution?'

'He said he'd write to you. Hasn't he?'

'Not a word.'

'Well, I'll talk to him again.'

'What sum would you suggest to him?'

I thought hard. I was getting forty-five guineas (all guineas at the BBC, then) so I said, 'Well, twenty guineas would be about right, yes?'

Ted looked happier. 'It'd do, lad.'

The BBC Copyright Department sent Ted a contract for Two Guineas.

He tore it up and wrote to the Director General of the BBC, whom he'd known years before, as a young journalist on the old *Manchester Guardian*, on toilet paper, relating his complaints. Very properly too, in my view.

This news was relayed to me by a green-faced Joe, in his office in Manchester. 'He's written to the DG! On Toilet Paper!'

'He's annoyed,' I said. 'Send him thirty quid now and he'll forget all about it.'

Joe looked at me pityingly. 'It's out of my hands. They've called the legal people in.'

'That's stupid, Joe. Pick up that phone and talk to the man. He's all right. You could sort it out in five minutes.'

'Are you mad?' said Joe. 'It's out of my hands. I daren't speak to him!'

'Is the programme off, then?' I asked.

He looked horrified. 'Of course it isn't!'

'No "of course" about it. The man could sue. Why let it get that far?'

I had total sympathy for Ted Arkle. But he was up against the BBC.

'It's out of my hands now, old boy. I have to write a bloody report,' said Joe.

I was getting a lesson in how things were done. I didn't like it.

The production, with a dozen actors and actresses playing Gypsies, all fully scripted, was a revelation to me. I hadn't realised how quickly you can become drunk with exhilaration on hearing your words spoken aloud for the first time. The Read Through, with all the cast present but rather bored, as they had all done this before, was but a prelude to the two days In Studio, all the work moving inexorably towards the 'live' performance to go out to the Nation, on the second night, at eight o'clock in the evening.

I sat in the glass booth next to Joe and drank it all in, particularly the small details I would put into my in-work novel, which was about broadcasting, adultery, sex and money and Attlee's England. I realised, sitting there, watching the actors and actresses turning the pages of their scripts delicately, so that they would not rustle, breathing into the microphone as if it was a living thing, that I really knew very little about broadcasting at all. I was, as they say nowadays, on a learning curve.

After it was all over (and the actors had dressed in their best clothes for the live broadcast, although nobody could see them) we all went to the Queen's Hotel across Piccadilly and ate cold salmon and drank white wine. Gazing at the rapt faces of the actors, I admired their bravery and high spirits. I had already realised theirs was a risky occupation but that they did it for the same reason I wrote books and plays. They loved it.

The programme was generally regarded as a success. The *Manchester Guardian* and the *Observer* wrote of it kindly and I only hoped that Ted Arkle had forgotten and forgiven. I said as much, months later, to yet another producer. He told me he had brought up my name with the Head of Programmes, BBC North Region, saying, 'I have an idea here from that young writer who did that Romany thing. I wonder if you know him?'

Said the Old Etonian, a veteran of much Colonial Service in the Old Empire, 'I should think I do know him! We let him loose amongst the Gypsies eighteen months ago and we've been in the hands of the lawyers ever since!'

Then he approved the idea. I have forgotten what it was.

So the BBC didn't kick me out. And they didn't let me down.

And the Old Man obtained for us a Council House, on the strength, as he told it, of the broadcast about Blackpool, saying idly to the Chief Housing Officer at the Town Hall (whom, inevitably, he knew): 'The lad is doing a bit for the Town. Isn't it about time the Town did something for the lad?' Accompanied, of course, by a Masonic handshake.

Only the Old Man would have thought of that.

Arrivals and Departures: Marthaann

The Old Man had a very healthy respect for women. So much so that, although he always went through the then accepted middle-class courtesies – the raising of the Woodrow, the standing-up when a lady entered the room, the polite holding of the chairback if she should sit down anywhere – he always performed these actions as if sleepwalking.

Quite simply, women were not real to him. They were creatures apart, to be treated (if they were *ladies*) in the correct officer-like fashion, which somehow created a distance between himself and them. Into this category came any well-dressed woman of a certain age and manner, speech and dress. Also, to qualify as a *lady*, the woman had to be of absolute probity. Such was his influence on me that I treated all women as ladies until I discovered otherwise, and, to this day, still do.

Women, on the other hand, were something else.

Women, as far as the family women went (that is, women married to the Brothers), did not come in the *ladies* category. The Brothers had all married mettlesome, argumentative women, and, to hear them tell it, made a profound mistake in doing so. As the Old Man said, 'As a family we are not lucky with women.' The possibility that the women had all been turned into what the Old Man described as 'a set of viragos' by the errant behaviour of the Brothers never seemed to occur to him.

Marthaann, naturally, was the prime subject of his misgivings. Upon hearing that she was proposing to go on a trip to the Isle of Man with her sister-in-law, Clara, he had opined, 'Those two never got on for more than twenty-four hours at a stretch in their young days. How do they expect to spend a whole week closeted together in some boarding-house in Douglas?'

'Harry will be there,' I said. 'It's his seven days annual holiday.'

Harry Warrington was Aunt Clara's Fancy Man, although hardly deserving of the term, with its intimations of romance. Harry was fifty-five, walked with a limp from the First War, and had married but was now living apart from his wife, who was a barmaid at Feldman's Music Hall, opposite Blackpool's Central Station. He was not divorced from her, that being the ultimate, shaming disgrace. Harry spoke with a stutter, brought on by excitability rather than infirmity. He was a wealth of information on the old Music Hall artistes. He worked for the Tower Company as a sign-writer, and his double-crown original posters, all painted by hand, hung in the foyers of the Tower and the Winter Gardens Pavilion. They were in demand by all artistes, whose portraits also adorned them. They were brilliant works of craft. Harry had no idea how good they were; nor did anybody else. He had been a sign-writer all his life and had painted the sides of very tall mill chimneys in his apprentice days.

'N-nowt to it,' he declared, when awe was expressed at such dangerous work. 'You get used to it, d'yer see? If the platform swung in the wind, it used to bother me a bit at first. But you get so you can eat your dinner up there and enjoy it.'

By dinner Harry meant sandwiches and cold tea at noon. He

also meant two hundred feet up in a swinging platform of wood held only by knotted ropes slung over the chimney top.

When the Old Man pointed out he'd be in more danger going to the Isle of Man for a few days with Marthaann and Aunt Clara, he replied, 'N-nay, I've never been to the Isle of Man sin' I were a lad and went to Camp there. I reckon it'll be a good do.' Harry paused, warily adjusting his wire spectacles on his plump, reddish nose. 'Of course, it means going on a boat from Heysham to Douglas. It can be rough, tha knows.' Harry spoke as if they were embarking on a big adventure. They were, to him. He had never been off the mainland since he had served in the First War, as a boy of eighteen.

The Old Man, who would have put down a considerable amount of betting money rather than be closeted with Aunt Clara and Marthaann for a week, uttered under his breath, 'Rough will hardly be the word.'

I couldn't see what the problem was. The trip got Aunt Clara away from under his feet – the Old Man found his sister a wearing companion on a daily basis, although nobody would have guessed it from his everyday attitude towards her, which was polite but offhand, as it was to all women, no matter what their station, be they ladies or, as he put it, 'Members of John Knox's Monstrous Regiment of Women'.

In that he was a typical man of his class and generation. Understanding and toleration between men and women had not yet been invented and Political Correctness was not even a gleam in anybody's eye.

Aunt Clara was still selling her spectacles to the boarding-house landladies on an introduction-by-customer basis. The Old Man commented, 'She sells the things by pattering away to these women – and all those farm-women out on the Moss – about the minutiae of their lives. The woman has an infinite capacity for gossip and tittle-tattle, all of it absolute nonsense. She asks them all about their families and so on.' He shook his head in astonishment. 'Then she sells them a pair of spectacles they could get free on the National Health.'

'Yes, but her spectacles have fancy frames,' I said.

The Old Man sighed. 'That,' he said, 'is the price of it. The women buy these spectacles to look pretty. I ask you, how can any woman who wears glasses look pretty?'

'When she takes them off?' I hazarded.

'Different thing,' he replied, briskly. 'But when you get to that stage, who's looking at her eyes?'

It was not a sexy remark. The Old Man never made sexy remarks. He had heard every blue joke in the book, when he had worked in the public houses in Newcastle as a young man before the First War, and his face bore an expression of instant pain if anybody tried to tell him one.

After Marthaann, he had not sought out women on an emotional level, or any other as far as I knew. He had, his manner conveyed, done his duty, married and begat, and that was that over with. Marthaann had, with their long-ago parting, turned from a lady into a woman and had accordingly to be treated with caution in all things.

He repeated, 'Harry must be mad. Clara is enough for any man, never mind Marthaann as well.'

Not that Aunt Clara was any kind of brake on the Old Man's natural instincts to gamble and generally go his own way. Her life as a Music Hall artiste, married to an irascible Scotch comic, had made her, in the end, extremely independent. She had money squirrelled away, and added to it weekly small sums or large, the Old Man never knew which. For his sister was secretive. Such a parsimonious way of life offended the Old Man, but she had his grudging respect because she always had money in her purse. She was there in an emergency. And the Old Man was always in a state of emergency where money was concerned.

'The woman,' he muttered of his sister, 'sticks to her few miserable shillings like shit to a blanket.' This remark was normally uttered when he had not been successful in, as he put it, 'parting her from her silver'. In truth, she didn't mind lending him small sums, since it gave her a hold over him, and was also a useful topic of complaint to any other woman.

Which number included, of course, Marthaann.

Marthaann had written to Aunt Clara, saying she would certainly go to the Isle of Man with Clara and Harry on the one condition that they stay at a good-class private hotel. They must not cut corners in that regard, as food and comfort were what she, Marthaann, looked forward to most of all – that and rest from the strain of running her shellfish shops in Newcastle, which she could close for a week over the August Bank Holiday without losing much trade. The idea of leaving the shops in the hands of her girls (women of all ages in the Fish Trade were called girls) never even occurred to her.

'They'd rob me blind' was her firm assessment. 'Never leave employees with a chance to take your money or they will. Never do it. It isn't fair to them.'

Marthaann was a stern task-mistress, like her father, the tycoon Isaac. 'A fair day's work for a fair day's pay' was her attitude to her employees.

'What she means by that,' explained the Old Man, 'is they work six days a week for twenty-five shillings, if they're lucky, and perhaps a crab that is going off to take home on a Saturday night.'

'Not now the Labour party's in,' I told him. 'Anyway, her girls have been doing War Work for top money. It's all changed.'

'Whatever,' said the Old Man, 'she won't be paying them a penny more than she has to.'

Marthaann, a smart businesswoman, had several bank accounts, being under the impression that it was safer from the eyes of strangers like the Inland Revenue. It probably was. A trade that dealt only in cash did well in those years. Money, like fish, sticks to the fingers.

Marthaann could therefore afford a good holiday and it was accordingly booked. Soon afterwards, she appeared in Blackpool and stayed overnight at a private hotel. She wouldn't dream of staying in any establishment owned by the Brothers, on grounds of propriety. So she met Clara and Harry, by appointment, at Yates's Wine Lodge to work out the details of the momentous trip to the Island, which was in fact only a couple of hours' sailing from Heysham, a few miles up the coast.

Said Marthaann, as Harry reported to us, 'First of all, we must have a place that gives us full board, all-in. That way we are not wandering about Douglas or anywhere else looking for cafés at dinner-time.'

Said Harry, stuttering slightly, 'M-Marthaann, they're all all-in, in Douglas. It's not the French Riviera, tha knows!' Harry had not been to the French Riviera but he knew it existed because he'd seen it on the pictures at the Waterloo or the Rendezvous Cinemas in South Shore.

Instead, as the Old Man said, he should have heard the first whisperings of a storm.

Marthaann was a mite unhappy about Harry. She did not seem too sure of the propriety of having him on the holiday at all, but since he came with the package (as they would say today) she had to accept it or not go.

Aunt Clara would obviously not go anywhere without a Man. She had never gone anywhere without a Man in her entire life.

Men, always of a gentlemanly sort (an elastic description, said the Old Man), had danced attendance on her ever since she had pirouetted and sung on the Halls at seventeen years of age. Aunt Clara had had coquettish good looks, large dark eyes and boundless vitality. She still had the vitality.

Said the Old Man, mildly, 'To look at her makes me tired, sometimes.'

This was an exaggeration. The Old Man never, ever, seemed tired. 'When I'm tired, I go to bed,' he said. It was usually midnight. Bedtime for Aunt Clara was even later, since her nocturnal habits, a hangover from her stage days, still dominated her day.

'What will you do,' asked Marthaann, 'about going to bed in a private hotel?' She meant a genteel boarding-house.

'I'll go to bed when I usually do,' replied Aunt Clara.

'That might be all right in a theatrical boarding-house but not in a good-class place. They want lights out at eleven,' said Marthaann.

'It's a good place we're booked into,' replied Aunt Clara, finishing her third Guinness. 'It comes well recommended.'

Harry later said he felt a slight tingle of reservation at that remark but, as he also said, he'd had nowt to go on, so he said nothing. He was looking forward to his annual week's holiday, the only one he would get all year, apart from Easter, Whitsun and Christmas and they would be only the odd day off.

Harry had worked that way all his life but didn't resent it. Nobody did. Everybody worked a five-and-a-half-day week. On Harry's Saturday afternoon, his only free time, he took his station on the Kop at Blackpool Football Ground.

There, as the Old Man said, a total sea-change overtook him. 'From being a mild and affable fellow he turns into a raging demon,' reported the Old Man, who had on one occasion attended a match with Harry. 'It is safer not to stand next to him,' said the Old Man, 'since the fellow quarrels with everybody in sight, about anything and everything. The Players, the Referee, the State of the Game.'

It was all true. I'd been with Harry to the Kop. Once, like everybody else.

'A minor eccentricity,' said the Old Man, being careful not to go to a football match with Harry again. 'Forgivable in an otherwise excellent fellow.'

Thus it was arranged, the trip to the Island.

Marthaann tried to recruit me, in order, as she said, to make up the numbers. I pleaded family responsibilities, but she was not impressed.

'About time,' she sniffed, much offended.

That was the thing about Marthaann. She had a skin too few as far as people were concerned.

Onkel Frank put it another way. 'The woman,' he said, 'would rather have a row than have her breakfast.'

These were but storm warnings fluttering in the Blackpool Promenade breeze, a long way away from the Isle of Man.

Marthaann persisted. 'If you come, it'll mean we'll have a few days together. We don't get that very often these days, do we?'

I was always an easy touch for emotional blackmail from women, then as now. Besides, what she said was right. She had put the shellfish business first and her family second, but I guessed she wasn't very happy about that, although, as the Old Man said, wild horses would not have dragged such an admission from her.

'Percy got you all to come to Blackpool and leave me,' she asserted. 'I had to keep the business going, your father being what he is.'

'Yes, I know,' I said, 'but you're wrong about him wanting us

– Ted and me and Peg – here. He'd have been happier on his own.'

'He's always been happier on his own; that's the trouble with him.'

Marthaann looked embattled and hurt and her beautiful skin flushed red. Despite her expensive clothes and shoes and the gold rings on her fingers, she plainly felt wronged, and I said yes, I'd go, for a few days anyway, adding that I'd finished my novel.

'Will you get some money for it soon?' she asked, never far away from the practical nub of any problem.

'Without a doubt,' I said, confidently.

'You sound like your father,' she said.

'Well, I'll come if you like,' I said.

When I told the Old Man he yawned and stroked the warlike Smout stretched on his knee. 'A mistake,' he opined, 'but at your age you're entitled to make a few.'

'I don't see why. It's only a few days.'

'A few days,' he replied, 'can seem like a lifetime under certain circumstances.'

I said no more. There was no more to say.

Douglas was very quiet after Blackpool. Marthaann approved of that, as she considered Blackpool to be noisy and lower class, and she had the Methodist disapproval of licence in anything, particularly drink and sex. Not that she was alone in that. Everybody in the North of England paid lip-service to, basically, the teaching of John Wesley. The ones who didn't were the Lancashire Catholic Irish, who had come over to work in the cotton mills a generation or two before and were still regarded as incomers.

Marthaann's lineage was Presbyterian, but as the Old Man

said, 'Wesley got at them and made them even more puritanical than they were before.' He added, 'There's nothing puritanical about Marthaann, only she doesn't know it, and that is the trouble, you see?' I didn't, but now I do. Then he said, 'Marthaann has a lot of emotion she can't get rid of, so it all goes into the shops and what's left over goes into criticism of other people.'

By that he meant, amongst other things, himself. But then that had always been so, or anyway during their brief few years together, interrupted by the First War and, of course, his nomadic life on the Race-tracks, culminating in his moving to Blackpool when the Dog-track there was, as he said, a Gold Mine. Now, it was a lot less than that.

Still, as long as Marthaann was living on Tyneside and occupied full time with her shops, that was fine. Her short trip to Blackpool, in which all they had done was exchange wary courtesies, keeping well away from the explosive subjects of money, imagined emotional slights (on Marthaann's part) and unfinished business (Marthaann's habit of using his name to rent new shop premises), was on the whole peaceful. Or, more properly, seemed so.

The Old Man didn't know the half of it.

'I like Douglas,' said Marthaann, snapping her crocodile handbag shut on an unspecified but, to me, extremely desirable sum of money. 'It's got more class than Blackpool.' She gazed at the horse-drawn trams and the clean and quiet streets. Well, clean and quiet compared with Blackpool.

'I don't know that I could live here,' Marthaann added, settling down in her deck-chair, price sixpence for the whole day. 'It's a bit too out-of-the-way.'

Marthaann had never, ever, lived anywhere but Newcastle, then still a bustling industrial port. She had literally never worked anywhere but in her father's shops, apart from her short stint as wife to the Old Man. Marthaann was to herself a Geordie born and bred, but Scots on both sides, in actuality. Her remark surprised me.

'You aren't thinking of leaving Newcastle?'

Marthaann pursed her lips. 'I must admit, young fellow, that the shops are getting a bit too much for me. I've only got three now and it's hard work getting up in the morning at six o'clock to go to North Shields and buy stock, see it on to the train, and then work all day selling it.'

'I see,' I said, but I didn't; I was nonplussed. I couldn't imagine her not standing behind her marbled counters, facing a large crowd of customers with a smile that was absolutely genuine and never wore off, crying, 'With you in one moment, Sir,' to any customer who might look impatient.

'The woman,' the Old Man had said, 'lives for those fokkin prawns. She's Isaac Henderson in female form. It's as simple as that.'

'But you're not serious about it?' I asked her, uncertainly. 'I mean, the shops have been in the family for ever.'

Marthaann's extremely penetrating blue eyes bored into me. She was instantly in one of her hurt moods, which could soon boil over into real anger. '*You* don't want them. *Ted* doesn't want them. To tell you the truth, I'm thinking of selling them.'

I sat, staring at the Irish Sea lapping the sand, and tried to make sense of it. The truth was, it made no sense at all.

'Where would you go?' I asked, in some dread. There was always, as the Old Man had reported to Edith, who had been stung by some remark of Marthaann, the probability of 'words' when Marthaann was about. He had added, hastily, that she had not been like that when they had been together. Edith had, anyway, retorted and Marthaann had reported her to me as being very sharp. I wished no repetition of that. But Marthaann was replying. 'Well, to tell you the truth, young fellow, I'm thinking I *might* move to Blackpool. After all, all my family's there.'

'But,' I protested, 'you hate Blackpool.'

'So I do, in many ways. But I could live at Bispham, a mile or two away from all the crowds, or even at St Anne's.' Marthaann spoke with conviction, nodding her dark head; she was never to go grey, even in her eighties. She always spoke with conviction and power and usually loudly, which is why Onkel Frank avoided her whenever possible. Being half-deaf, he hated people who shouted, and usually rebuked them sternly. Not Marthaann, though. Nobody ever rebuked Marthaann.

Except the Old Man, when she had lived with him. Even now, she showed him the respect due a husband, by, as they used to say, holding her tongue. Well, she was still his wife, and to her that mattered.

Thinking of how he would react, I persisted. 'But if you moved to Blackpool, who would you have for friends?'

I realised, somewhat guiltily, I didn't really want her to move to Blackpool, and tried very hard not to be influenced by the Old Man's statement that 'Wherever Marthaann is, there soon follows a whole host of trouble. That has been my experience.'

Then Marthaann turned her head and spoke to a gentleman of a certain age (small, in a blazer, and balding of head) who had asked her the way to the Central Hotel. He had fixed her with an admiring eye. Marthaann was bonny and an armful, a big woman. Such women were admired then. Marthaann pointed out the way in a cursory fashion (she did not give suitors any quarter and only the very bold even approached her) and, much shaken, the bald man retreated and headed off gloomily along the promenade, in the opposite direction to the Central Hotel.

It occurred to me that no man, this side of her beloved father, the tycoon Isaac (sixteen stones of bone and muscle, as high in the Masonic Order as a man not of the Blood Royal could be), would really do for her. She would simply crush them underfoot, like the small bald man in the blazer.

Except for the Old Man. She had loved him, given her all to him, very young. Ever wayward and, when a young officer, a glamorous figure, he had briefly answered her needs. But, in the end, the Old Man's steely determination to live his own life was nothing she could, as they say in Lancashire, throle.

But Marthaann was talking on. 'Friends? Well, I have Clara. She's my sister-in-law, after all. She's not my sort, with her drinking and goings-on' – she meant Harry the sign-writer – 'but that's her business, not mine.' *Not much*, I thought. 'Also,' she said with emphasis, 'there's you and Ted in the town.'

'I don't know how long I'll be there,' I said, defensively. 'I suppose I'll go to London some time – I'll have to.'

'Well, you can't go until you've got enough money, can you? To buy a house and set up home down there? Shall I tell you what I think? I think, young fellow, all that's a pipe-dream.'

And her grip on the crocodile handbag seemed to me to stiffen. No hope there. I'm becoming just a little bit like the Old Man, I thought, not liking the notion at all. I said, 'Well, Ted's got his family, too. And Peggy's only in Blackpool at holiday-time or weekends.'

'I'm not sure I'm interested in seeing too much of Peggy. She's very odd since she turned Catholic and married Matty.'

'I don't think that's got anything to do with it.'

'Of course it has.'

Marthaann's word was law on matters religious. Again, I was reminded of her father. Once, when in drink, and feeling holy, Isaac had entered St Nicholas Cathedral in Newcastle, attired in his Sunday best (top hat, frock-coat, rolled umbrella on his arm), and had cried out, in a huge voice, 'Papists! Idolaters!'

And that, as the Old Man reported it, was only to the Anglicans.

'What happened to him?' I had asked.

'They threw him out, of course,' reported the Old Man, 'his hat and umbrella after him!'

That was long before people thought of Speaking In Tongues.

To Marthaann, such behaviour was acceptable in a man, if he was any sort of man. 'Further,' reported the Old Man, 'Marthaann expects everybody else to behave like that. Nonsense, of course, but there you are.'

I said to Marthaann, blinking in the sunshine on the Promenade at Douglas, 'Do you really want to live in Blackpool?'

'Yes, I think I do.' Marthaann spoke with defiance. 'Nobody need worry about me. I have money enough to see me through to the end. I won't want anything from anybody. If nobody wants me or nobody wants to talk to me or visit me, well, I'll just have to lump it. It's up to you and your brother and sister, after all I've done for you, young fellow.'

I was hard put to work out what that was, but I didn't feel much one way or the other. I was trying to work out how the Old Man would react to the news.

But first I had to talk to Aunt Clara.

I found her in the Boarding-house, chattering to the landlady about money and men, both topics near to her heart. I broke in to tell her I wasn't staying the full week but catching the boat home on Thursday as I had a producer at the BBC in Leeds to meet. That was not quite true but I felt that, as the Old Man said, enough was enough, of Clara and Marthaann. He had remarked that the two of them together would give a hippo the headache. Until now (it was only Monday), things had gone well enough between Clara and Marthaann. That was soon to change. But I didn't know that yet.

'Aunt Clara,' I said, 'what's all this about my mother wanting to live in Blackpool? Surely she isn't serious? She hates the place.'

Aunt Clara examined her face in the large gilt mirror over the fireplace in the sitting-room. 'I know that's what she has in mind. She's on her own in Newcastle and she's worked a lot of years at the shops. It's time she had a rest.'

'She never rests,' I said. 'And she'd be lost without her shops. They're her life.'

Aunt Clara applied a thick sludge of very red lipstick to her full lips. 'You don't want them. Ted and Peg don't want them. And she has a fair bit of money put past her.'

'Money?' I wondered, aloud. Aunt Clara now applied a thick layer of powder to her face. She always made-up as if going directly on stage, as she had been doing since she was seventeen.

'Of course, money. It's what makes the world go round, isn't it?'

'Yes, I suppose so.' I was touchy on the subject of money, not having any.

'You'd better learn that lesson, young fellow,' said Aunt Clara, breathing on her recently lacquered nails. 'And get your hair cut – you look like an out-of-work old Pro.'

By that she meant an actor, or, more probably (since she thought actors an even more penniless crowd), Music Hall Artistes. Sometimes *they* had money. Aunt Clara approved of money, whoever had it. So she approved of Marthaann. Simple as that.

I pressed her, none the less. 'Where will my mother live? She can't live with us. We haven't room.' Get your retaliation in first, I thought.

'She'll buy a little house. She's looked at one or two places. Didn't she tell you?'

'No, not exactly.'

'Well, I think by the end of the year you'll see her in Blackpool.' Aunt Clara jammed her bright-red tammy firmly on her black-blue-dyed hair and was ready for what the day would bring. 'So you'll have to get used to the idea, won't you?'

I said, 'I suppose you'll be thinking of going to whist drives and so on with her? If she comes to Blackpool?'

'Well,' said Aunt Clara, with a total disregard for the truth, 'we've always got on, Marthaann and me, so why not? She's be company – more than I can say of Harry. He's asleep on his bed upstairs and he'd only been up two hours.'

I said, 'I'll wake him up for you.'

Said Aunt Clara, always impatient of any delay, 'He'll be an hour pulling himself round. You go and wake him and tell him I'll see him on the Promenade, usual place, in an hour.'

And with that she flounced out in a mist of strong, cheap perfume. She seemed in a hurry to get to Marthaann. They were, of course, sisters-in-law, and had one or two things in common, including an unnerving ability to pick the wrong men.

Harry was heavily asleep on his single bed in Room 12. He was fully clothed and still wore his wire spectacles. It occurred to me he had come on holiday for a sleep, being deprived of it for most weeks of the year. People worked very long hours then. Harry probably put in fifty-five hours a week, with no paid overtime. He did not grumble. Nobody did. The Depression was only a decade away.

He wakened as I put my hand on his arm.

'W-what's to do?'

'Tickle's gone to meet Marthaann. They'll see you in an hour on the Prom. Usual place.'

'Oh, right.' Harry took off his glasses, breathed on them and polished them on his necktie.

'You're on your own here?' I said, without thinking.

'I am that,' sighed Harry, putting his spectacles back on his reddened, fruity nose. 'Tickle's in with Marthaann. I'm a spare prick at a w-wedding, tha knows.'

'Ah,' I said.

'Mind, this way I can have as much bevvy as I want and no complaints.' I looked uncomprehending, so he added, courteously, 'I like me beer, as you know, but it gives me the wind. Both ends.'

'Ah,' I said again.

I looked around the room. It contained only the bed and a tiny dresser and, of course, a magnificent po under the bed. Sounds of wind and waves came softly through the window, mixed with the cries of children. Harry, I thought, might as well have stopped in Blackpool.

'Makes a bit of a change, Douglas,' he said, lighting a Craven A.

'It does,' I said. 'No doubt of that.'

Harry drew on the cigarette and seemed anxious to confide. 'Tickle told you Marthaann's thinking of coming to Blackpool?'

'Yes,' I said. 'Will anything come of it?'

'B-buggered if I know.' Harry shook his head. 'You can never tell with the women, can you?'

'No,' I said. I had been married only a couple of years (being now twenty-four) but I knew that for a truth.

Said Harry, 'I'm none bothered what Marthaann does or doesn't do, but if she comes it'll change things a bit, it will that.'

I waited. There was more.

'Dostasee?' said Harry. 'If Marthaann comes she'll know

nobody but Tickle and they'll be out together a lot.' He drew deeply on the Craven A. 'It takes thinking on, does that.'

'It does,' I said. It did.

Harry was paying me a big compliment, confiding in me like this. It meant he was regarding me as grown-up, not a felly-lad any more. Well, I was grown up, but perhaps not as grown-up as I thought I was.

'Dostasee?' repeated Harry. 'Percy's all right – he's none bothered if I go into the flat and sit and have a cuppa tea with Tickle, any hour of the day or night. Percy's very easy that way. But wi' Marthaann around, well, it could be very, very different.' Harry drew particularly deeply on his Craven A. 'P-put it that way,' he said.

I knew it was my turn to say something helpful, but I couldn't think of anything but the truth, which was: 'The Old Man won't want Marthaann in Blackpool at all, never mind around the flat, will he? I mean, he went to Blackpool fifteen years ago to put a few miles between them both.'

Harry appeared to find this remark comforting. 'I-I think tha has a chance wi' yon writing that you do,' he said. 'It doesn't seem to have harmed thy brain at all.'

I nodded, aware of the compliment.

'The fact is,' said Harry, struggling to the edge of the bed and putting his misshapen, wounded foot into his surgical boot, 'if Marthaann comes to Blackpool, it's domino wi' Tickle and me.' He paused. 'I'm relying on Percy to nip it in the bud.' He laced up the awful boot. 'P-put it that way,' he said.

As we went downstairs to join Marthaann and Aunt Clara on the Prom, I noticed some framed theatrical playbills on the wall of the boarding-house.

I said, 'Does Tickle know these people?'

'I don't know,' said Harry. 'I think she's stayed here before the War with Harold the Comic, when she was on the Halls.'

'Are there any Pros in the place?'

Harry shook his head. 'You'd hear 'em if any Pros were in. You know what they're like. Stay up till all hours talking and boozing. Tickle's like that.' His voice held a note of regret. 'I–I sometimes wonder if she ever goes to bed.'

I said nothing to that, but I wondered.

On the Prom we found Aunt Clara, whom Marthaann never called Tickle, considering it vulgar. She actually considered Aunt Clara vulgar in all sorts of ways, had said so times without number, as they used to say, yet now she was linked arm in arm with her sister-in-law, calling her Clarrie and warily buying a drink or two with silver from the formidable crocodile bag.

Harry and I walked behind them into the various bars and drank strong beers. Harry refused to buy me shandy, which I preferred, considering it 'nobbut a lad's drink'. Marthaann and Clara sipped Gin-and-Its and crème-de-menthe and got tiddly and laughed immoderately at the mildly obscene comics in the Pier Shows, as Harry and I sat in the row behind, Harry gloomily counting his change.

'At this rate I shall be coppering-up before the week's out,' he whispered to me, in a beer-breath. 'I didn't reckon on paying for Marthaann as well.'

I made clucking noises to show sympathy, causing Marthaann to turn and hush me up. Harry took more and more drink the following two nights, plunged into gloom at the sight of Marthaann and Aunt Clara as they strode out in front of us to the best seats on the sightseeing trams and the best seats on the Prom and, ominously, the best seats in the theatres and Music Halls, paid for by Harry.

'It's costing me Pounds Ten, is this, lad,' Harry confessed to me as, somewhat emotionally, he bade me farewell at the ferry-boat pier. 'I shall be drawing out me life savings when I geet home.'

Harry was at Douglas, an hour's sail and another hour's train ride from Blackpool, but he spoke like the Outcast of the Islands.

Said Marthaann warningly, as I got on the boat, 'I've made up my mind, young fellow. You'll be seeing a lot more of me in the future.'

'Yes,' I said. 'I imagine so.'

'Well, you might show a little bit of enthusiasm!'

I kissed her cheek and said, 'I do. Of course I do.'

She didn't believe me, saying only, 'You take after your father a lot, you know.' From her point of view there was little more in the way of criticism to be offered.

I waved to the three of them from the deck, affected by the parting moment. Well, they were still the family and I had been away for four years and hardly ever thought of any of them during that time. I was being selfish, wishing nothing to change. Life changes, all the time, I told myself.

It didn't help.

The Old Man listened with patience to all I had to say. We were on the tramcar on our way to play a Snooker match (or, rather, the Old Man was) at the Talbot Arms on Talbot Road. Onkel Frank joined us, carrying his billiard-cue in a tin case. As he sat down with us on the upstairs of the rattling tram, the Old Man said, 'Marthaann is On the Ball.'

'What?' said Onkel Frank, deaf as ever.

'What I said was,' repeated the Old Man, furious as always at Onkel Frank's inability to hear him, 'that Marthaann is thinking of coming to Blackpool to live. What I am saying is that she is On the Ball.'

Onkel Frank thought about this for a full minute. 'She can be Ten Thousand Bloody Balls,' he said and got off the tram.

'Why did he do that?' I asked the Old Man.

'Because every time he sees Marthaann he has a row with her. She's a very argumentative woman, as you know.'

'Well, I think she has plenty to argue about with you and Onkel Frank. It seems to me you both took advantage of her when she was a young wife – you in your usual way and Onkel Frank living in the place as a lodger.'

The Old Man was silent a long moment. Oh God, I thought, now I'm defending her. 'This is our stop,' said the Old Man.

I waited for him to comment on my remarks, but he didn't. That was one thing about the Old Man. He always wrong-footed you.

He left his single comment on the subject until the end of the evening, after he had, as he put it, 'disposed of' his opponent and Onkel Frank had, through over-confidence and foolish and risky shots, lost.

'The thing is,' said the Old Man, 'Tickle and Marthaann are alone on the Isle of Man with plenty of time to get used to each other. Or not.'

'What?' I said, but he had bounded on to the last homeward tram with alacrity. Frank, too. They were a damn sight quicker and fitter than I was, I thought, and I was only half their age.

Of course, I had not led their lives.

Harry it was who told us the tale of woe on his return from the Isle of Man. We were sitting in the Billiard-room of the Grand Hotel when Harry came in, burnt bright red and peeling and smoking his inevitable cigarette. He sat down and ordered drinks all round, presenting Onkel Frank with a large whisky and myself with a pint of brackish mild I didn't want.

'To what do we owe this, Harry?' asked the Old Man, mildly. 'We didn't expected you until tomorrow. Where's Tickle?'

'S-she's in the flat,' said Harry. It occurred to me he had been drinking all day. 'The bar was open on the boat for them as had strong stomachs. I thought I'd tell you what went on,' he added.

'What?' asked Onkel Frank, impatiently.

'Well,' said Harry, indicating me, 'it went on as this young fella here will have told you, me paying for everything and the two of them laughing, and carrying-on, as you say, Percy, and you have it right when you say together they'd give a hippo the headache.' Harry paused. 'Dostasee, I got right sick of it, I tell yer. A-anyroad, the thing was, a troupe of Pros from the Pier Show came to stop in the Boarding-house and a right boozy lot they was. Tickle knew one of them and she got to talking and yattering away with them until all hours of the mornin' and goin' to see their show an' that, an' going backstage afterwards, and she got right chummy with them all.' Harry paused again, deeply offended. 'S-specially the manager – he were a buggeroo, but never mind.' He drew on his Craven A. 'Marthaann's nose got put well out of joint. She never went anywhere with Tickle without the Pros being there, one or other of them, and then . . .' Harry paused, savouring the words '. . . Marthaann took umbrage.'

'Umbrage?' enquired Onkel Frank.

'Umbrage,' said Harry. 'They had a big row day before yesterday and they haven't spoken since. I-I tell yer, I'll be glad to get back to me work. P-put it that way.'

'The woman is easily offended,' said the Old Man, with, to my astonishment, a tender note in his voice. 'But when she lived with me she was the best wife a man ever had, you know.'

I stared at him. Onkel Frank stared at him. Harry stared at him.

'Not now,' said the Old Man, hastily. 'I'm speaking of long ago.'

'Longer than that,' said Onkel Frank.

'Where is she now, Marthaann?' I asked.

'She's got the train to Newcastle.' Harry consulted his steel pocket watch. 'It goes in ten minutes.'

I took a taxi but I was only in time to wave to Marthaann from the platform.

Marthaann didn't wave back so I didn't know if she was still umbrage-taken or just hadn't seen me.

The Vent and the Cockerel

The Old Man was interested to hear Mo Beck's proposal, since it involved an animal. Anything involving an animal had his instant attention and sympathy, whereas a human being's behaviour, even that of his own family, was only of distant, even academic, interest to him.

'You are telling me,' he said to Mo, glass of whisky-and-water in hand, sitting in the Billiard-room of the Grand Hotel, which virtually served as his office and place of business, 'you are telling me that this Bird can talk and sing?'

'That's what we'll tell the Punters, Percy.'

'You have to back it up with more proof than that,' said the Old Man, 'if you are going to put up a notice saying, "Come In! See the All Singing All Talking Bird! Admission One Shilling!" ' The Old Man paused. 'One thing is beyond dispute. The Bird must be able to talk. And sing!'

'It can do both. As well as you or me.'

'Is it a parrot, then?' the Old Man asked, curious.

Mo Beck shook his head.

'Is it a parakeet or a budgie?'

'Neither one.'

The Old Man pondered, intrigued. 'Is it a macaw? I've heard of macaws that are better imitators than parrots.'

'It isn't a macaw, Percy.'

'Then what is it?'

Mo sipped his gill of brackish mild. 'I can't tell you that. All I can say is, I've got a stall booked on the Golden Mile for Easter.' Mo put a finger along his nose, which was prominent. 'Mum's the word as to how I got it. If it does well over the Easter weekend, then it's mine for the Season.'

'Easter is only three weeks away,' the Old Man reminded him.

'I know that,' said Mo. 'That's why I'm asking you to invest. I need a hundred quid, in addition to what I have in hand.'

The Old Man hadn't got a hundred pounds but he behaved as if he had. He always behaved as if he had a hundred pounds. A hundred then was a thousand now.

'I can't see why you need all this money for a Talking Bird,' said the Old Man, plainly intrigued. 'Either it talks or it doesn't. Does somebody else own it, not yourself?' The Old Man, as ever, had divination.

'Something like that.' Mo gazed into his beer, plainly reluctant to say anything more.

The Old Man then said, 'I might go to fifty, if I knew a bit more.' He hadn't the fifty, either.

Mo thought about that for a moment. 'I'll tell you what, Percy. I'll open the show myself on Good Friday. Come to the show and if you want to put in then, you can. I'll keep it all open for you but it has to be a hundred and it has to be by midnight on Good Friday or all bets are off.'

The Old Man extended a brief Masonic handshake but it was wasted on Mo. He was a member of no club, but of a very rich Jewish family, big in furs in Manchester, who had cut him off without a shilling when he married a shiksa. In those days that was a very big thing to do.

Mo, as a boy (he was the same age as I was but looked ten years older and was already losing his hair), had been a teenage sexual wonder, the envy of every other boy in South Shore. For a very good and simple reason. He had sex with the Mill-girls.

No other boy still wearing a school cap had been willing (in living memory) to take on these hoydens: turbanned, lipsticked and scornful girls from Wigan, Bolton, Blackburn, Colne, Burnley and all the industrial towns of the North. These creatures came in their droves to Blackpool once a year for one week's holiday. Seven Days of Heaven, as they used to say.

The whole town (say, Bolton) went to Blackpool at Wakes Week, having first prudently tucked a pound note under the clock on the mantelpiece to see them through the following week, when, penniless and hung over, they returned home on the Saturday night, with fifty-one weeks at the Mill looming ahead of them, before they came to Blackpool again.

They thought Blackpool was Paradise. After Wigan or Nelson, it was.

In Paradise you do as you want.

To Mo Beck that represented, as he put it to me, stuffing his school cap in his pocket, Corn In Egypt, sexually speaking.

'You aren't really going with those girls, are you, Mo?' I had asked him, scandalised. We all despised the trippers, regarding them as people to be laughed at, rooked, robbed and fooled. We hated their drunkenness and their habit of pissing in dark alleys behind the boarding-houses. To us, they were trouble. We couldn't get on the trains or buses for them. We couldn't get a drink in the pubs or bars because they crowded out such places. Of course, we kept away from their favourite haunts, the Tower Bar, and the Winter Gardens and Yates's Wine Lodge, which were always full. We went to quiet pubs on the outskirts of the town or somewhere like the Grand Billiard-room where, if a tripper did come in, he was not served in a hurry and ignored until he went out, to the Public Bar where he belonged.

The trippers were as common as clarts.

Of course, most people in Blackpool got their living from them. They had to put up with the trippers. Those of us who didn't (Jack, Norman, Peter and myself) found them, as Jack said, a pain in the arse.

Not so Mo Beck, at fifteen years of age. Looking with a lingering and frankly sexual eye at the long line of Mill-girls on the Prom wearing 'Kiss Me Quick' hats and singing 'It Ain't Gonna Rain No More', Mo said, 'They're on offer – anybody can see that. And they don't go with fellas from their home town because that can get them a Bad Name back home and spoil their marriage chances.'

I had looked at Mo with new respect. How did he know things like that?

'Just the same, they're always together,' I said. 'They stay at the same boarding-house, they eat the same meals, they go dancing at the Tower or the Winter Gardens together.'

'There you have it,' said Mo.

'What?'

'They *go* dancing together. But they don't *dance* together, do they?'

'Well, no. I suppose not.'

'You suppose right,' said Mo, running a broken-toothed comb through his wiry black hair. He never wore a school blazer and now I knew why. He took off his school tie and substituted a very loud red Tootal number in its place. 'In the right light I can pass for eighteen.'

'Seventeen,' I had said.

'That'll do. The ones I'm after are younger than that.' He added, 'But I've had older ones. I had a married one last week who was twenty-seven.'

I didn't believe him. 'Where?'

'Under the Central Pier, where else?'

'But it's all sand under there.'

'Nice and soft, is sand. As good as a bed.'

My curiosity had got the better of my disdain. 'Are many people there at night?'

'Dozens.' He lit a Player's and puffed it nonchalantly. 'Most of the population of Lancashire are conceived under the Central Pier. Don't you know *anything*?'

Now, this selfsame Mo, only ten years older but married with two kids and worried about money, and losing his hair, was negotiating about fifty pounds with the Old Man.

Truth to tell, I was sorry to see the change in Mo. He had married the shiksa and much good it had done him. He was now devoting his time and energy to getting money instead of getting sex. It seemed a poor swap.

He got to his feet. 'See you at Easter, Percy. Good Friday night?'

'As ever was,' said the Old Man.

Mo nodded to me and went out.

'An All-talking, All-singing Bird? It's a lot of rubbish, isn't it?' I asked.

'I don't know,' said the Old Man. 'We must wait and see.'

'Besides,' I said, 'you haven't got the hundred pounds.'

The Old Man ignored that, as he ignored all facts that did not suit his mood of the moment. 'Plenty of time before Easter,' he said.

There were two meetings at the Dogs on Good Friday, one in the afternoon, another in the evening. The Old Man, following Onkel Frank's tips for once, won twenty-five pounds in the afternoon and, thus armed, he went along, with me in tow, to see the Talking Bird.

We filed into the marquee on the nod (that is, we did not pay) and were gratified to find the tent full of trippers. The sign on the marquee had invited us to 'See the Amazing All Singing All Talking Bird!' We had arrived in time to see Mo Beck go through his pitch.

'We are not here today and gone tomorrow,' he told the becapped punters and their womenfolk. 'We're here today and gone tonight, if we can get the money!'

The punters did not laugh but regarded him stoically. Their white nylon shirts (their only concession to the fact that they were at the seaside) were folded outside the collars of their best Sunday suits. Their hands and their money remained in their pockets. They had worked hard for it and were wary.

Said Mo – who was surprisingly attired in a light-grey double-breasted suit (to the eye of the *cognoscenti*, from Burton the Tailor) and who wore a white shirt with a red tie – 'Friends, the Good Book tells us about the fowls of the air; it tells us that the fowls are many and different, but nothing in the Good Book will prepare you for what you will be seeing if you step up and pay your shilling to see the Wonder of the Orient, the Fowl that has been presented before Three Crowned Heads of Europe!'

'There aren't any Crowned Heads of Europe left,' I said to the Old Man, but he was watching Mo with great interest, no doubt working out how Mo would react when he discovered that only twenty-five of the promised hundred pounds would be forthcoming.

Mo, meantime, was whetting the Punters' appetites. 'This Bird,' he yelled at the silent trippers, 'is the Eighth Wonder of the World! You've heard of the Cat with Nine Lives that lived six months trapped in a sewer? You've heard of the Elephant that trekked five hundred miles to its grave in Equatorial Africa! You've heard of the Tigun, the cross between a lion and a tiger, a thing that all the Professors and Scientists said could never be done!'

The trippers gazed at him unblinkingly.

'Now,' yelled Mo, louder than ever, 'you will *see* a Bird that is able to talk to you in English! And, what is more, this Bird will Sing!'

'Rubbish!' called a drunk man in a Big Cap standing at the front, adding, 'It's a parrot, i'n't it, be fair?'

'No, sir,' said Mo loftily. 'It's not a parrot or a macaw or a budgerigar or any other kind of mimic bird. It is something very different, and the price is not half a crown, not two bob, not eighteen-pence but *One Shilling*! Go in now, Ladies and Gents. The show is about to commence, in one minute only. Obtain your seat now! The young lady will give you your ticket. Thank you very much, Ladies and Gents!'

The tripper with the Big Cap went in first. It occurred to me he was a plant. There was a long, long moment when it seemed nobody else was going to go in, then we did, on a sudden desperate gesture from Mo. The girl taking the tickets was local, faintly familiar to me, and for some reason dressed in a cowboy outfit. We went inside the marquee. The girl smiled and winked at Mo and I realised that nothing had really changed in Mo's life.

There was always a place for a pretty young woman, under the Central Pier or here, on the Golden Mile.

We sat in the back row of folding chairs that filled the tent.

It probably held sixty people, so there was a gross profit of three pounds every session. There could be any number of sessions per day – twenty, thirty, fifty – depending on the weather, the crowds, and the stamina of the Barker: in this case, Mo.

Now, Mo stood proudly at the back, his arm negligently around the slim waist of the cowgirl.

'Very good turnout, Mo,' observed the Old Man.

'Been like this all day,' said Mo.

The trippers coughed and hummed and hawed and lit cigarettes, waiting for the All Talking All Singing Bird to appear.

But first, Mo sprang forward and vaulted on to the stage. He turned to address his audience. 'Ladies and Gents, you see behind me a Box. In that Box is a Surprise!'

The cowgirl, now at side-stage, played a roll on the drums. Obviously she was not purely ornamental.

Mo held out his arm, stiff as an iron bar.

A lad of sixteen with ginger hair opened the box, which was very large, and stepped hastily back.

Again the cowgirl rolled the drums. Then came the surprise.

A huge Anaconda whipped out of the Box, sprang through the air and coiled itself around Mo's outstretched arm.

Mo remained absolutely still.

The trippers did not.

Uttering a collective 'Nay' they shrank back in their seats. One or two at the back, near us, left the tent in a hurry. Mo called after them, 'It's all right, Ladies and Gents, he's been fed! This is Arnold the Anaconda and he lives on live white mice and a rabbit every Sunday. He doesn't eat human beings. He only squeezes them to death if they annoy him! Don't you, Arnold?'

Mo then stroked the Anaconda's head and the ginger lad

stepped forward, coiled the snake like a piece of rope and put him, adroitly, back in his box.

The trippers let out a collective and relieved sigh.

'Nay!' they said to each other.

'That's some snake,' said the Old Man.

'Where's Singing Bird?' asked the little man in the Big Cap.

Mo ignored that, and held up his hand. 'Please allow me to introduce the Eighth Wonder of the World, the Singing Bird, and his Master!'

The cowgirl gave us a blast of music on a turntable and from the side walked a dark, seedy-looking man in a dusty, ancient evening suit. He was about fifty years old and needed a shave. On his arm rested a white chicken.

'Nay, it's nobbut a cockerel,' said the little man in the Big Cap, in total disgust.

'Not only is it a Cockerel,' shouted Mo, 'it's an All Talking and All Singing Cockerel!'

'I don't believe it,' shouted the little man in the Big Cap.

'Then let us demonstrate!' cried Mo. 'Ladies and Gents, The Great Marco!'

The dark and greasy man, needing a shave, bowed.

Mo stepped down, the lights, operated by the cowgirl, dimmed, and a single spot played on the Great Marco and the Cockerel.

Said the Great Marco to the Cockerel, in a hoarse and whisky-soaked voice, 'Well, say hello to all the nice people who've come to see you this afternoon. They've come in here to see you rather than go on the Dodgems or up the Tower. What do you say about that?'

'Fook 'em,' said the Cockerel.

'That's no way to behave,' said the Great Marco. 'These Good

People are on their holidays and they've paid good money to see you. Be Nice, say Hello.'

'Sod 'em,' said the Cockerel.

'These good people,' said the Great Marco, 'think very highly of you or they wouldn't be here. They think you're a very talented bird.'

'Balls to 'em,' said the Cockerel.

'They've paid a shilling each to hear you sing,' said the Great Marco. 'So sing for the Nice People!'

The cowgirl changed a record on the player and the loud music filled the tent. The Great Marco coughed theatrically. There was absolute silence. The Cockerel then sang in a whisky-soaked voice.

> 'Little Sir Echo, How Do You Do?
> Hello, Hello
> Little Sir Echo, I'm Very Blue
> Hello, Hello . . .

The Great Marco motioned for the trippers to join in. They didn't.

The Cockerel sang on:

> 'Hello, Hello
> Won't you come over and Play?
> You're a Nice Little Fellow
> I know by your Voice
> But you're always so Far Away!'

The Cockerel sang the verse again and the trippers, at Mo's urging, finally joined in the chorus and the Great Marco bowed, the Cockerel still clamped to his arm, and the show was suddenly over.

'Thank you very much, Ladies and Gents,' called Mo. 'Thank you for your Patronage!'

The trippers filed out, dazed but not feeling particularly robbed, as far as I could see. After all, they had been frightened half to death by the Anaconda and amazed by the Cockerel and now they were outside, blinking in the spring sunshine of the Golden Mile, only a shilling a head worse off.

'Total time,' said the Old Man, 'five minutes.'

'Not bad,' I said, 'but it's a trick. That isn't an All Talking All Singing Bird. That's an ordinary cockerel. The Vent is an old hack from the Music Hall and it's all a fraud.'

'Nobody has asked for their money back,' said the Old Man.

'They should!'

'No,' added the Old Man. 'At home, in Burnley or Bolton, they won't part with a shilling to save their lives. Here, on holiday, they expect to be robbed. They'd stand for the Three Card Trick.'

The Three Card Trick, to wideheads like the Old Man, is the most barefaced robbery in the book. Yet even today, in Oxford Street, punters bet on it, to the flyman's cry of 'All Together Now, One Two Three, Where Oh Where Can The Little Lady Be?'

To stand for the Three Card Trick, in the Old Man's book, was to be worse than mad.

Mo left the cowgirl after a friendly pat on the rump and came towards us, lighting a cigarette from a flash new lighter. A conspicuous flash never did any harm with the women, observed the Old Man, and of course he was right, as ever.

'Well, Percy, are you In?' asked Mo.

There was a hint of impatience in his voice. I understood that. He was trying to pin the Old Man down. It wasn't easy.

Mo perhaps didn't any longer feel he needed the Old Man's contribution, given the success he had witnessed. I hoped so. The Old Man never had any luck in these sort of scams. Had Mo known it, the best thing he could do was forget the Old Man.

Of course, he didn't know that.

'You're in for a hundred, yes?' he asked.

'Not exactly a hundred,' said the Old Man, his eye on the box containing the Anaconda. 'Is that snake properly looked after?'

'Of course it is,' replied Mo. 'The Ginger Lad's in charge of it. It travels all over the country, does that snake. The Vent has a longer act when he does the clubs. He does a lot more with the snake in his full act.'

'Aren't you scared?' I asked.

Mo shook his head. 'He's as good as gold, is that snake. The thing is, he mustn't get hungry. He gets edgy on Friday and Saturdays because he's hungry, like. He's looking forward to his rabbit on a Sunday.'

The Old Man said, 'I didn't expect the Ventriloquist.'

'Nor did the punters,' said Mo. 'But nobody objected, did they?'

We shook our heads.

'It's a good con,' said Mo.

The Old Man agreed that it was, adding, 'The thing is, I'm in for the hundred. Here's twenty-five on account; the other seventy-five before you open again at Whitsun.'

Whitsun was six weeks off.

Mo looked dissatisfied but the five flimsies were in his hand by now. The Old Man had made sure of that. Nobody, especially Mo Beck, likes to hand money back.

'All right, Percy, I trust you.'

Famous last words.

And that is how we left it.

Now, all the Old Man had to do was raise the Seventy-five Pounds, with which Mo would pay his summer rent, in advance, for the 'Concession'.

I asked the Old Man how much it would be.

'Probably Five Hundred Pounds for the Season.'

'As much as that?'

'Of course. That's why Mo needs every penny he can get.'

'What are you on?'

The Old Man was evasive, as ever. 'I should do all right, all things considered, if Mo does well at Whitsun and is in profit by the end of June.'

'But first you have to find Seventy-five Pounds?'

'There is that, of course.'

A week before Whitsun, the Old Man still didn't have the Seventy-five.

But an odd thing happened, as, in the life of the Old Man, odd things were inclined to do.

The Warrant Officer in the Air Force Headquarters went off duty, sick. The Old Man inherited his Betting Book – that is, the right to collect bets in the Headquarters Offices. He only had it a week but it was enough to get him the Seventy-five Pounds, because the RAF Officers and men were terrible pickers of horses and every favourite that week went down the Swanee, as they used to say. So the Old Man now had the money to go into partnership with Mo Beck.

It was a miracle, if you believe in that sort of thing. But, as he said wonderingly, it had been a hell of a good week for the Book.

That should have taught him a lesson, of course – like the Book always wins. But, of course it didn't. He gave Mo Beck the Seventy-five Pounds.

So, there we were on Whitsun Saturday, waiting for a repeat of Good Friday, and to all extents and purposes it was just that.

The trippers were the same.

Mo's pitch to them was the same.

The cowgirl was the same, only prettier, owing no doubt to Mo's sexual attentions.

The Anaconda came out of the Box exactly as before.

The trippers called 'Nay' in shock, as before.

The Anaconda went back in the box, put in adroitly by the Ginger Lad.

The Great Marco appeared with the Cockerel and Mo introduced him as The Great Marco.

'Tell the People how much you love them,' said the Great Marco to the Cockerel. 'They're on their holidays – give them a nice word of welcome!'

'Fook 'em,' said the Cockerel.

'These Good People have come a long way to see you,' said the Great Marco. 'The least you can do is be polite. Now, try again!'

'Balls to 'em,' said the Cockerel.

Then, suddenly, the Great Marco clutched at his side as if in pain. It occurred to me he was ill. He put the Cockerel on the floor.

'Ladies and Gents,' said Mo swiftly, moving towards the podium. 'I fear that the Great Marco has taken sick.'

The Great Marco staggered. He wasn't ill. He was drunk.

The punters waited.

The Cockerel stood still, on the floor.

The Great Marco swayed, hiccupped, but regained his composure.

Too late.

A large wandering black Tom Cat appeared from the wings, took in the scene in one glance and attacked the Cockerel. The Cockerel flew up in the air, losing some feathers in the process.

The Great Marco, suddenly revitalised, swiftly kicked the Tom Cat into the wings. He picked up the Cockerel and put it on his arm, unsteadily, but obviously in command. We sighed in relief.

The Great Marco said in a slurring voice to the Cockerel, 'As I was saying before I was so rudely interrupted, these Nice People have come on their holidays and they have taken time out to see you – so be nice and say how pleased you are to see them!'

There was a long pause, as the Great Marco drew breath.

Then the Cockerel bit deeply into his arm.

The blood rose in a fountain.

The Great Marco stood alone on the stage a long moment, then he collapsed, slowly, in a heap on the floor.

The blood still flowed in a spray of red.

The Cockerel walked about the stage.

The punters ran out of the tent in alarm.

The cowgirl telephoned for an ambulance. The Great Marco went to Victoria Hospital but refused to come back to the show. Not only that, Mo reported sorrowfully the next week, he demanded payment for injuries received while in Mo's employ and was threatening court action.

'Will you pay him?'

'I've had to,' said Mo.

We didn't know if he was telling the truth. I felt he was.

'About my Seventy-five . . .' said the Old Man.

Mo raised his hands. 'Had to use it to pay him off, Percy.'

The Old Man sighed and sipped his whisky and said no more, except, 'What happened to the Cockerel?'

'Had it for Sunday dinner,' said Mo.

A Day Out with Joe Locke

'I paid five quid for these bananas,' said Josef Locke, the famous Irish tenor. He held up a hand of green Fyffes. 'Was I done?'

'Of course you were,' said his wife good-naturedly. 'It was after one o'clock when you got home! God knows where you bought them!'

Since it was now eleven-thirty the following morning and Joe was still in his pyjamas and dressing-gown, having just risen from his bed, the remark was really of a general, rather than a specific, kind. Joe took it in good part, as they used to say, by ignoring it.

'Sure, I was done. No doubt about it.' He inspected the bananas again as he descended the stairs. 'I may have had a wee drink taken when I bought these fellas, for sure I don't remember anything about them except they were five pounds, and since that works out at ten bob a banana any old eejit can work out that's too much, so it is!'

Joe, although he had not yet greeted me, was putting on his Irish act for me – for sure wasn't I going to write him up in the newspapers?

''Morning, Joe,' I said, as he came downstairs into the hall. Joe was a very large man but he bore his bulk lightly, as athletes and singers usually do. He had been in the Palestine Police and the Ulster Constabulary in his time, an unusual training for a tenor. He quite simply had a magnificent voice, especially in the highest and lowest registers, and had absolutely no idea how good he was. Joe should have been at Covent Garden but he was quite happy to be at the Winter Gardens in Blackpool, where he was said to earn a Thousand Pounds a week. If he was, he made a decent fist of spending it, for Joe loved life, not art. Art started when he began to sing, at which time, if you had any ear at all, the hairs on the back of your neck stood up.

''Morning, young fella. Come away in,' said Joe, gesturing I should follow him along the hall of his palatial house on Blackpool's North Shore. It was surrounded by large boarding-houses but he didn't mind that. He probably didn't notice. Shaving with a newfangled electric razor while he walked ahead into the drawing-room (expensive, silk-covered suites and heavy-shaded lamps), he talked cheerfully, as if on cue.

Joe had obviously done many interviews with journalists before. The trouble was, I wasn't a journalist, not really. I had to fill a column about Radio in the *Gazette* and I had looked at the other journos doing the same thing in the Nationals and discovered that all they wrote about were programmes that had already been broadcast. Since those programmes were rarely repeated, I couldn't see what the notices were for. Then I realised that the feature editors were following the example of 'Mr Precedent' (who, as the Old Man said, was always present at any committee meeting, and always the most Important Person there) and were 'reviewing' the BBC's output of radio plays as if they were *stage* plays and had a continuing life.

I told Sir Harold, my editor, that I didn't propose to do that, and would instead *forecast* what programmes would be like, as best I could. That way, the readers would at least be interested and might even listen in. Sir Harold nodded approvingly and said, idly, 'Never a bad idea to lead with something personal. About some Actor or Personality?'

I had thus landed myself with beginning my column with an interview, and I had not the slightest idea how to do that, but I soon learned two things: never make notes, for the subject stops talking. Never ask the subject how much money he earns.

Professional journos had already all asked me that question about my radio plays and my novel (still in writing) and when I replied 'Bugger all!' they looked satisfied and made no mark in their dog-earned notebooks. I decided it was a self-lacerating question and never did answer it, not even after suffering, many years later, the immortal headline WRITER DENIES EARNING TWENTY THOUSAND A YEAR!

Joe Locke was certainly earning a great deal more than that, even then. The day was yet to come, however, when a singer calling himself Jose*ph* Locke was tracked down by the Inland Revenue and presented with Joe's Income Tax bill. The man denied that he was *that* Josef Locke and readily gave as proof Joe Locke's telephone number in the Irish Republic, which had no machinery for returning people who owed tax into the hands of the British Inland Revenue. Joe answered the telephone himself.

'Is that Josef Locke the singer?' asked the Inland Revenue Man.

'It is so,' replied Joe, safe in the Republic.

'We have a man here in Bolton,' said the Inland Revenue Man, 'who says he's not the Josef Locke who owes us a very great deal of money. Is that *you*?'

'It is so,' said Joe, again.

Said the deflated Inland Revenue Man, 'Have you anything to say to me regarding the very large sum you owe to the British Inland Revenue?'

'Yes, I have,' said Joe. 'Since yon fella's using my name and singing and being paid for it, would he like to pay my tax for me?'

The Inland Revenue Man put down the telephone, sadly.

Of course, that hadn't happened yet.

Joe, his shave completed, downed a large cup of black coffee and changed into a clean shirt and trousers as he did so. He slipped on a jacket.

'Where's me shoes?' he asked.

Said his wife, 'Wherever you took them off last night.'

'Jasus,' said Joe, 'I wonder where that was.' His tone was one of earnest enquiry.

'They're under your nose,' said his wife.

'Ah, so,' said Joe, and slipped his feet into a pair of newly cleaned and very expensive black shoes. He consulted his equally expensive gold watch. 'The car should be here any minute.'

'Car?' I said. 'I didn't know you were going out or I'd have come another time.'

'Not at all!' Joe took me by the elbow and, avoiding his wife's stern eye, bustled me out of the room, through the hall, along the garden path and into a long black American saloon, somewhat resembling a hearse, that had just come to a halt in the road outside the house. The chauffeur held a door open for us and we were inside.

It had all happened in less than a minute. Joe called out, 'Back lateish, dear.'

Then we were spinning along the North Promenade.

'Where are we going?' I asked.

'Sure, we can chat while we're going there. Do you take a drink?'

'Well, it's a bit early for me. And where -?'

But Joe had already taken two glasses and a decanter from a tray which unfolded from the thick leatherwork at the back of the driver's seat. Joe had given no instructions to the chauffeur, who drove steadily along the Promenade and turned inland. I felt a little uneasy. Where were we going?

Joe handed me a very large Bushmills.

I didn't care for Irish whiskey. I sipped it warily, recalling the Old Man's advice. 'Don't drink whiskey until you're forty: you won't appreciate it. And not brandy until you're sixty, because there's nowhere to go after that.'

Joe said, 'What do you think of the car?'

'It's very big,' I said. It was – a vast cavern of very soft leather. 'Is it American?'

'It is so,' said Joe, stretching his legs and winking. 'Plenty of room in the back.' He added, 'I bought it off Tony Vittorio.'

Tony Vittorio was only a name to me. But I felt that I knew it.

Joe enlightened me. 'Tony's a bit of a gangster, y'know.'

'Not really, is he?'

'He is so,' said Joe. 'But he's a very decent fella. He made me a good price on it.'

I didn't ask how much; I didn't want to ask any questions about money. Instead, I said, 'How did you get started as a singer, Joe?'

'Ah, sure, I've always sung a wee bit,' said Joe, closing his eyes and kicking off the expensive black shoes so lovingly polished by his wife. 'Always done it, y'see.'

'Yes, but, er, exactly when and where?'

'I wish,' said Joe, unexpectedly, 'I had a catch in me voice as good as that Tauber man!'

'Richard Tauber? The Austrian tenor?'

'The same fella. He's the master at the catch in the voice. And him with a paralysed arm and a limp and a glass eye, so they tell me – did ye know that?'

'No,' I said. I didn't. I knew only that Tauber was reputed to be the finest singer of Schubert and Lehar in the world. Even Onkel Frank had pronounced him a fair tenor. Of course, Onkel Frank judged everybody against Caruso, whom he had heard in person.

'Sure, the fella just stands there and he has a catch in his voice, so,' Joe brooded. 'Meself, to get that effect, I have to get down on me knees and sing "Christopher Robin is Saying His Prayers". That Tauber, he's the great one, sure enough.'

'Where,' I asked again, 'did you start singing, Joe?'

The answer was a gentle snore. Joe Locke was asleep.

The limousine turned on to the Preston New Road. Were we going to Preston, then? Preston was fifteen miles. It hardly seemed likely.

I looked at Joe's slumbering form and felt a pang of sympathy. His was a hard life, despite the money. Joe was doing a twice-nightly act at the Winter Gardens, performing before two thousand people, singing half a dozen or more songs during his thirty-five-minute act, including, of course, 'Hear My Song, Violetta'. Joe was Top of the Bill and the trippers expected their money's worth. They had paid as much as seven-and-sixpence (some even more) to see him, and they were a knowing audience where a voice was concerned. These were the sort of people, Lancashire and Yorkshire working class, who listened to Handel's *Messiah* two or three times a year, for pleasure. They had also heard Heddle Nash, and Count John McCormack, who was a Papal Count and modestly billed as The World's Greatest Singer of Songs.

There were a lot of very good popular (as opposed to classical) singers about, then. Joe was one of the best. He had about him the aura of all the great star tenors, Mario Lanza and even Sinatra – a sexual pull with audiences of the kind that McCormack, a technical singer of great competence, never had.

I'd heard McCormack sing a whole concert at the Tower Ballroom when I was twelve. We stood, packed, as they used to say, like sardines, on the dance-floor. We had to take our boots off (if we wore boots) so as not to damage the priceless floor. The Old Man and I were excused because we wore shoes.

McCormack sang his Irish songs in a very clear metallic voice, very different from Joe's, which was warm and clear and full of humanity. Listening to Joe, you felt there was a man behind the Voice.

The automobile cruised along the Preston New Road, showing no sign of stopping. I thought of calling out to the chauffeur but that would have woken Joe, so I drank the rest of my large glass of Bushmills and relaxed in my seat as we entered the outskirts of Preston.

Soon, obviously, we would stop and my interview with Joe would get underway again. Wherever we were going, plainly it was some place we could talk, or why arrange a meeting over the telephone the day before?

I wondered about tenors. Why were so many of them Irish? I recalled uneasily that the BBC producer Barney Colehan had recently, for some reason I couldn't fathom, invited me to judge an Amateur Night Television programme with him. It was called *Top Town* and I was introduced to the contestants and the audience as the *Evening Gazette* Television Correspondent, which I sort of was, but I didn't wish to be so publicly known as such! In any event, people afforded me respect, which they certainly would not have done had I been described as a radio playwright or a would-be novelist.

I was introduced to my fellow-panellists, two Blackpool Councillors, heavy, meaty, jovial men, who were without doubt Tories, since the Blackpool landladies thought Socialists would take their hard-earned money off them (and they could have been right) and always voted Tory. The Councillors said they read my column in the paper.

As far as they were concerned, there was only one paper, *The West Lancashire Evening Gazette.* And, of course, the *Daily Mail,* but that was a London paper and therefore not to be entirely trusted.

This *Top Town* audition was held at the self-same Tower Ballroom, with the two Councillors sitting between Barney and myself. The contestants were ten in number, from which we, the panel, had to select five. Barney had put before us a list and we had to tick off what we considered the five best acts.

Barney winked conspiratorially at me, which made me think he was relying on me to choose what he did. But how was I to know which acts he would consider the best? I raised my eyebrows questioningly, but if Barney gave any other signal it was smothered by his moustache, which was vast, a relic of his Army days, when he had been Major Barney Colehan of the British Forces Network in Germany. Barney was an enthusiastic producer, that much I knew, and was known to go as far afield as Romania and Egypt in search of the Best Variety Acts in the World.

Which was most decidedly not what we were seeing at the Tower Ballroom, in *Top Town,* that evening.

The first competitors on show were a local dancing team, twenty strong, the men in evening dress, the girls in short white skirts and tunics in the Twenties style, singing and dancing the famous Fred Astaire routine *Top Hat.*

That was the trouble with amateurs, I thought: all they do is copy. Also, there were too many of them for a live performance in a television studio.

I wrote 'No' against the *Top Hat* dancers.

The Councillors, stimulated by the long legs of the girls (they were men who came from a time when dance routines were known as Leg Shows), put down an enthusiastic 'Yes' on their forms.

Barney closed his eyes in despair, and his busy eyebrows signalled 'No'.

The next act was a tap-dancer with bottle-blonde hair who had obviously been a pro at some time or other. She danced to the strains of 'Who's Sorry Now?' She was thirty-five at least, which is old for a dancer, but tapped well until her obviously borrowed leotard-cum-stockings started to slip slowly down her legs. She ended almost in tears. I put down a 'Yes' out of sympathy.

I hoped Barney had done the same.

What the Councillors made of it, or of any of the acts that followed, I didn't know. The point was that the last act was a local Irish tenor, who gave us a spirited rendering of 'The Rose of Tralee' that I'd heard *ad infinitum* in clubs and variety halls and what used to be called 'Smokers'. I gave him a 'No'.

It was the only act on which, I divined through osmosis, I differed from Barney. Dismissing the woman whose borrowed stockings had slipped, Barney whispered, 'They love an Irish tenor, you know.' He was, of course, ignoring the views of the Councillors, who must have been bewildered by the final choice, announced later in the evening.

The young Irish tenor had received a warm round of applause from the audience.

Barney was right. Irish tenors were popular.

The proof of it was Joe, still asleep, snoring gently, as the limousine cruised through the centre of Preston and out the other side. I had given up wondering where we were going and sat, slightly bemused by the enormous Bushmills, waiting to see when, if ever, we would stop.

I wondered what I was doing, apart from earning a modest fee, writing about variety performers, comics, the sort of people I was beginning to interview for my column, like Joe. All I had to offer was a rough-and-ready knowledge of such people and only that because I'd been going to Music Halls since I was four years old, when I saw my Uncle Harold, the Scotch Comedian, in Panto at Wallsend, singing 'In and Out The Window' and performing a soldier skit in which the phrase 'I tapped the Colonel on the Chest with a Woodbine Packet' was spoken by my Uncle, a diminutive Glaswegian wearing, most of the time, a kilt two sizes too big for him.

Since then, in the company of Marthaann, I had seen such now-forgotten luminaries as Harry Lauder (very confident, wonderful voice, used all the stage), an obvious star before he opened his mouth; Will Hay and Graham Moffatt, the Headmaster and Boy of Whakem Academy who were very broad and wouldn't seem funny now. Humour doesn't often travel across the generations. It relies on comic and audiences having the same experiences. Norman Evans, appearing at Blackpool that summer, the finest Dame I ever saw (but I hadn't seen Dan Leno because he was dead by then), was typical. He didn't talk about how he was the finest female-impersonator of the time because he had no words to explain it. Like all the Music Hall comics, including Rob Wilton (like W. C. Fields, a lot funnier Off than On), he was at a loss to tell me how he did it. The nearest any of the comics got to the truth of their talent was that some gags and routines *worked*, so they kept them in. That way, over a period of months and years, they refined an act, so that it was pure gold. Nobody can do that now. There isn't the time. Now, a television comic has a script cobbled together the previous week, or even the day before, by three or four desperate gag-men and throws it at the tame studio audience more in hope than confidence. The producer puts a clapometer on it and manufactures the laughs. In the Music Hall, if an audience didn't laugh you were dead.

The Old Man had seen all the Great Ones. He'd seen the clown Grock, who'd had him laughing his heart out even though, come what may, at the end of the show he'd have to get on a Boat Train at Victoria for France and the trenches. George Robey, too, singing 'If You Were the Only Girl in the World' to an audience that would, most of them (the young men, anyway), be dead in a few days or weeks.

The Old Man had seen Harry Tate, whose golf clubs W. C. Fields had stolen for drink. (He stole his act, too.) Tate was the greatest 'sketch' artist of the Music Hall, said the Old Man. His 'Get Out and Get Under (Your Automobile!)' and his aforesaid 'Golf' sketch were imitated by everybody. I asked the Old Man what it was Harry Tate had that made him great.

'Presence,' said the Old Man, surprised that anybody should ask so obvious a question.

Of course, his father, Edward Prior, had owned Music Halls, and lost all his money, eventually, through investing too wildly in them. 'Overreached himself,' said the Old Man, bearing no discernible ill-will against a father who had left him and his two brothers penniless, in their teens.

There had been compensations.

The Old Man had once seen his brother, the Bookmaker Edwards, aged nineteen, blindfolded, sit on the shoulders of the most famous acrobat in the world, Blondin, as Blondin walked a rope from the gallery to the stage at the Empire, Newcastle-on-Tyne, with no net. He did that with a brave youngster every night. Edwards had reported it as being 'like sitting in an armchair'. If they had fallen both would have been killed. Probably the people they landed on, too.

But, as the Old Man said, Blondin had walked across Niagara (the only man ever to do it) so it was unlikely he'd fall in his tight-rope act in a theatre.

Still, because it was 'live', it had an element of danger. That, the Old Man said, was what made the Speciality Acts, Houdini, Leotard, The Daring Young Man on the Flying Trapeze (dead at twenty-seven, famous), Cinquevalli, who caught a heavy glass bowl in the nape of his neck every night, so *good*, so unlike a modern, packaged, artiste on television.

Then, some artists actually risked their lives to amuse the audience. Some were killed doing it. Houdini, with an unexpected punch from a punter that burst his appendix; the illusionist Chung Ling Soo with a gun trick that went wrong and put a fatal bullet in his lung.

Nowadays, acts so dangerous would be seen as incorrect, akin to the Roman Circus. Yet, I had heard comics say that is how they felt when they went on to face a packed house at the Winter Gardens or the North Pier or at Feldman's, next to the Old Central Station. 'Go On, Mek us Laugh', the audience seemed to be saying, as the sweating, apprehensive comics waited for their opening music from the orchestra.

'It takes balls to go out and face them, they're like live animals,' Norman Evans told me.

Marie Lloyd didn't have balls but she had told the Sheffield audience that gave her the Bird, 'You know what you can do with your knives and forks and your circular saws as well!'

The Bird: the shrill, chilling chorus of whistles. It happened to the worst and the best. Even Max Miller narrowly avoided it at Blackpool. He was a Cockney and that was enough to put him in danger.

It was, I suppose, knowledge of this sort – acquired, much of it, from the Old Man and Aunt Clara, who seemed to have been on a bill somewhere with *everybody* – that enabled me to take on the hoary old comics and venerable Speciality Acts who packed Blackpool's many venues in the summer (and its two remaining Variety Houses, the Palace and Feldman's, in the winter) and somehow get a 'star' interview out of them.

It never occurred to me that I was doing anything that literary critics, editors and publishers might have thought odd, or, as they say nowadays, downmarket, in an aspiring young novelist. I liked talking and listening to these men and women, the rump of the old, live Music Hall tradition, then almost gone, now entirely lost.

Joe Locke at this moment was entirely lost to me. He was still snoring gently.

I wakened from my Bushmills-induced reverie to discover that (a) I was very hungover and (b) we were in Manchester. I recognised the streets and the road signs. There were very few people about because it was Sunday.

'Is this Manchester?' I shouted to the chauffeur.

Unable to hear me through the glass panel, he made no reply, but I had woken Joe.

'Are we here already?' he asked, yawning and rubbing his eyes. In the same movement he reached for the Bushmills in the leather container and poured us both a liberal measure. 'I could do with a stiffener, so I could,' he added, by way explanation.

'Manchester?' I asked, accepting the Bushmills as I was now, I realised, accepting anything and everything, there being no point in doing anything else.

'Sure enough.' Joe consulted his watch. 'We're a bit late but that won't matter at all. They work on a loose schedule, so they do.'

'Do they?' I wondered who we were talking about. Plainly, Joe had it in his mind, as they say, that he'd told me. The possibility crossed *my* mind that he didn't quite remember who I was or why I was there. This was borne out in the next statement.

'You'll get a fair bit of copy from the Boys!'

'Who?'

But the limousine had drawn up outside a very large Victorian church of blackened stone in the best mock-Gothic tradition. It had obviously been rained on, snowed on and sooted on for a hundred years. Despite the fact that it was Sunday, there appeared to be no worshippers about. I swallowed the rest of my Bushmills, which had a curious, stunning effect, and followed Joe out of the limousine, the door of which the chauffeur held open for us. I put the empty glass in his hand and walked on air into the church.

It seemed rather bare for a church and there was still nobody about. Possibly, I thought, we were between services.

'Joe, what sort of church is this?'

Joe didn't seem to hear me. He pushed a door which gave on to the body of the Church, and a blinding flash of light hit us in the face.

I thought: *It's a miracle.*

But it was only an arc light.

I stood and stared as Joe strode forward, to be greeted by a middle-aged man in two sweaters under a dark waistcoat, horn-rimmed glasses and a battered, black Homburg hat. 'This,' I was told by Joe, 'is Mr Brierley.'

I shook his hand. 'From the *Gazette*,' said Joe. 'Come to write us up.'

'Ah,' said Mr Brierley, not unkindly. He pointed to a table covered with bottles. 'The booze is over there, Son.'

'Fine for now, thanks,' I said, aware I was slurring my words.

'Well,' said Mr Brierley, 'we've just going to shoot the parade-ground scene with Frank and Jimmy and Ben.'

'Right,' said Joe.

'You're in it, Joe. Your uniform's in the dressing-room and your script is in there as well. Say, five minutes?'

'Sure enough,' said Joe, and disappeared.

All around my bemused head carpenters hammered and people shouted for more or less light, and men in cloth caps and overalls carried props made of wood and cardboard (sides of Army huts, sentry-boxes) on to a brightly lit sound-stage.

The cameras, very large and immobile, sat like large crabs at each end of the sound-stage, manned by men in sports jackets and sweaters. Despite the season, it was cold in this bright and airless place.

Two make-up girls (both over forty) fussed around the male performers, all in Army uniform, putting 'cake' on their already orange faces and dusting it off again with large feather-brushes.

Blinking, I realised that we were on a film set. I said – or, rather, shouted – to a man moving what I later discovered was a sound-boom, 'What's the picture you're making here?'

'*Girls in Khaki*,' he said, without looking up.

'I can't see any girls.'

'You will.'

And soon, there they were. From a Pantomime chorus, probably, *en masse*, but dressed now in ATS khaki skirts (very short) and ATS tunics (very tight) and totally ignoring the ATS's and WAAF's and Wrens' wartime rule that no service-woman's hair may touch her collar.

The Girls, none of whom was older than twenty, were heavily lipsticked and most of them bottle-blonde. In several scenes they sported 'silken undies', which were worn by nobody (except possibly an Air Vice-Marshal's mistress) during the late War, the setting for the film. However improbable the portrayal, to me the Girls looked very good.

To the camera crew they were just so much flesh to photograph. Some of the crew, wrapped in jerseys and scarves and caps, actually yawned as these fleshy young beauties (no slim girls these; there was, obviously, No Call for Them) cavorted saucily with the craggy, leering old comics who shared the unutterably silly story with them.

I asked one of the crew, who seemed to have a spare moment, 'Is there a script for all this?'

'There used to be one but the comics keep changing it.'

'Why?'

'They think of new bits of business, you see.'

'But it's all terrible.'

'Yes, but it's what the punters want.'

'Is it?'

'Must be or they wouldn't be making it, would they?' He sipped his hot tea. 'Anyway, they're paying me, so what do I care?'

I found this attitude shocking after my small experience of BBC Radio. There everybody seemed to believe in everything they did. I had never heard anybody (producers, sound-men, actors) talk about punters. I'd heard the Old Man and the Brothers talk about punters, but it was always in a derogatory way. Punters, to them, were mugs, ignorant dupes, fools, idiots. To consider pleasing the punters the first priority seemed to me immoral (and still does), but most practitioners in Light Entertainment – Clubs, Cabaret, Variety and the Old Music Hall – had to think that way because if the punters didn't like what you did they didn't pay to come in and there you were, on the street corner, unemployed.

Only the BBC in those days had this other attitude: that the production of good work *of any kind* was what mattered. Some people used to say that the old BBC gave people what they thought was good for them rather than what they wanted. Paternalism, they would call it nowadays. It was the legacy of Reith, who also gave the nation the Scottish Sunday when nothing moved except to pray.

The English never wanted the Scottish Sunday, and eventually got rid of it. It took a long time. Television finally buried it.

But Television then was just the glimmer of a few programmes in Black and White on Ten-inch screens and only a very few people in the North of England had a television set. I had one because I had to have one if I was going to write about it.

Thereby hangs a tale of the times. The Government had decided that if you couldn't pay half the purchase price of a television set in cash and the rest in instalments you couldn't have one. So nobody except well-to-do people had a set. I wasn't well-to-do but I went to see a dealer, Mr Dewhurst, whom I remembered from the days of my incarceration in the radio and electrical firm before the War. Mr Dewhurst I remembered as a dark man, too busy to shave, who loved to do a deal, even if it cost him money. I outlined my case to him and he listened sympathetically. I waited there in his back-street shop, surrounded by old radio chassis and valves and Halicrafter's kit and electrical wire and more wire, while he thought deeply about how to 'do' the Government.

It didn't take him too long.

'You're prepared to pay the extra money monthly over a longer term? Your problem is you don't have the half price to put down?'

'That's it.'

'Have you got a second-hand radio set at home?'

'No.'

Mr Dewhurst put an old, broken-down Philco People's model (now worth a fortune as an antique) in my hands. 'Now you have.'

'Do I?'

'Yes. It's worth, let's say, exactly half the price of the Television set.'

'Is it?'

'Let's say it is.'

'Oh. Right.'

Mr Dewhurst was scribbling on an invoice. 'You want a Ten-inch Set at a hundred pounds. I've given you fifty on this Philco radio.'

'It isn't worth that, is it?'

Mr Dewhurst looked disappointed in me. 'Lad, second-hand stuff is worth what you say it's worth. Now, all I do is extend your payments to me over an extra twelve months, with extra interest, and hey presto!'

'How much is it a month?'

He told me.

It sounded a lot but I had to have it. Television was the future. Anybody could see that. 'Right. Done. I'll write the first cheque now.'

Mr Dewhurst looked doubtful. 'Is your cheque all right, lad?'

'Only just,' I laughed.

'That'll do me.' He added, 'You'll need an aerial, that's fifteen quid cash, and five to install it is twenty, is that all right?'

It was. Anything was.

I shook hands with Mr Dewhurst. I said, 'You drove a Coach and Horses through something that all the Whitehall Mandarins and the politicians took months over.'

Mr Dewhurst scratched his nose. 'None of their own money at stake, had they, lad?'

Girls in Khaki had money at stake.

Presumably the producers, represented by Mr Brierley, the director in the horn-rimmed glasses and the black Homburg hat, which gave him the look of a disbarred city accountant rather than a man in charge of an artistic project, wanted the film to please the punters. Sweating profusely under the hot glare of the arc lamps, he lined up the shots, displaying the busty girls to the most salacious advantage, rather like a butcher arranging meat on a slab.

To the Comics he had nothing to say. It would have been futile, if he had.

Frank Randle, for a start, was a law unto himself. I had already interviewed him for my column and had naïvely expected him to be something like his stage persona – that is, eighty years of age, impotent, incontinent, *sans* teeth and hair and attired as a hiker in baggy shorts and ankle socks. In his famous sketch of that title, he reduced Lancashire audiences to helpless, exhausted laughter, using nothing but innuendo and dialect, speaking the English of Beowulf.

Example: a young, sexy, woman hiker (hiking was the cheapest way to see England then) walks past him, wearing very short shorts, on the stage.

Randle, to audience: 'I believe hoo's a bit of a Hot Un!'

Hoo is Beowulf-speak for Her.

Showing his gums (he always took his teeth out before he went on-stage), he called after the sexy girl, 'I'll catch thee up in a minute, lass, and then I'll . . . [the dreadful truth of his age and impotence slowly showing on his face] I'll . . . I'll . . . I'll . . . *play thee at Dominoes*!'

Frank, off-stage, was thin, fifty, shy and so nervous he threw up in a bucket in the wings before he went on. Every time. No matter what the occasion. Ensa. Concert Party. Panto. A Kid's show. *Every time.*

'Why do you do it,' I had asked him, 'if you're so nervous about it all?'

He looked pityingly at me. 'I'm all right once I'm *on*!'

He was. He was *now*, in this draughty, disused church, in this awful caricature of a film. He was turning it into pathos and comedy and tears of laughter. He was enjoying himself too, a wicked sexy gleam in his gargoyle eye as he ogled the saucy Girls in Khaki, and attempted, vainly, to lay hands on their tempting, busty figures.

The tragic look on his toothless face when they scornfully eluded him had even the bored technicians smiling.

Other members of the 'Awkward Squad' were the comics Jimmy Jewel and Ben Warris, who were first-cousins in real life. They had worked together for years and were so in tune that if you saw them from the side when they were dancing they looked like one person. Jimmy Jewel, unlike Frank Randle, was a deadpan comic, who, when in doubt, had recourse to but one single word, uttered in a hundred different nuances: '*Gerraway*?' He was later to be a wonderful straight actor, an achievement nobody could have predicted then.

Jimmy James, the Geordie Comic, made up the Comedy Team. He had with him his assistant, the Gormless Man, who would ask him questions like, 'Are you Putting It About that I'm Barmy?' Jimmy, a straight-faced, elderly man, did a silent 'Drunk Scene' as well as anybody in The Business (to the tune of 'Three O'Clock in the Morning'), and he was doing it here. It didn't fit in with the story-line of *Girls in Khaki* but all the other Comics wanted to see Jimmy do it. Comics, unless they are touring together, *never* see one another's act. They had probably all seen Jimmy James's Drunk Act before because it was a classic. But they insisted, loudly, that he fit it in somehow. So he did.

It was miraculous to see, the last of a thousand performances, as he peeled off his evening gloves and coat, took off his hat, found a cigarette, tried to light it, set fire to his scarf, tripped over everything on stage, *tried* to remember where he was, failed. Finally discovering he was in the wrong bedroom (a Fat Woman covered with face-cream suddenly sat up in the bed), he crashed through the window (sugar-glass accompanied by sound of breaking glass) and spoke the only words of his Act.

'God, it's the Wife!'

Everybody applauded, except the Director in the Homburg, who looked at his watch and said, 'Lovely, Jimmy, can you get into your uniform now for the Parade Scene?'

And now they were in a line, with Joe Locke dressed as the furious, bullying Sergeant-Major (all Sergeant-Majors were furious and bullying in these sketches, as indeed they were in real life), and very well Joe did it. His years in the Palestine Police and the Ulster Constabulary, both paramilitary forces, had not been wasted. He bellowed, sweating, eyes popping out of his head, at the straggling line of Comics.

Being po-faced by profession it wasn't difficult for them to remain po-faced, no matter what insults he shouted at them.

Finally, he fetched up in front of Frank Randle, the oldest-looking of the line of soldiers. He inspected the sorry scarecrow in the ill-fitting uniform and hissed, in a low, ferocious whisper, 'I said, Stand To Attention!'

Replied Frank Randle, *sans* teeth, 'I *am* At Attention! It's me uniform that's At Ease!'

Only a man who's worn an ill-fitting uniform and been a recruit really understands that joke.

Joe came over when a break was called. The shooting, he told me, would go on until eleven o'clock that night. 'It's a Quickie,' he said. 'I come over for a couple of hours in the mornings or the afternoons. We all do. We're all playing some theatre or other at night.'

'It's a long hard week, isn't it?'

'So it is,' said Joe. 'But it's been good having your company coming across.'

That was it, really. Joe, as a true Irishman, loved company, even when he slept or worked through it. It is the Irish gift for making all work a social occasion.

'You got what you wanted?' he asked anxiously, as the Director called him for yet another farcical scene, involving Frank Randle straying by mistake into the hut in which the Girls in Khaki slept in their silk undies.

'I did, I did, thanks a lot, Joe, very helpful.'

His face broke into a wide, relieved grin. He felt he had maybe neglected me, shown bad manners. He had obviously forgotten all about the interview.

'Enjoyed every minute,' I said. I had.

'See yez soon now!'

And he was gone, on to the set for another scene of *Girls in Khaki*, the oddity of making a silly, mindless comedy about the most horrible, bloodthirsty war in history never occurring to him, or to anybody else connected with it. All of them were giving their talent and magic to a production patently not worth it, yet investing it with a humour and a hope that said something about the human ability to make the best of things, to carry on smoking, no matter what; to – in the last analysis – laugh at it all.

I said no Goodbyes; everybody was too busy. I let myself out, into the late summer evening. Cold sober now, but very hungry, I tried to work out the way to the Railway Station.

A Clean-living Lad

The Old Man had found a protégé.

His name was Lewis, he was a Gas-meter Reader and he came from St Anne's, along the coast, a mainly residential little seaside town with none of the raffish and garish glitter of Blackpool. The thing about Lewis, the Old Man imparted in a confidential whisper, was that he could make One Hundred breaks at snooker.

'Not now and again. *Regularly,*' whispered the Old Man, as if he might be overheard. Which was not likely in the hubbub of the Grand Hotel Billiard-room. Snooker-fourhands are noisy with congratulation and criticism.

There was a long moment of silence as Onkel Frank digested this. Then, 'How is it we know nothing of this man? Is he up here for the Tower or what?'

Blackpool, after the War, had become famous for the yearly Tower Snooker Knock-Out Tournament, the final match of which was played inside the four legs of the Tower itself, where the summer Circus took place. That is, in the building that houses the foundations of the huge edifice. The area could also be flooded with water for swimming competitions. There was nothing else in any other seaside resort like the Tower (tallest iron structure) and the Winter Gardens (biggest indoor-entertainment area, comprising dance-hall, two theatres, restaurants and four large bars) or the Pleasure Beach (largest outdoor Amusement Park in the World) or the Piers (accommodating more people than any other similar structures) or the number of excursion trains; or the number of people who came on holiday every year; or the Illuminations (a bigger concentration of electric-light bulbs than anywhere else in the world). Blackpool had all these attractions pre-war and had them still.

The Tower Snooker Competition was a Special Event because it was something new. It attracted only Amateur Talent, but from all over the country. If a player had been registered as a Professional he was not eligible to compete. All the same, many players entered who had competed for large sums of money in their time. To all intents and purposes they were professionals, so the standard was high. But as long as they did not perform on the professional circuit with the likes of Joe Davis and Melbourne Inman and Rees and Newman they were not barred from the Tower. If they did not play at Thurston's in Soho Square in London or any of the professional venues up and down the country they were free to enter the competition.

'If a man can make a hundred break regularly,' suggested Onkel Frank, 'we would have heard of him, for sure. What you are saying is, he's a dark horse. If he is, somebody will know him.'

'The man has just come to St Anne's from somewhere in Wales,' retorted the Old Man, glancing round again. 'Nobody knows him.' The Old Man paused, so that his words would sink in. 'I tell you, the fellow reads gas meters for a living.'

Onkel Frank placed his cigarette, butt down, on the drinks-table. That way, it burned very slowly. (I have never met anybody else able to do this trick.) He said, 'I've met first-class snooker players who were drunks or whoremongers or gamblers or tea-leaves or ponces. I've never yet met a first-class snooker player who was a gas-meter reader.'

'There's a first time for everything.' The Old Man lowered his voice even more. All around us the local snooker-players flitted, the balls click-clacking into the pockets. 'This man has a wife and two kids, he doesn't drink, he doesn't back horses, he doesn't smoke and he doesn't chase women. All he does is read gas meters and play snooker.' The Old Man's voice dropped until it was all but inaudible. 'He is a Clean-living Lad.'

There was a profound silence at this statement.

Onkel Frank spoke for anybody who knew anything about the Game when he said, 'There's no such thing as a Clean-living Lad in this business.'

Even I knew what he meant. Proficiency at billiards is the sign of a misspent youth, yes. But a great skill at snooker cannot be learned without weeks, months, years, of work: thousands of balls potted, night after night, in smoky public billiard-halls and Workmen's Institutes, for small stakes or large, on slow tables or fast. It cannot be learned at all without a great natural talent, allied to a temperament patient and steady, because the only things that make a naturally talented snooker-player a great snooker player are: one, a great teacher; and two, practice, practice, practice.

And *more* practice. Practice from morn until dawn, practice ten hours a day, practice against all manner of other players: potters, safety-merchants, spoilers, con men, drunks who are has-beens but can produce one frame that would beat Joe Davis, gamblers who up the ante during the game or drop their cue on the floor as you shape up to strike a vital ball. As the Old Man said, 'To be a top snooker-player you have to know every lodging-house trick in the Book.'

A low-class lodging-house, then, was a place of peril. You

could lose your money or the very boots on your feet in such an establishment. Learn all the low-class snooker tricks: the sudden very slow table on which your opponent has been practising all day or the fast one, just ironed, that plays like a skating-rink. Learn all that and much, much more and still you might not be ready for what might be thrown at you. The sort of so-called amateur who played at the Tower had without doubt played for cash-money, which the real professionals like Joe Davis did not. Joe Davis played for a fee, or purse-money, as did all the members of the Pro Circus. They still do, but nowadays for huge fees on television.

The real blood-and-guts Snooker was – and is – played for cash-money under, generally speaking, dubious circumstances. Onkel Frank shook his head as the Old Man further explained, 'This man's famous in his part of Wales but he tells me he's never played for money, ever. He's simply won local tournaments and so on.'

'You're telling me he's a total amateur?' Onkel Frank shook his head even more vigorously. He had himself only made three or four one-hundred breaks in a lifetime of play. He was constitutionally unable to accept the Old Man's story. 'He can't have made the breaks where wideheads might see him. It would get out.'

'Of course he didn't make them where wideheads would see him,' said the Old Man impatiently. 'That is the whole point.'

'You insist he's never played for money?' demanded Onkel Frank.

'Never. He's against it on religious grounds.'

Onkel Frank's black and burning eyes, always protuberant, almost popped out of his head. 'Then we're wasting our time talking about him.'

'Not necessarily.'

'How so?'

'All this man has is his wages from the Gas Company. He won't beat seven quid a week. He has a small family. He is amenable . . .' The Old Man hesitated, obviously wondering how much he should say. 'He's amenable to reason.'

Decoded, that meant Lewis needed and wanted the money.

'What about the religious thing?' asked Onkel Frank.

'Now he's away from Wales, he doesn't seem to be so bothered about it.'

Onkel Frank lit a fresh cigarette from the butt of the one anchored to the table. 'Even so, he remains, however good, an amateur who has never even played for a ten-bob note?'

Confirmed the Old Man, 'Always been dead against it. But now he's away from the Chapel and all that, he is, as I say, amenable.'

Said Onkel Frank with great emphasis, 'None the less, you know nothing of billiards unless you have played for your breakfast!'

The Old Man bowed to the truth of that, but said, 'I have seen this man make a break of ninety-six, another of seventy-eight, another of one hundred exactly.' The Old Man paused, again for maximum effect. 'And I have seen him clear the table. All the reds, all the colours.'

Onkel Frank put down his glass of whisky. 'Are we speaking of One Hundred and Forty-seven?'

'We are,' said the Old Man, signalling to the waiter for two more whiskies and also a Guinness for me. The Old Man felt I needed a stout or two per night to combat the exhausting ravages of my War. Well, *he* had, after *his* War. 'Do you good,' he said. It was easier to drink it than to argue. I had grown to like the taste of it by now. I rarely drank more than two in an evening.

Now, I sipped at the creamy foam and wondered: *Why was*

the Old Man telling us all this? If true, it was far better kept to himself.

'Where,' asked Onkel Frank, wonderingly, 'have you seen this man clear the table from breaking-off?'

'In his own house.'

Onkel Frank stared at him. 'He has a full-sized billiard-table in his house?'

The only person I know who had one was my Uncle, Edwards, the oldest of the three brothers. He'd always had one, but he had a very large Victorian house in Hampton Road.

The Old Man said, 'This man has converted a greenhouse in his garden that will fit a billiard-table. He plays on it for three hours every night and I tell you he's the steadiest snooker-player I've *ever* seen. He misses nothing.'

Onkel Frank was very curious but nowhere near convinced. 'Have you seen him play anybody good?'

'I've only seen him play me.' The Old Man held up his hand. 'And before you say it, I left him nothing to pot. I went safe every shot, to try to stop him scoring. I never was able to do it.'

There was another long silence.

Onkel Frank said, 'Who knows besides you?'

'Only Bob Curl, manager of the Beach.'

Onkel Frank grunted. He knew Bob Curl – who didn't? Bob Curl was twenty-two stones in weight and had been the landlord of the Beach Hotel for as long as anybody in Blackpool could remember.

'Did Bob Curl tell you to go and see this fellow Lewis?'

'Yes, he did, and it's all between us and him for now.'

'Why are you telling me?' asked Onkel Frank.

'Because,' said the Old Man, 'I don't entirely trust my own judgement. I want a second opinion.'

'Mine?'

'You're a far better player than I am. You can tell me if I'm wrong.'

Onkel Frank pondered. 'You have some sort of speculation in mind?'

'Let us say,' said the Old Man, distantly, 'that there will be an opportunity to make a decent profit out of all this, if we keep it under our hats.'

Onkel Frank pondered again. It was almost possible to hear his brain working. One half was assessing the truth of what the Old Man was telling him, the other half wondering exactly what the Old Man *wasn't* telling him.

That was, and had always been, their relationship ever since they had been left to fend for themselves on the bankruptcy and death of their father forty years before. Onkel Frank was totally, almost painfully, honest; his vast intelligence forbade him to be anything other. The Old Man was, quite simply, less so. Onkel Frank's decisions were always based on logic. All the Old Man's decisions were made on the hoof – driven, as it were, by necessity.

At last, with enormous reluctance, but still consumed by curiosity, Onkel Frank asked, 'When do I play this man and where?'

'Now, if you like. There's a taxi standing outside this place. We can be in St Anne's in fifteen minutes. You can know in an hour or two whether I'm right.'

'Why a taxi, why not a bus?'

'He's a clean-living lad, but he's no fool. Arrival in a taxi will impress on him we're serious people.'

'Has there been any copsy, as yet?'

By 'copsy' Onkel Frank meant money.

'I've paid him a small sum to maintain his interest, that's all.'

Onkel Frank digested that. 'And the idea is, if I have all this right, that you and Bob Curl want to enter him for the Tower, get a good price about him early on, and make a killing?'

The Old Man looked crestfallen. 'I didn't say that.'

'None the less, is that the position or is it not?'

The Old Man sighed. 'Yes, it is.'

'Then why,' asked Onkel Frank, 'didn't you say so in the first place?'

Lewis was a very nice young man. Well, not exactly young compared with me, but young in those days for a good snooker player. Nowadays, Hendry and Steve Davis and O'Sullivan are great players at twenty years of age but they have not had a cue out of their hands since they were six or seven years old, and they have had great tuition because television has made snooker a big, public sport with a paying audience and vast purses at stake. Then, snooker was still a low-class game, played by thousands for sport and for hundreds for small sums and for a few dozen for big money. In that, they were like bare-knuckle fights are now. Illegal but thriving and nowhere to be if you were faint-hearted, lily-livered, or young.

If you were young you hadn't learned the Money Game, or the lodging-house tricks that went with it. You needed years to learn them, but had not grown too old learning them that your eyes had gone.

Lewis was about thirty and had been, he said, in a Reserved Occupation during the War. He'd been a Time-checker in an office in the Welsh Coalfields. In short, a clerk. He looked one. Cheap clean shirt, cheap grey suit, soft hands, an ingenuous, almost innocent expression.

'It's good of you gents to call in.'

Lewis did seem genuinely pleased to see us. His wife, a dark good-looking girl, also Welsh, gave us tea and biscuits and then left us alone. The house was like a thousand others. Furniture by Utility, lino and carpets by the Co-op, cups by Woolworth's. A wooden clock ticked on the mantelpiece.

The whole house exuded decency and no money whatever.

Asked Onkel Frank, as soon as the tea was drunk, 'I understand you've played some snooker?'

Lewis nodded. 'I've won a few amateur knock-outs in Wales.'

'Never played in a money match, Mr Lewis?'

'No. Never.'

Onkel Frank sighed. He still could not envisage anybody who could play snooker at all never having played for money. 'Shall we knock a few balls about, Mr Lewis?'

Lewis nodded, after first looking at the Old Man, who smiled encouragingly. Then he led us first into the back-garden and then into a long glasshouse, explaining as we went, 'The man who had the house before me was a keen gardener. This used to be a greenhouse. All I did was take out the plants and cement the floor and board up the windows. You'll find it a bit draughty but I keep the heating on and the table seems all right, so far.' He switched on the light and there it stood, a very old Burroughs and Watts billiard-table, with a good light above it. Onkel Frank selected a cue and the Old Man racked-up the balls into a triangle. The place was cool and there was no atmosphere at all, as there is always around any billiard-table, put there by the occasion and the people. The converted greenhouse seemed airless and calm. I wondered how anybody used to playing in such a place would respond to a roomful of noisy punters.

Onkel Frank took off his hat, mackintosh and then his jacket, exposing crisp cuffs held by armlets. His waistcoat was navy blue and his dark hair gleamed. 'Shall I break off?'

'Yes, please,' said Lewis. He wore a home-knitted brown pullover under his waistcoat. He didn't look at all like the accepted idea of a good snooker-player. Onkel Frank did. For one thing he was what the Old Man described as a magnificent cueman. That is to say, he had style. The cue was an extension of his arm. Onkel Frank got down very low, in the correct fashion, eye along the cue, and remained absolutely still, only his right arm moving, before, during and after he played a shot – almost always the sign of a good player, which he was. Not as good a money-match player as his brother Edwards the bookmaker, because he was prone to take risks, believing he could pot anything. Onkel Frank was famous, locally, for having beaten the professional Tom Newman, who was one of the best five snooker-players in the whole world. The occasion had been an Exhibition by Newman, to open a new table at the Grand Hotel, ten years before. Newman had demonstrated a lot of trick shots and then was expected to decimate a good local player, to score a couple of big breaks and amaze the locals, thus earning his hundred guineas fee.

It had not happened.

The best player by common consent in the hotel was Onkel Frank, and he was chosen to stand around and hold his cue while Newman demonstrated what a great player he was. That, after all, was what people had come to see.

They did not see it, because Onkel Frank broke off, smashed up the reds and potted Newman for the game, that being the only way, he explained later, to beat a world-class player. No point in trying to play safety, because there was no red ball that was ever safe from such a great talent.

Newman was surprised at the confidence and expertise of Onkel Frank and found himself playing before a suddenly silent and attentive crowd. He also found, as soon as the reds had gone, that Onkel Frank was playing him ball for ball – that is, not any longer trying to clear the table, but making sure Newman didn't either. Before a now profoundly silent house, not a word being spoken, Onkel Frank found himself looking at the final Black, needing it to win. It was tucked close to a cushion half-way down the table, between the centre and bottom pocket. Onkel Frank's White cue-ball was in exactly the same position between the middle pocket and the top pocket. Newman had put the balls there, knowing them to be safe.

They were not safe.

Onkel Frank went for the pot, very, very slowly.

The Black trembled on the lip of the pocket and dropped in. The place erupted and Newman stood still for a long time, finally offering Onkel Frank his hand.

'You've played before,' he said.

Onkel Frank explained his winning shot later. 'I had no choice. If I'd tried to play safety, Newman would have potted it, almost certainly. I happened to have seen the table ironed that morning. I knew the ball would run in, if I hit it right, which I did.'

Newman did not hang about, the Old Man reported, but collected his money and left.

Onkel Frank was the hero of South Shore. That match had happened ten years before put people still remembered it. On hearing my name, they would ask if I was related to the man who beat Tom Newman.

That was Onkel Frank's reputation. The fact, as the Old Man said, that he wouldn't do it again in a Month of Sundays was neither here nor there. He'd done it.

And now, older, and with his eyes not quite so good, but nevertheless a redoubtable opponent, he struck off against Lewis, leaving him nothing except a solitary Red, disengaged from the triangle, and stood back to see what Lewis would do.

The Red was just pottable but no Money Match player would

have tried for it. Lewis, who had no style at all but did keep still before, during and after his stroke, put it in the top right-hand pocket, his white cannoning gently into the triangle of Reds. This disturbed four Reds and the Black and Lewis potted the four Reds and the Black each time. Then he took a Pink and then he took a Blue, after getting into a good position each time. I had an idea he had done that deliberately, to open up the game. He didn't want us to think all he could do was shop Blacks. A lot of players can do that. To play for difficult positions on the Pink and Blue and the other colours is another skill, altogether rarer. Lewis had it.

He made an Eighty-two break.

When he had finished, Onkel Frank put down his cue, having played only the one shot that opened the Frame. 'I've seen enough. You're a very fine player, Mr Lewis.'

'Thank you,' said Lewis without smiling. He did not smile at all, I realised. He seemed to be without emotion, either playing snooker or just talking.

The Old Man said to Lewis, 'What we'll do is, we'll sort you out some kind of special match, just so people can see what you can do. Is that all right?'

Lewis nodded. He seemed ready to agree to anything. I wondered how wise he was, but it was no part of my business to warn him. It was just obvious, to me anyway, that he had a talent and was in need of disinterested advice on how to use it. One thing was certain. The Old Man and Onkel Frank were anything but disinterested, and other people involved might be even less so.

The Old Man shook hands with Lewis and we went out and got into the waiting taxi. The Old Man knew the driver but there was no possibility of credit. However, he agreed not to charge 'waiting time', on receipt of the names of two Dogs to back at Saturday's meeting at St Anne's Road. The Old Man was no longer clerking at the Dogs, having the Air Force job and the income from it. Mostly it went on Dogs that Onkel Frank did *not* tip. It was ever thus.

The brothers now reported to their elder brother at the Grand Hotel. Sipping a Brandy-and-Soda, Edwards listened gravely to all they had to tell him. The Old Man did all the talking but it was to Onkel Frank that Edwards turned.

'Would this fellow give Billy Crumpsall a game?'

Billy Crumpsall was a local professional. I knew him, a tall, heavily built man, yet very light on his feet – as all great players are. He was about fifty years old but had once been good enough to be offered a place in the Professional Circus (of Davis, Inman, Rees and the others) who travelled the country playing each other, endlessly, in Exhibition Matches.

'Billy is a drinker, likes the women and didn't want the discipline of touring about and behaving himself.' Onkel Frank's tone as he first told me about Billy Crumpsall had been disapproving. 'He's got a name, now, for doing what he's told.' Onkel Frank meant Billy might win or lose to order. Of course, nobody could ever prove a thing like that.

Onkel Frank had then said, 'Ten or fifteen years ago, when I was playing at my best, Billy could give me two Blacks in a frame and beat me more often than not.' Two Blacks is fourteen points start. 'That,' added Onkel Frank, 'took some doing in those days.' He further added, 'The man has pissed his talent away.'

I never asked for more information on these occasions. It was apt to dry up if I did. I was still suspect, not being, as it were, in the Family Business but writing for a living, which did not seem to offer the rewards that racing might bring and created a lot less excitement.

Well, that was true.

Of course, I never heard any words of encouragement from Onkel Frank where the writing was concerned. I tried to tell him once or twice that if it had not been for him getting me interested in Darwin and Nietzsche and Winwood Reed and all the other Rationalist writers I wouldn't hold the views I now did. Also, Marx and Engels and Kropotkin. He had made a political animal of me but I had discovered fiction and drama for myself. He did not take those subjects seriously. They seemed to him frivolous and not a proper subject of study for a serious man. But he had taught me to read at four years old and had subjected me to a rigorous questioning ever since, whenever I said something he thought stupid. It was a harsh educational regime but it prepared me for a lot of things that came later. It was all of a piece with his handicapping skills, which were profound.

'Lewis would give Billy Crumpsall a game,' said Onkel Frank. 'He might or might not beat him. I don't know how Lewis would play in front of a crowd, since he says he's never done it.'

Asked Edwards, mildly, 'Do you believe him?'

Onkel Frank studied his whisky in some irritation. 'Yes, I do.'

'Why?'

'Because of his domestic situation and the fact the man reads gas meters for a living!'

'So he can be trusted, you think?'

The Old Man intervened. 'I've told you. He's a clean-living lad.'

'And nobody knows him?' asked Edwards, studiously.

'Nobody in this town.'

'And the idea is to enter him for the Tower and back him for a fair bit of money, early doors?' To Edwards all this was everyday.

'Yes it is, and for that we'll need money, and we'll need to handle the man very responsibly,' warned the Old Man.

'Before I put money in this,' said Edwards, toying with his B-and-S, 'I'd have to see him for myself playing against an opponent who can stretch him like Billy Crumpsall could. And under something like match conditions. Then we'll know if he can do it.'

The Old Man said, 'If you do that and he beats Billy, then the whole world will know how good he is and we won't be able to back him with bad money.'

'He won't beat Billy. I just want to see him try.'

'How do you know he won't?' demanded the Old Man.

'How many people in the North of England can beat Billy when he's trying?' asked Edward, still mildly. 'Billy's not eligible for the Tower because everybody knows he's a Pro and plays strictly for money.' He thought for a moment. 'What we do is, we set up a Challenge Match between Billy and your man. Joe Curl, since he's involved, could arrange for it to be held at the Beach Hotel. Say, on a Saturday night, very soon. To all intents and purposes it will be just a match between two very good players who have a bit of needle going between them. Then we'll see what we'll see.'

'If he's beating Billy at some point,' asked the Old Man, 'what then?'

'Then you ask him to stop beating Billy, obviously.'

The Old Man looked upset. 'I don't want to do that.'

'No choice.'

'Just the same, he isn't like that.'

'He'll have to be, won't he?' added Edwards without emotion, signalling for a replenishment of drinks. 'Anyway, it won't happen, will it, Frank?'

Onkel Frank shook his head. 'How can it? Billy is still a great player.'

The Old Man sipped his whisky-and-water. He looked unhappy about it but this was obviously the best deal he was going to get.

'All right,' he said. 'But I'll need a few quid to sweeten Lewis.'

Edwards reached for his wallet and smiled. This, at least, he understood.

The Beach Hotel was crowded, as if for a presentation. Set on the South Promenade, it had once been a hotel, but it had not taken in guests for many years. Travellers had stayed in hotels with public bars since Dickens's time. Indeed, the only alternative had been dirty and flea-ridden common lodging-houses. But the rise of the seaside boarding-house after the First War (due entirely to paid holidays for the working-class) had transformed those Dickensian sleep-overs into clean, well-lit places for a man to take his family. This development had reduced most of Blackpool's older hotels to large public houses. The Beach was such a casualty. Others can be seen all over the country, even today. 'Just look at their empty rooms and think of the Victorian families who used to use them,' said the Old Man. 'I've stayed in hotels of every possible kind,' he added, 'but never in a Seaside Boarding House. Seventy guests to one lavatory. Incredible.'

That had not stopped him (in a bad season) selling much-needed lavatory fresheners to the seaside landladies, who, acutely conscious of the need, were prepared to pay sixteen-and-six-pence a pint for the liquid to put in the attachments to their lavatory chains. When you pulled the chain, you were immediately enveloped in a lung-choking, eye-watering cloud of lavender, pine, or mint.

The motto of the firm that made this indispensable product

was *Let us Spray.* The legend appeared on all packets and containers of the product. For a season or two before the War it had kept the Old Man gainfully employed. He had sold many, many hundreds of pints of this vital fluid on a commission-only basis. Such desperate times were now behind him, as they were for most of the men (almost no women) who were crowding the Beach Hotel that night.

These men were all snooker enthusiasts. Most played in the local Pub League, in one division or another, and also entered the Christmas Handicaps of various public houses. They bet small monies (sometimes not so small) on every game they ever played, in the same manner that most of them backed a horse or two every day. They were small gamblers but they knew a lot more about snooker than they knew about racing. In snooker only one man can win. No matter how you bet it, it is even money really. In a horse-race a lot of other horses are trying to win. You rarely back a winner but when you do the odds are long, sometimes twenty-to-one or more. In snooker the odds have, classically, to start at even money. After that they are dictated solely by the way the money goes. If there is a lot of money for one player his odds shorten. How the spectators know the way the money is going is a kind of miracle when they get it right and a fix when they don't.

That night in the Beach Hotel the money was heavily for Billy Crumpsall. There was an avalanche of early money for him, struck by one spectator against another (usually known to him) in five or ten-shilling and one-pound bets. There were much bigger bets going on behind the scenes but the spectators knew little of that.

Billy Crumpsall stands in the pool of light and chalks his cue. He is a portly man with immaculate white shirt-sleeves and a dark waistcoat (the uniform of any serious player) and he is smiling. This is his milieu. He has played Money Matches in public houses almost all his life. The noise of the spectators – some in rows of seats around the table, but the rest standing, craning for a view, those at the very back soon to stand on the small drinks-tables – does not disturb him at all. But it is an intimidating atmosphere.

There is from the spectators an expectant buzz. These men (almost all married to, or in some way connected to, a Boarding-house landlady, be she daughter, daughter-in-law, aunt, sister or elderly mother) have, as the Old Man remarks, 'a few bob in the winter because that is when they spend the money they have slaved for during the Summer. Often,' he adds, 'making beds and emptying chamber-pots and sometimes even cooking.' The Old Man shudders. Such menial work is beyond his imagination. The Husbands, as everybody calls them, join in the work of the family Boarding-house during the summer, unless they have a job on the Pleasure Beach or the Golden Mile or on the trams. The Civil Service apart, there is little else. In the winter the Husbands paint and repair and renovate the Boarding-houses for the coming summer. At around Christmas-time, they are carrying, the Old Man said, and ready to bet their hard-earned money on anything that moved.

Hence the florins, half-crowns and pound notes changing hands in a flurry of betting immediately before the first ball was struck. This event did not mean that the betting was over; anything but. Punters would bet on each frame as it went along, or on the whole match, but most had to elect a favourite early, and they had.

Billy Crumpsall.

They knew him, suspected he was bent, but still thought him a brilliant snooker player who won far more games than he lost.

Most of the audience were middle-aged (the young ex-service men with wives and families had no money to gamble with) and had won money, at one time or another, on Billy Crumpsall.

They didn't know James Lewis from, as they used to say, Adam. Of course, they murmured suspiciously to one another, he might be a dark horse. Lancastrian peasants, removed from the soil or the mill by only a generation or two, they ran to many pullovers and weskits (some still wore their cloth caps indoors) and shirts they changed but once a week. Nobody had central heating yet, so all bedrooms were freezing-cold; the only heat in most houses was in the kitchen or living-room. Many wore overcoats. Body heat upped the temperature in the room unbearably and there was a strong smell of beer-breath and male perspiration, alleviated by tobacco smoke. Everybody, without exception, smoked, if only in self-defence.

In this atmosphere Lewis seemed a mild and wan figure. 'He looks,' opined Onkel Frank, 'like a refugee from a Bible Class.'

The Old Man, who, in Onkel Frank's words, Had The Rent on Lewis, was disposed to argue. 'As soon as he pots a few Reds we'll be in business!' he declared with the glee he showed whenever there was a big risk in prospect. We were sitting in the front row of chairs and the hubbub behind us was deafening. Everybody of any consequence in South Shore was present and others from afar (bookies, boxers, footballers) were pointed out as distinguished visitors.

The Word was Out that Lewis could play, but nobody knew how well. So much was obvious: the money wagered on him as yet was small.

Edwards sat, in open Crombie overcoat and silk scarf, Brandy-and-Soda in hand, on the window side of the table, a spot reserved for those who did not, because of their local eminence, sit with the *hoi polloi*. Amongst them were local snooker-players of repute. It was an important occasion. Any man who challenged Billy Crumpsall to a Money Match had to be brave and confident and by definition an outstanding cueman.

But Lewis had come from nowhere, so maybe he wasn't? And he was a total amateur so far as anybody knew. 'This,' the Old Man said, 'has lengthened the odds against him.' The Old Man had obtained, he told me, Three-to-one on the Match. He would bet his remaining monies on the Seven Frames as they progressed and according to how the game was going.

I asked him. 'How is this match going to help Lewis to win the Tower?'

The Old Man closed his eyes at such ignorance. 'It isn't. It's going to help his backers to decide if he *can* win the Tower.'

'But if he beats Billy Crumpsall tonight, won't it shorten his odds in the Tower?'

'Of course it will, but people will still wonder about him. He'll still be a player most people don't know. They'll hesitate to back him to win it. After all, there are only a hundred people in this bar. The first round of the Tower starts on Monday. This is Saturday night. We can get on him early doors tomorrow and on Monday.'

'You seem pretty sure he'll beat Billy Crumpsall.'

'I am,' said the Old Man. 'Billy is a Pro and I respect that. But his great days are behind him. He plays for money and nothing but money.'

'What does Lewis play for?'

The Old Man pondered. 'Glory, what else?'

I looked at Lewis. He looked anything but a contender for glory. His face was pale and his brown home-knitted pullover was not reassuring. Nor was his expression, which was stoical, as if he was ill at ease but concealing it. I said as much to the behatted Onkel Frank, who sat at my left.

'Naturally. Matches are very often won or lost on how you feel before the off.'

'Isn't all this a bit too much for him, since he's never played under these sort of conditions before?'

Onkel Frank pondered, cigarette between lips. 'It's make or break for him. Simple as that.'

'But can he beat Billy Crumpsall?'

Onkel Frank stubbed out his cigarette and leaned towards me. 'This young man is capable of beating any player I have ever played against or seen. Whether he can do it when it is required, only tonight will tell us.'

'Have you had a bet yourself?' I was breaking protocol by asking anybody what they had their money on, but I didn't care. I had to know what Onkel Frank thought. After all, he'd played Lewis. Only in the greenhouse, of course.

'A small investment,' he admitted.

'On which player?'

A long silence while the black eyes bored into me, in astonishment.

'On Billy Crumpsall.'

'You don't think Lewis can do it?'

'It would be a Turn-up if he did. Just look at the thing logically.'

I saw what he meant. Everything in the room was against Lewis. The occasion, the noise, the crowd even. Most of all Billy Crumpsall himself, the magic Money Match player supreme, a man who had renounced fame and honour for money and women, a people's choice.

Standing there, sleek and brilliantined, Billy Crumpsall smiled and I was reminded of a seal in water.

I said, 'I'm having ten bob on Lewis, for the match.'

The Old Man heard that and struck the bet at Three-to-one with a man in the row behind.

Onkel Frank said, 'A fair bet, but it'll go down.'

I didn't reply because Joe Curl, the landlord, was making the announcements. All twenty-two stones of him quivering, he needed only to hold up his hand and he had silence.

'Gentlemen! This is a Seven-frame Challenge Match between Billy Crumpsall, who needs no introduction [loud cheers from the company], and a newcomer to competitive snooker in this part of the world, James Lewis of St Anne's.' He pronounced St Anne's *Sintanns*, as it should be pronounced, not *Sayntawns* like them as talked Far Back did. Lewis received a few scattered hand-claps.

Joe Curl added, po-faced, 'As you all know, these Players operate under Amateur Rules. There will be no purse to be played for and all Gambling or Betting is forbidden Under Law!'

There was loud laughter and cheering at this.

The Old Man had told me that Billy Crumpsall and Lewis were playing for two hundred and fifty pounds, winner take all.

'Who's putting up the money?' I asked.

'Well,' said the Old Man, 'Billy has his usual backers, Chizzy the Bookie and a few others. Edwards and his friends are on Lewis.'

'Do you have any of that?'

'I have a small interest with Edwards's syndicate, no more.'

Decoded, that meant everything, including the kitchen sink. But Onkel Frank had hazarded that already.

'So Edwards thinks he'll beat Billy?'

'Of course he does, or he wouldn't support him.'

'When did Edwards see Lewis play?'

'He went down the next night and saw Lewis make a hundred break in the greenhouse.'

'And that was enough?'

'Yes. He says he's never seen a steadier player than Lewis.'

I wondered at that. Edwards was notoriously a careful gambler. He'd been making a very good living as a Bookmaker since he was nineteen. Everybody in the Racing Game knew that he was good for a touch (a loan) on anything except the price of horses, dogs or billiard-players, where his odds were, properly, iron. If Edwards was that impressed by Lewis, who was I to argue?

I doubled my bet to one pound, at three to one. The Old Man nodded approvingly. Perhaps I was, after all, growing up and starting to enjoy life?

That wasn't it. I just wanted Lewis to win.

Joe Curl, who was acting as Billiard-marker, called for silence. He got it.

Lewis won the toss and stooped down, in a deadly hush, to break off, quite calmly. The triangle of Reds moved hardly at all and his White came down the table and rested behind the Brown. It was a perfect shot.

Billy Crumpsall had a long hard look at Lewis, not at the balls. Then he thought for a long moment, standing absolutely still as the whole assembly looked breathlessly at him. Then he smashed the Reds all over the table.

It was a brutal declaration of War.

Onkel Frank said, 'He's out to break Lewis's nerve!'

Replied the Old Man, 'If anything drops.'

A single Red hovered on the brink of a pocket. Then it dropped.

A relieved sigh went up from Billy Crumpsall's supporters. He now had a clear sight of a lot of Reds, with colours to follow them. There was the prospect of a very big break ahead.

If that solitary Red had not dropped, it would have been Lewis who would have been looking at a big break.

Instead, Billy Crumpsall made forty and just failed to pot a Black that would have given him the first Frame, without doubt.

Lewis potted it instead, and every other available Red and all the colours, and did it all calmly and with such lack of style and flourish that he could have been playing in his greenhouse.

There was a stunned silence.

All the time Lewis was in play, Billy Crumpsall was watching him. His face showed nothing whatever. He had himself played against the very best and he was no doubt wondering what else Lewis had, besides the ability to pot whatever was in front of him.

As the balls were racked up for the second frame the Old Man searched his pockets for spare notes and silver and put everything that he had loose on Lewis to win the second frame. The odds were now evens.

Lewis won the second frame. Billy Crumpsall tried to slow him down, playing a lot of safety-shots, but to no avail. Lewis just potted his way steadily through them, scoring every time he went to the table.

The room was now almost silent. Most of the money was on Billy Crumpsall and therefore most of the throng were on what was beginning to look like a loser, made worse when Lewis ran out a winner of the third frame (narrowly, on the Blue) and Joe Curl declared an interval for, as he put it, 'Refreshments!' adding, 'I want to sell some ale and I won't do it while this game's on, will I?'

He sold a lot of ale because the interval lasted forty-five minutes. As everybody smoked and all the windows were shut – and, very soon, the door, too – and as Closing-time came and went, the air became almost clear blue with tobacco smoke. The Old Man grew fractious.

'This is a lodging-house trick,' he said to Onkel Frank.

'Certainly it is!' agreed Onkel Frank, without surprise.

'What is?' I asked.

'Lewis doesn't smoke or drink,' said Onkel Frank. 'He is sitting over there, bored. Nobody's talking to him. The delay isn't doing him any good. He can lose his concentration.'

'You think it's deliberate?'

Onkel Frank looked at me pityingly. 'Of course it's deliberate. What have I just told you?'

I looked at Billy Crumpsall. He did not look like a man who was three frames down in a Money Match of seven frames. He was drinking large whiskies and he was smiling and listening quietly to his backers, who seemed, to Onkel Frank at least, to have been busy in the crowd. I asked about that.

'They're backing Billy to win by the frame from now on. It's correct betting. Billy's too good to lose all the frames and they can get odds to cover. He's now going at Four-to-one the Match but only Two's the Frame.'

'What,' I asked, 'of the plot to tell Lewis to lose, so you'll all get a better price about him for the Tower Competition?'

'Gone out the window,' said the Old Man. 'The man's won the first three frames. Nobody can ask him to lose the last four.' He shook his head. 'Not that I think he could or would do it anyway.' He sighed. 'He's a Clean-living Lad and that's not his style.'

The Old Man spoke of Lewis as if he was a rare but wonderful animal. Which, in the Old Man's world, he was.

Said Onkel Frank, 'There are four frames yet to go. Anything can happen.'

'Not it,' said the Old Man. 'Lewis is Home and Dry.'

None the less Onkel Frank placed a bet of two pounds on the next frame, Billy Crumpsall to win. Which he did, in a breath-taking hurry, nominating (by pointing with his cue) into which pocket he would put a difficult ball, in a brilliant exhibition of sheer potting.

Lewis had but two visits to the table and scored neither time.

The next frame was Billy's too. He simply carried on where he had left off in the previous frame. The Reds were scattered, Billy got amongst them, potted, potted, potted, leaving nothing, and ran out again, a comfortable winner.

'I told you,' said Onkel Frank to the Old Man. 'The pace is too hot for Lewis.'

'This isn't a billiard match, it's a fokkin riot,' said the Old Man bitterly, as the punters began to cheer Billy Crumpsall's every pot. Lewis's efforts were met with total silence. He did not so much wilt as stand helpless before the tornado that was Billy Crumpsall. Billy was terrifying, a confident, swiftly moving, machine-like player at the top of his form.

'The man,' said Onkel Frank, 'is unstoppable.'

Said the Old Man, 'It will all be on the last frame.'

For Billy Crumpsall had sunk the final Black of the sixth Frame.

Only one Frame remained.

As we all waited for it, the Police hammered at the door, demanding entrance. There was a brief altercation between them (a Sergeant and two constables) and Joe Curl. It was now almost midnight. The drink extension was until eleven o'clock.

The Policemen weren't arguing about that. They heard it was down to the last Frame and had come to see it. Bob Curl found them pints and a vantage point. They took off their helmets and watched, with us, the last historic Frame.

Billy Crumpsall broke off and smashed up the Reds in total confidence, his tactic of the very first Frame, which seemed like several hours ago now but was in fact only two, snooker time not being Real Time. All were agreed that hardly a bad shot had been played all night by either player. Both had given their best and it had been a magnificent best. Now the Reds lay scattered, for the taking. It was now, as Billy Crumpsall had designed it to be, a simple, brutal test of nerve.

Did Lewis have it?

'Get them potted!' breathed the Old Man, his confidence in Lewis unshaken.

Lewis scored a twenty-five break to Billy Crumpsall's thirty, Billy Crumpsall twenty-three to Lewis's twenty-six. Both played safe after these breaks. Breathlessly, they fought for every Red, every colour. The Yellow, Brown, Blue and Pink went down and they were looking at the Black. They both needed it to win. And it was Lewis's turn to play.

The Black was almost on its spot at the far end of the table; the White cue-ball at the near end, but at a slight angle. 'A safety shot is advisable, of course,' the Old Man whispered as Lewis leaned over the table, imperturbably. Billy Crumpsall was now standing still as stone, his shirt clinging to his back. He suddenly looked old, and defeated. There was, truly, nothing more he could do.

Slowly, Lewis cued, sighting the Black, perfectly positioned. He struck the Black hard, so that if he was a millimetre out it would not settle gently in the jaws of the pocket but might come out to relative safety, such was its pace.

But he meant to pot it, above all other considerations.

And pot it he did.

The room was in sudden uproar as the Black disappeared. Of cheers. Of roars of pain. Of sheer animal growl.

Billy Crumpsall's shoulders slumped.

His backers stared at their vast losses.

Then, there was a sudden silence.

The White ball had gently rebounded off the top cushion and

was, very slowly, rolling down the table. It seemed harmless, it was just the spin that Lewis had put on it (besides potting the Black) to prevent it coming down and running into the bottom pocket, always a danger in a shot like that. Lewis had taken proper insurance, in putting spin on the White.

There was a hush as everybody in the room watched the progress of the White ball.

Edwards' calm voice broke the silence.

'He's *In Off*!'

And so he was. The White ball rolled and rolled ever so gently into the jaws of the pocket, hesitated and ever so gently dropped. There was a total, amazed silence. Lewis had lost the frame and the game.

'A chance in a million, to go In Off like that,' said the Old Man in deep anguish.

Billy Crumpsall walked round the table and shook hands wordlessly with Lewis before he was engulfed by his own frantic, frenzied backers. The whole place was, as the Old Man said, 'In a fokkin uproar!'

Which went on for some time.

When we looked for him, Lewis had gone. It was reported he had got into a taxi, carrying his cue-case, within five minutes of losing. Alone.

He never played competitive Snooker again, in the Tower or anywhere else.

He is still a Gas Meter Reader, as far as anybody knows.

The Fancy Man

Marthaann turned up in her Ford Popular.

She wasn't driving it. Jake was.

None of us had met Jake. We had only just heard of him through Aunt Clara, who was the only one who had met him, on her recent trip to Newcastle.

'He is,' said Clara with enormous emphasis, 'A Fancy Man.'

There was a sharp intake of breath all round.

Fancy Men, as anybody who had any knowledge of them would attest, were feckless, good-looking and never, ever, worked at any honest job, preferring to live off a woman who had money rather than work for a living.

Well, Marthaann had money and therefore she qualified.

Fancy Men were not liked. They were avoided, sneered at, made fun of. They were sinful, for a start: their style of living showed a disregard of people's feelings about marriage and the family, feelings which were still very strong amongst ordinary people in the Forties.

Then, it took character to mess about with a marriage, your own or anybody else's. Divorce was still shameful, which is why Marthaann and the Old Man had never gone in for it, in the Old Man's phrase. The fact that they had not lived together as man and wife for almost twenty years altered the situation, as seen by other people and themselves, not at all.

The situation, as I saw it, was that the Old Man was too lazy to bother and Marthaann was ashamed to. Simple as that.

As Aunt Clara told the story, Jake had been a butler to Mr Thompson, the Thirty-Shilling Tailor. Mr Thompson's retail outlets (shops, as they were known then), sold men's suits at the amazing knock-down price of thirty shillings each. Or had, pre-war. Now, with rationing and Utility clothes, his suits were the same price as everybody else's. That was Socialism and we all approved of it. Mr Thompson's feelings were not known.

Jake went into Marthaann's shop to buy a lobster or two for Mr Thompson. Lobsters were off the ration and expensive but Jake knew Mr Thompson didn't care about that. Jake had been impressed by a bustling, bonny woman who knew fishmongering as well as he knew buttling, and, as Aunt Clara put it, one thing had led to another. Although too old for the Army, Jake had soon left Mr Thompson's employ and got a job as a van driver for the Post Office, this being the kind of National Service he felt comfortable with. Well, it beat going into a shipyard or a factory, the only alternatives on offer.

When the War ended, reported Aunt Clara, pouring tea and buttering teacakes with Black Market butter, the job at the Post Office ended. Not wanting to go back to buttling, Jake offered his services to Marthaann as a general handyman around her shellfish shops and at the Fish Quay. Now that stocks of shellfish were more plentiful, Marthaann, getting no younger, required assistance of a new kind. She needed somebody who could cope with buying and transporting her prawns, crabs, lobster and oysters from the Fish Quay at North Shields to her shops in Newcastle, and taking care of the hundred and one things (insurance cards, wages, sicknotes, working conditions) that suddenly, with a Labour Party in power, concerned staff and employers, even in catering – the sink-job, traditionally, of the unskilled working-class trades.

In short, Jake moved into Marthaann's business.

And, inferred Aunt Clara, it was but a short step, if taken delicately and with proper decorum, into Marthaann's bed.

So spake Aunt Clara with her tammy and scarf still on, so anxious was she to impart the news to all and sundry. With this vital step, she said, Jake had attained the comfort of a good home: good food, satin eiderdowns, ham and egg breakfasts, a motor car and a fair bit of money flying about. In short, said Aunt Clara, Jake had struck lucky.

Her voice held a grudging admiration.

'The man is an adventurer?' asked Onkel Frank, hat on head, as ever, looking up from his cup of strong, boiling-hot tea and about to bite into a teacake.

'Hardly that,' said the Old Man, who seemed unsurprised and unconcerned at the news. 'No adventurer would want to take on the job of going down to the Fish Quay at seven o'clock of a morning.' He winced at the idea. 'Bloody cold place, North Shields. East wind cuts right through you. And then there's all that fish, d'you see? A fellow would have to be worse than mad to want it.'

The Old Man hated the smell of fish.

I often thought that the fact that he had refused to go into Marthaann's shops was a much more valid reason for their split-up (as they would say now) than any emotional trauma or anything modern and fashionable like that. The Old Man, now fifty-five, was no nearer being Marriage Material than he had ever been, even as a young Infantry Officer in the First War. But, as he himself often said, he *had* married the woman. In his generation that was thought to be enough. Togetherness, like counselling, had not yet been invented.

In those days, a man was a Husband and found the Wherewithal (money) to keep the Establishment (home) going, and the Wife ran it. That was the Old Man's declaration on the subject. Of course, Marthaann had broken that golden rule by inheriting her Father's shops and running them, so she had no time to run a house and family as well. Neither did it help that the Old Man had never been known to 'provide' well, partly because he didn't have to. In short, it was a Nineties marriage in the Twenties, with all the modern problems of Male and Female roles, such as who looks after the children and who does what and when they do it. It was tangled up and wrong, for the time. Marthaann genuinely thought marriage mattered. The Old Man genuinely didn't care one way or the other. He regarded all man-made institutions as inherently fallible and unsatisfactory. He had, in fact, dropped out from most of them long before the Sixties made dropping out fashionable. He did it without the aid of booze or drugs, that was all.

'Marthaann,' said Aunt Clara, with emphasis, 'doesn't like people thinking of her as having a Fancy Man and I think she pretends that she and Jake are married!'

'The woman's a fool,' said Onkel Frank. 'Everybody will know that isn't the case. So why do it?'

Onkel Frank did not censure Marthaann. He was simply applying his famous logic, which, as the Old Man remarked, more often than not got him nowhere.

'She's doing that,' said the Old Man, 'because she's a Methodist and she cares what people think.'

'Not enough to stop her doing it!' said Aunt Clara, who had always had a Fancy Man in her life since her husband, the Scotch Comic, had gone. Her current beau was Harry, the sign-writer with the Tower Company, who had a wife from whom he was separated but (of course) not divorced. She worked as a barmaid at Feldman's Theatre. That was how people did it then. They found their own accommodations, as they always had. They had a care of the proprieties. I found all this subterfuge and messiness of living foolish, but then I was only twenty-five and I hadn't learned that life is almost always emotionally messy, no matter whose life it is.

This did not apply to the Old Man, who never allowed emotion into his life, since it would have interfered with racing and living the way he wanted to. Hence his stoical reaction to the news of Marthaann's Fancy Man. Nowadays, a Samaritan on the other end of a telephone would doubtless have told the Old Man and Marthaann to Talk It All Out. Given they had never talked to each other about anything, such advice would have been ridiculous.

The way things were, the Old Man felt unthreatened (as they would say today), and that was enough. Marthaann, after all, lived two hundred and fifty miles away. Just, as he said, a nice distance.

Except now she was here, in Blackpool. With a Fancy Man. Who didn't sound all that fancy, since he was apparently prepared to get his hands in amongst the fish.

Aunt Clara had a thought on that. 'My belief is that he's after her money.'

This remark alerted the whole company, which included – since it was midsummer – my sister Peggy and her husband Matt, along with their young son, Little Matty. Big Matt, his father, was still in the Fire Service but now a Senior Officer, and since he was no better at picking winners than the Old Man he was often in a state of being short, as the Old Man would say, of the necessary. Matt was paid monthly, and a large sum at that. He was free with loans to the Old Man, which, of course, were never repaid. The Old Man would have considered, if you had asked him, that providing Matt with Onkel Frank's tips for the Dogs was worth whatever monies he had temporarily borrowed from Matt.

The point was, it was never temporary.

Matt didn't seem to mind. His attitude was what we would nowadays call 'laid-back'. This easygoing philosophy, coupled with his physical courage born of a love of sport, had been useful in the War when burning buildings were collapsing all around him in the Liverpool Blitz.

Now, all that was over. He smiled amiably at the news of Jake. He wasn't going to worry himself about Marthaann's doings. As a Catholic, he did not judge people as the Nonconformists do, leaving all that to God. His wife, my sister Peggy, was a cradle Nonconformist who had 'turned Catholic' to marry Matt – provoking the fury of Marthaann, who was not only a Nonconformist but a bigoted Nonconformist. Her attitude would have been much the same towards *anybody* who was not a Nonconformist. That might be thought very strange now but tolerance in religious matters had not yet been invented.

Peggy, a dark-haired young woman of spirit, was stung by the mention of money, which she never had enough of. That was because she had, to all intents and purposes, married her father.

'I gave Mother my savings – Two Hundred and Fifty Pounds – to put down on her new house! That was fifteen years ago. I've never had a penny of that back!' Peggy's dark eyes blazed. 'I don't like the sound of this Jake one little bit!'

Breathed Aunt Clara, 'There you are, then!' Her theatrical instincts were satisfied. Somebody had at last responded dramatically to her story, which until then had been falling on unresponsive male ears. 'You'll see him for yourselves tomorrow,' she promised, 'when they arrive.'

'No hurry for that,' grunted Onkel Frank.

The Old Man asked, mildly, 'Does this fellow have a bet?'

Nobody knew.

So, Marthaann and Jake arrived in Blackpool in some style, in her Ford Popular. In the Forties and Fifties not many people had a motorcar. Only Ted and Matt, in the entire family, had one. Matt because he had never been without one since passing his driving test at the age of seventeen and now drove a Fire Service Austin Saloon, *circa* 1938, free of charge because of his rank of Column Officer. He was one of only two men to reach that rank during the War from the starting point of Auxiliary Fireman. The other was Lord Brabazon, which, remarked the Old Man, was only to be expected. 'The English way of doing things, class prejudice, that's all' was my own Socialist response.

The only other person in the family with a motor car was Ted, who had bought a fourth-hand Railton for a hundred pounds a month or two before. It looked good and would have gone at eighty, in Matt's hands. In Ted's it went at fifty.

Ted was not a speed merchant but he rather liked looking like one. The Railton was a purchase designed to 'Show the Flag', the Old Man said.

'Why?' I asked. I hadn't a Railton, or any possibility of getting one, so I was out of sympathy with Ted on that score.

'Looks good for his business. You have to look the part, you see.'

'How will a Railton help him to sell suites of furniture?'

'Gives creditors and customers confidence in you if you look the part.'

'I thought his problem was getting hold of anything to sell.'

That *was* Ted's problem. Since Marthaann had staked him to the tune of Three Thousand Pounds six months before, he had found that making a million in business (and what is anybody in business for, if not to make a million?) was not so easily done.

In the Attlee years, when nothing much was being produced for the Home Market, it was harder than ever. Everything that could be sold abroad was being sold abroad, to pay off the enormous debts the country had incurred winning the War.

Onkel Frank had an emphatic view of it all. 'We worked ourselves to death to stop Hitler. All our factories are clapped out. All our workers are clapped out, too, after grafting twelve hours a day for six years. We're broke and the Americans, who wouldn't have come into the War unless they'd been bombed into it by the Japs, will take all our old markets. We'll give the Empire away because we lack the will to keep it and we'll be a Fourth-rate Power very soon.'

'Labour has to release some consumer goods on to the Home Market,' I said, repeating what I'd read in *Tribune*. 'We can't go on with Utility furniture for ever!'

I couldn't even afford Utility furniture, which everybody in Blackpool hated anyway because it was made by modernist designers who didn't realise what ordinary people wanted, which was overstuffed three-piece suites and fitted carpets and flying ducks on the wall.

Ted sold those items, when he could get them, and prospered. He did not stock Utility but often bought, second-hand, the effects of people who had recently died. In St Anne's and Lytham and the North and South Shores of Blackpool that very often meant people who were, as they say in the North of England, Living Retired.

Such people usually had good, if old, moquette-upholstered suites, oak dining-tables, brass coal-scuttles, heavy mahogany dressers and wardrobes, delicate occasional tables and magnificent, roomy, cedarwood beds, built for women to have babies in. Fortunately, the relatives of those recently bereaved advertised the fact in the local newspapers.

Ted and his wife Gladys were at their doors within the hour. A price was arranged, and Ted's vans arrived and took the furniture away the same day, before any competitor could offer more money. The furniture went into Ted's workshop, where his craftsmen set about cleaning, polishing, repairing and reupholstering – whatever was required to make them as good as new. To be sold, naturally, at a profit.

As Ted said, all he ever bought was the cream of the crop. He now had a largeish house, not in a fashionable district yet, but comfortable. His suits were handmade (and bought without coupons) and he looked what he was rapidly becoming, a successful young businessman. He no longer went to the Dogs.

'A loss,' said the Old Man, regretfully. 'He would have made the best Bookie in the North of England.'

'Doesn't want it,' said Onkel Frank. 'Anyway, the Game's finished. The Totes have spoilt it.'

The Totalisators now gave better odds than the Bookies, on Racehorse or Dog-tracks. Sometimes I wondered why punters bet with Bookies at all. I decided that it was because they liked the personal touch. It was the difference between buying from a large store (no Supermarkets yet) and Off the Barrow.

So, Ted, who had been first a naval draughtsman (from which time he had only his beautiful printing to show) and then pursued a short career as a Bookie's clerk and door-to-door canvasser and shop assistant in the Depression, was now using his rich experience of life to sell furniture and make money. Probably the Dog-track experience was most valuable. If you can make a living at the Dogs you can make one anywhere. Ask anybody.

Onkel Frank asked the obvious question, as we listened to Aunt Clara's news of Jake the Fancy Man and Marthaann.

'Why is she coming here?'

'I would have thought it obvious,' said the Old Man.

'How so?'

'Ted owes her money. The lad here owes her money.'

'Only a hundred,' I protested. 'And it's well spent!'

'The thing is,' the Old Man said, wise in the ways of creditors the world over, 'she has come to collect.'

'She'll be lucky,' I said. 'I haven't finished my novel yet.'

'She won't care about that.'

'It's no sort of money at all, a hundred pounds!' I hated owing money but I had hated working at the Min of Ag and Fish even more. I hoped I wasn't developing the Old Man's ways. I had a suspicion, hastily stepped on, that I had a little more of his temperament than I would care to acknowledge. Or maybe it was just example. I hoped so.

Marthaann would have called the Old Man a Bad Influence. People nowadays would say it was Genetic.

I was in fact living like a professional gambler with no stake-money to speak of and I didn't like it. I'd been in a War for the sake of people like Marthaann. They ought to be grateful.

'What does she want?' I asked, angrily.

'Money,' said the Old Man. 'Or just to lord it over everybody for a bit.'

As ever, he was close. For Marthaann, fox-fur around neck and attired in a splendid Costume (nowadays called a Suit) of dark-blue worsted, had not been sitting long at the family meeting she'd called at her private hotel on the South Promenade before she made her attitudes and intentions plain.

'Business has fallen off,' she asserted. 'The good times for the War Workers – ten or twelve pounds a week, most of them – are over. Even when I can get prawns and crabs, I have a job to sell them.'

'All this is new, isn't it? I always thought the shops were little gold mines.' As the only one of the triumvirate (Ted, Peggy and myself) who had not been under Marthaann's thumb during her reign as a stern mother with a heavy hand, I was unafraid of her and didn't care, really, what she thought. It was tough but true that her business came before everything else. Which was why she had never, ever, thought of following her family to Blackpool.

I felt at some level she was guilty about that. If she was, she didn't show it.

'Young fellow,' she said, eyes flashing, 'when you're a bit older you'll know money doesn't grow on trees, in the shops or anywhere else. Men are back from the War and they have only six or seven pounds a week to spend. They have families to keep. Or the responsible ones do.' This was a dig at me, but I said nothing. There wasn't much I could say.

Marthaann went on, pouring tea with plump, beringed hands: 'My old gentlefolk customers, who bought my lobsters and oysters, are selling up and going to Kenya or some such place.'

It was true. Half the upper-class families were selling their country houses for what they could get and hightailing it out of the country because the Labour Party's inheritance tax was beggaring them. This was hard luck, since so many of them had lost sons and brothers in the War. They had come a cropper like those in the Lloyd's débâcle of the Nineties.

Of course, I had no sympathy to spare for such people. Nobody had. They'd had it too good for too long. We were all building the New Jerusalem, as Nye Bevan rightly said. And about time too, we thought. The trouble was, it was slow in coming. The Pits had been Nationalised but the owners seemed to have been paid off handsomely. Medicine had been Nationalised but even Nye had had to buy off the Harley Street consultants, by giving them the right to run private practices as well as work in the new, crowded hospitals, where a huge backlog of ill and old people queued for help.

None of that seemed right. Nor did the mechanics of Naked Capitalism, as outlined by Marthaann.

'I've been looking at things a bit closely,' she said, 'and I believe I'm right in saying that you owe me money, all three of you. I'm here to ask you: when are you going to pay me back?'

We stared at her, astonished.

With all her faults (too easily hurt, too narrow-minded, too wedded to her shops, too afraid, as I see now, of failing the memory of her father Isaac, the tycoon), this was not Marthaann, it simply wasn't. Her way, as the Old Man said, was to lord it over the rest of the family but to stop well short of bringing about a breach, because the family, really, was all she had.

Now, there was a difference. Now, Marthaann was obviously ready to risk that breach. We all three of us exchanged glances and, without a word spoken, came to the same conclusion: this was Jake's doing.

Nothing was said as Marthaann handed round a plate of cakes. In the dining-room of the private hotel (a glorified boarding-house with no drinks licence) the first rush of visitors since the War ate their High Teas.

Peggy it was who spoke first. 'You owe me two hundred and fifty pounds. With interest, that is three hundred. I'd like to know when I can expect that.'

People say that money causes family rows. It doesn't. Emotion does, and money just stands in for emotion, that's all. That, anyway, was true then and, I imagine, still is, except that now people hide it behind psychological explanations. Well, whatever, there it was: emotion, a lot of it.

Marthaann fielded Peggy's retort with aplomb. 'Peg, that house housed you for years. You had money from me when you got married. You've had large sums from me whenever Matt was short of cash. I think you owe me two hundred and fifty pounds at least and I'm not including that *car*.'

The car was an old Ford Marthaann had sold to Matt before the War. It was worth, then, perhaps ten pounds. He had given her a new Singer Sewing-machine for it. The retail price of the Sewing-machine was thirteen pounds. What Matt had omitted to tell her was that the Sewing-machine was on Hire Purchase and only one instalment had been paid. That instalment had been of one pound and another twelve was due.

The Old Man had nodded his head to the sagacity of this. Marthaann had been understandably furious. That, in part, was the reason Matt was not present. He had not yet been forgiven. Even the intervention of the War had not lessened Marthaann's anger. But in the Depression anything went. We all understood that – all of us except Marthaann, who was listening to Peggy without sympathy.

'I worked in that shop for you, day in, day out, for four years and all I got was a shop assistant's pay. And I was your daughter!'

Peggy's voice held anguish and hurt. The trouble was, she loved her mother. There was only seventeen years between them. They'd gone to dance-halls together, posing as sisters, doing the Charleston. Peggy was sentimental about that. Foolishly, because her mother wasn't.

'Well, you would get married. The shops were there for you, after I'm gone.'

'Were? Or *are*?'

Marthaann sipped her tea, imperturbably. She had won and she knew it. 'Things change, Peggy.'

Peggy sat back, tears misting her eyes, hurting. She had never won an argument with Marthaann in her life and this evening was no exception.

Ted, in his splendid handmade suit, was tiring of this. 'I take it you be including me in this?'

He was hurt, too, but wouldn't show it. His long apprenticeship with the Old Man, whom he so much resembled physically, had hardened him quite a lot. Marthaann, to whom he was, as they used to say, the Apple of Her Eye, was instantly disarmed.

'No, not you, not at all, Ted.'

'Why not me?'

Marthaann looked at him with love. 'You'll pay me back. I know that. It's just I'm getting a bit worried about money.'

'Or somebody's worrying you about it,' I said.

'What's that supposed to mean?' she asked, taken aback, which I meant her to be.

'This Jake,' I said, 'whoever *he* is!'

It was unkind but at twenty-five you are unkind if you feel menaced, and I did. I had enough on my plate struggling with my new life as a (self-declared) writer, plus, as everybody in the world seemed to be reminding me, a wife and child to look after, without added aggravation over a mere hundred pounds. The fact that, apart from my long-spent gratuity, I never had a hundred pounds in my hand at any one time was beside the point. Marthaann was too flustered to make a riposte. She was, also, too alarmed to think of anything but the shame.

'Jake's only helping me with my business,' she said, colouring and looking down at her rings. There was a long, disbelieving silence. I felt sorry for her but I didn't feel sorry for Jake, whoever he was.

Ted broke the silence. 'Mother,' he said gently, 'you'll have all your money from me by Christmas. Will that do?'

Marthaann nodded her head, not looking up. I guessed she was close to tears. In this sort of situation, she always was. It was her female strength and power of recovery you had to look out for. Peggy knew that better than any of us and struck at once.

'*You* still owe *me* money, not the other way round, and that's a fact!'

Marthaann still didn't look up. I felt sorrier for her than ever, but she had brought it on herself. I did not bring up my hundred pounds and she didn't either. After all, she'd got Ted's promise and that was what she wanted most, if money was what we were talking about. Which is wasn't, really.

'Hello, people. I'm Jake. I'm sure Madge has told you about me.'

We looked up. Jake was a tall, plump but muscular man, with a balding head, and he spoke with a butler's voice. That is, standard English, but not quite. He was confident and confiding in the manner of manservants from (as George Robey used to put it) Time Immoral.

There was a feeling of timeless immortality about him too, at that. But what struck me, at first, was his likeness to the Tory politician Sir David Maxwell Fyffe. Being around gentlefolk much of his life had made him look, almost, like one of them.

'Who's Madge?' Peggy asked.

'Jake doesn't like Marthaann,' whispered Marthaann, totally defeated by now. 'He prefers Madge.' I had never heard her whisper before. She always had a loud, confident voice.

'But Madge *isn't* your name,' said Peggy with pleasure.

Marthaann's voice was almost inaudible now. 'No, but he likes it better, you see.'

'No, I don't see,' said Peggy, sharply.

Jake sat down in the comfortable armchair and signalled to a harassed maid. 'More tea, dear, if you can manage that for me?' And he winked.

The maid smiled. 'In two ticks, Sir.'

'Thank you, my dear.' The eye was lecherous, no mistake about it. Marthaann was not the sole subject of Jake's attentions. Any woman was. He turned to Peggy but found her frozen-faced and hostile. None the less, he tried. 'Marthaann's a servant girl's name, isn't it?'

'Well, I suppose you would know!'

Jake looked surprised at the hostility but smiled, politely enough. I had the feeling he had been in situations like this before. 'I have been a gentleman's butler, yes, that's true,' he admitted.

'Isn't that a demeaning sort of job?' asked Peggy, going for the jugular.

Jake seemed even more surprised and to gain time lit a cigarette taken from a gold case, obviously new and just as obviously a present from Marthaann, and said, directing his gaze at Ted and myself and ignoring the women, 'I have buttled for several gentlemen but my last employer was Mr Thompson of the Thirty Shilling Tailors. That is to say, Mr Thompson owns the company, along with all its many branches. Now, while I was in Mr Thompson's employ I walked on the same carpets as Mr Thompson, I ate the same food as Mr Thompson, I drank the same wine as Mr Thompson, I smoked Mr Thompson's cigars and I had none of Mr Thompson's worries!'

I grinned, but Ted didn't. He said, in a neutral voice, 'How is the suite of furniture I sent?'

'Very good. We . . . *I* like it,' said Marthaann with a quick sidelong glance at Jake.

Jake ignored that too and, turning to me – since, after the

grin, he saw me as a possible ally – said: 'Ted sold your Mother a suite of furniture for a hundred pounds that I could have got for forty and your Mother could have got for thirty-five.' He turned back and drew on his cigarette. 'Smart work, Ted.'

'I sold it to Mother, not to you,' said Ted coolly but he had lost that round.

'You've been working for the Post Office?' I said, hoping to throw him.

'Gave it up. Terrible money, awful people.' He smiled magisterially, looking more like Sir David Maxwell Fyffe than ever. 'Nowadays, I'm helping your Mother with her business. She's got far too much to do, and since it seems nobody else wants to do the work . . . well, I'm new to it all but I'm learning.'

Said Peggy, flatly, 'Our Grandfather founded that business.'

'I know he did,' said Jake. 'But none of you want anything to do with it, do you?'

Another point to Jake. Plainly, he *had* been in this sort of situation before.

Peggy fired a last dart. 'You're not a young man, Mr . . . I didn't get your name?'

'Jake will do, my dear.'

'Have you ever been married?'

There was a shocked silence at this. Marthaann looked even more fixedly at her rings.

Said Jake, 'Of course I have. What man of my age hasn't? I went into the Army straight off the farm, in the First War – told them I was eighteen when I was only sixteen. Went to France. In the Artillery. I was married wearing khaki, like this young fellow here.'

I thought of the Old Man's reaction to anybody who'd survived the War. 'What were they *in*?' he always asked. Usually it was Army Service Corps, Medical, sometimes Artillery. Never, or hardly ever, the Infantry. So, Jake even at sixteen was a survivor. Unless he was lying, which he wasn't, since he brought out his wallet and took a faded monochrome photograph from it. He passed it to me, clearly confident that I would be impressed. It was him all right and I was. People were impressed by bravery and loyalty to country then.

I handed it to Ted but he passed it back to Jake with but a cursory glance. 'Long time ago,' he said, with finality.

The young harassed maid arrived with the tea for Jake. 'Thank you, my dear,' he said, and put a coin in her hand, holding it a moment longer than was absolutely necessary. 'Very kind of you.' And he winked again.

Marthaann didn't see it. She didn't see anything. She was still looking down at her rings.

Jake poured himself a cup of tea and ate a cream cake with a fork, which looked a difficult thing to do. Eccentric, too, in the North of England, then as now.

Ted glanced at his watch and stood up. 'Must go. Things to do.' He smiled at Marthaann, who was grateful for it. 'See you tomorrow evening for supper? At the house? Gladys is expecting you.' He pointedly ignored Jake but Jake was not offended. After all, he'd been ignored practically all his life; he'd been a piece of furniture, as he said later, to the Ladies and Gentlemen of his world. He had not minded that. Like most servants, he was a voyeur by training.

Ted waved his hand and was gone.

I felt like following him but Peggy was on her feet too, calling, 'Ted, drop me off, will you?'

I guessed she wanted to be first with her impressions of Jake to the Old Man. They, like Clara's, would not be good. I felt that there was a bit more to learn about Jake and no matter how much you thought you knew there would always be more. A Fancy Man had to have a history.

Jake shook Peggy's hand and gazed into her eyes, which were hard and unfriendly. 'I hope we get to know each other well, Peggy.'

'I doubt that,' said Peggy, and was gone.

Marthaann recovered a little and poured tea for Jake. 'Take no notice of Peggy. She's always like that. It's going to that posh school did it. I never should have let Percy send her there.'

'Which school was that?' asked Jake, idly sipping his tea.

'Newcastle Central High School for Girls.'

'That's only a posh school in Newcastle. Cheltenham Ladies College, that's a posh school.' Jake sighed. 'But in Newcastle nobody will have heard of it.'

'Which school did you go to?' I asked wickedly.

'The School of Experience and the University of Life,' responded Jake, in an avuncular manner. I laughed and he looked surprised and laughed too, and I saw the charm. It was a dangerous and wicked quality but I didn't mind it. There was nothing I had that he wanted, so he could show off, to me. Which he proceeded to do.

'Do you take a glass of whisky?'

'They don't serve it here. This is a non-licensed hotel.'

Jake took a leather flask from his hip-pocket. He hailed the harassed maid. 'My dear, could you find us a couple of small clean glasses? And a little water in a jug?'

The girl smiled and nodded. 'Clean glasses, clean jug,' she said in a flighty voice.

Jake pressed another coin in her hand. She wasted no time and in but a moment he had poured the whisky-and-water into two glasses and gave one to me. 'Young fellow, I hope you and I are going to be friends. Good health.'

I nodded and drank the whisky-and-water. I usually drank beer, but I wasn't going to tell Jake that. I guessed he already knew anyway.

Taking a long leather case from his pocket, he asked, '*Can* you smoke a cigar?'

I had never smoked a cigar. 'Yes,' I said.

'Good,' said Jake ironically, producing a silver cigar-cutter. He snipped off the end of the cigar before handing it to me. That was a kindness, I realised. He could have embarrassed me. I had no idea how to clip a cigar. Now I knew. I drew on the cigar and drank the whisky and thought that, well, Jake wasn't such a bad fellow after all. Which, of course, was exactly what he wanted me to think.

Marthaann excused herself, saying she felt tired and would have a wash and a lie-down in her room. Jake didn't get to his feet but he said, 'That's right, Madge, take it easy. I've booked for the Winter Gardens, Second House. We can have supper somewhere afterwards?'

'Whatever you like,' said Marthaann, meekly.

Usually, she made those sort of decisions. I began to feel even sorrier for her, but there was nothing I could do. People, as the Old Man often said, Go to Hell in Their Own Way.

The Old Man, for his part, was not surprised to hear of Marthaann's plight, as I saw it. When I suggested that perhaps he might have a word with her, tell her that Jake was, well, what he was, the Old Man answered testily, 'Don't you think she knows that already?'

'How can she know it? She'd run a mile if she knew it.'

'No, she wouldn't. He's Somebody. He's better than Nobody. Simple as that.'

I said, 'You sound as if you've been expecting something like this for a long time.'

'Let's just say it's no surprise.'

'If there's any money, Jake will get it.'

'He's welcome to it. You recall the old Arab proverb "He who marries for money earns it"?'

'Even if that's true, she's badly advised being with him at all, isn't she? It can only go wrong, can't it?'

'Depends,' reflected the Old Man, 'on what there is in it for him. If it continues to be worth his while, he'll stay. The moment it isn't, he'll go.' The Old Man paused, thoughtfully. 'Did you say the fellow's good at building walls?'

'He said he is.' Jake had, in an aside, admired the Guest-house exterior, built of local brick to resist the salt winds.

Said the Old Man, 'Then he's Done Time!'

'You mean he's been in prison?'

'Only place a butler would learn how to build a wall.'

'But a butler's job's a good one. Why should he get into prison?'

'Who knows? Because he got a chambermaid pregnant, then pinched some of his employer's money to pay her off? Got found out? Anything.'

'He's not a bit like a convict.'

'Con men aren't, are they?' The Old Man added, 'I've known a few Con Men around the Race-tracks. They always boast they con money out of gullible women by craft and cunning. In reality they go to bed with them then steal their jewellery while they're asleep.'

'Why don't you tell her that?'

The Old Man shuddered at the very idea. 'Look, one thing you must learn. Saying anything to a woman infatuated with a man is like talking to the wall.'

Being only twenty-five I had no knowledge of that, so I had to give up. But I wasn't sure the Old Man was right, so when Jake offered us a short holiday in North Wales I said yes, on behalf of Edith and the kids. We now had Maddy, our singing star, aged one.

It may seem odd to take a holiday from a place like Blackpool, but it isn't really. You get extremely tired of crowds and sea and sand. Blackpool is a noisy place and very wearing on the nerves. And my nerves were showing a bit, since all I seemed to do was sit at my desk and write, write, write – the novel, radio plays, my column for the newspaper, all of which Edith typed up on a Barlock portable. It was all somewhat ill paid, as most pleasurable work seemed to be, and the finances didn't run to holidays. So North Wales, all mountains and solitude, all presumably free, was a welcome idea.

Besides, I had wanted to see more of Jake at close quarters. I wanted to know what he was really like, what his intentions really were regarding Marthaann. I felt it my duty to find out, which was somewhat pompous of me but I didn't know that then.

The Old Man said, 'Take it easy. Just go along with it, if you must.'

'I think we know so little about him we can only benefit by knowing more. After all, the family shops are at stake!'

Said the Old Man, 'Can't think why you bother. Don't want 'em, do you? Nor does anybody else – Ted, Peg.'

'No,' I said, stubbornly, 'but just the same.'

I had to know more. I was curious in all sorts of ways. For one thing, I'd never met a Con Man before. If he was one.

First stop, Portmadoc.

The Ford Popular rolled into it around eight o'clock in the

evening, Jake driving, Marthaann in front, Edith and the kids and myself in the back. It was a crowded vehicle and a tiring journey but Jake had kept up a flow of fluent and interesting talk much of the way. He spoke of large dinner parties held by his various employers: of the guests, among them one or two Royals and several titled people whose names I had seen in newspapers. All this had to be true; nobody would be able to make it up. It was very informative, to me. There seemed to be a lavish spaciousness about these society-people's lives. They did as they liked, when, where and with whom they chose. The ordinary rules of lower-middle-class society did not apply to them. Nothing would shame these people, their marriage bonds were ignored, their duties to their children often disregarded, their loyalties given entirely to adult members of their families and their energy devoted to their own gratifications. I was surprised when Edith said, 'They must be lonely, never having anybody to really love. Their kids off at school, all those affairs, what's that but unhappiness?'

Edith always surprised me with statements like that. Hers was such a different perspective from my own. (I just thought: I wouldn't mind living like that for a bit.) I wondered if we thought along the same lines about anything. The point was, she usually saw the truth about a situation without having to experience something that explained it. It's a rare gift. A little like the Old Man's knack of forecasting people's actions through working out what they really wanted from any situation and basing all calculations on that.

One was an amateur view of human nature. The other was a professional one, because the Old Man lived by his judgements, which were often, of course, wrong. But more often than not they were right, and this talent, as Onkel Frank said, had kept him out of serious trouble all his life.

But Jake was talking, shocked at Edith's remark. 'But the rich *are* happy, my girl. They do everything that the poor only wish they themselves could do! They eat and drink what they like, they go to bed with whom they like, they work if they want to and don't if they don't feel like it. The poor have no choice. Believe me, I've been poor and I know.'

'When were you poor?' I asked, interested.

'When I was married to a young wife and had a young family, like you are now. I was poor then.'

'What did you do about it?'

'I got out.'

'Of the marriage?'

'Yes. Mind you, I had to run away at dead of night or they'd have killed me!'

Jake swerved the Popular into the little seaside town. Portmadoc had a breathtaking bay and hills behind the town, and a pretty little row of ex-fishermen's houses along the harbour, but I had no appetite for further scenic views. I'd been looking at scenery all day.

'Who'd have killed you?'

'Her brothers. Still would, I dare say, if they saw me.'

'You're not serious?'

'I am. There are a lot of shotguns in the country. Problem was, young fellow, I got another young woman pregnant as well, at around the same time, so I had no choice. I had to run for it.'

'You left them *both*?'

'Of course I did. Only thing a sensible man could do.'

Said Marthaann, quickly, 'Jake, don't fill his head with all that old stuff and nonsense.'

'Madge,' said Jake, bringing the car to a halt outside the row of cottages, 'the young man asked me a question and I answered it. We're on holiday, and we can talk frankly or what's the point?'

He got out of the Ford. 'I'll try this cottage here. Just been painted – probably nice, decent people.'

He walked across the road, knocked on the door and talked to the young housewife who opened it. She was pretty and smiling and we could hear her laugh at something Jake said. Marthaann said, to me, 'You should take Jake's stories with a pinch of salt.'

'You mean he tells lies?'

'No, but he has his own view of things.'

'Yes, I can see that.'

Jake came back to the car, having knocked on another door two cottages down, and said, 'Madge and me are in this cottage; you're two doors down. The name is Llewellyn, and it's five bob each Bed and Breakfast, half a crown for the kids.'

I had envisaged staying at a hotel and Marthaann paying for everything, but plainly that was not to be. Jake was a professional. Pros get value for their money and resent paying over the odds.

Jake and Marthaann's room was spotless, the breakfast scrambled eggs and bacon, beautifully done, the young woman childless and a mite too attentive to Jake, who squeezed her waist when they said goodbye, on the blind side of Marthaann.

Our room was hermetically sealed, had a dirt-encrusted lampshade over the bed, and the breakfast was foul – bacon swimming in grease with black specs from the frying-pan liberally sprinkled over it. Everybody ate fried breakfasts then, if they could get them. Nobody had had enough to eat for years, what with the Depression and the War. In the War, only RAF aircrew got bacon and eggs for breakfast every day.

The WC was at the bottom of a very long garden and I'd trailed the kids up there with the aid of a candle and a newspaper, only to find, to their delight, that it was an ash-closet. I had seen one before, in a miner's house in County Durham. To the kids, it was an unexpected treat.

On to Rhyl, where the water was so clear you could see the sand and seashells six feet down. Then to Colwyn, to stay with a shoe-shop manager who had won the Military Medal in Normandy and had it mounted on the mantelpiece. This was a luxurious house, for the time and place, full of expensive bric-a-brac. The wife, perhaps, had money. I tried to get the husband to reminisce about the War but all he wanted to talk about was shoes. We went to bed under a huge silken eiderdown. Pre-war, said my wife. They overcharged us the next day, despite seeing our two small kids. I wondered why they bothered to let rooms at all. They plainly didn't need the money. Perhaps some people always need the money.

It was, all in all, working out as quite an expensive holiday. When Marthaann asked me to contribute, on the last day, five pounds towards the petrol, I was more than a little affronted. Jake, I realised, made noises like an aristocrat but behaved like a peasant. Also, I learned much later, he had in his pocket a pair of knickers, a present from the young housewife in Portmadoc, discovered by Marthaann on her routine search of his jacket and trousers. But I didn't know that then.

Marthaann didn't mention the hundred pounds, which was just as well because I didn't have a hundred pounds. Our expenses had gone up to meet our income. We were just about surviving, the new Council house being cheap to run, but we still needed to buy more, and lots of coal for the fires, and the kids seemed to be growing out of their shoes almost every week. I finished The Novel, sent it off to Michael Joseph, and in three weeks back came a letter of acceptance offering a Seventy-five Pound advance, to be set against royalties.

I wasn't surprised.

Now, I'm amazed.

This was a time of shortage of newsprint. Publishers' Printing Orders were low. A new novel was something publishers said they wanted, but very few of my friends who had been writing in the Little Reviews (and who had, most of them, been to Public Schools or Oxford) had been able to find publishers. Neither had my BBC producer friends. So, for a long time, I kept the whole thing secret.

When Michael Joseph threw a party at Claridges for the Book I didn't go, pretending I had influenza. Of course they would have paid my fare and hotel bills, but I was growing touchy about being poor. Subsequently, good reviews and an option from Rank's at Pinewood Studios for The Book made me feel better. But that hadn't happened yet. My name was soon in the National newspapers (forty reviews, nearly all good – unlike today, when ten notices is a quorum), which I was sure would galvanise Marthaann into action regarding the hundred pounds. I hourly expected a letter demanding repayment. It didn't come, and for a very good reason.

Jake had gone.

Much later I went to see Marthaann at her newly purchased cottage in the West Country. It was strange to find her in such a setting. A village street, a thatched cottage: it wasn't *her*! I'd always known Marthaann against the bustle of her shops, the crowds of people on Saturday nights, the flashing knives of the girls opening crabs and oysters and prawns, the crustaceans piled in great heaps along the marble counters, the tills ringing up the money she was making.

Now, apparently, all that was over. The shops had been sold for what she could get for them, which was not very much, since to run shellfish shops you had to be brought up in the trade. There is simply too much to know. How much stock to buy, what price to pay, what stock will keep, what won't, all that. Even Jake's son (it was news to me he had anything to do with his offspring) had been given a shop free, but it had failed.

'But where's Jake now? And why are you here, in a place like this?'

Marthaann shook her head. She wore a print overall and seemed older. Yet she was very fit and did not have, as she said, a grey hair in her head. The Old Man said that was because of her lack of wisdom. Certainly, her story bore out his theory.

Apparently Jake had taken her unawares one Sunday morning in her opulent semi-detached in Newcastle, with the simple announcement: 'Madge, I'm leaving you.'

'I shouldn't have been surprised,' said Marthaann. 'I'd been a fool, I knew that. I'd stood for all his women because he only wanted them for you-know-what.' She wouldn't say sex. It wasn't polite then.

'Wasn't he really going off with a woman?'

Marthaann shook her head. 'Not him. He was going back to his wife.'

I said, 'How could he? He hadn't seen her for years and years. Had he?'

'He said he felt it was right to go back. He said he felt bad about not seeing his other son in all that time. His other Son's thirty now, with a family of his own.'

'What happened?'

'Well, he just went. Took the car and went. Of course, he had three cottages in his name. I'd given them to him. All in North Wales. We bought them when we all went there that time.'

'Yes,' I said slowly, 'I remember you looking at cottages.'

'And you remember that young married woman?'

'Don't tell me he was . . .?'

'Yes. Later on, he went down to see her again. They were Carrying On. Right under her husband's nose.'

I took a deep breath. 'What else?'

'Well, he did go back to Norfolk to his wife. But he never saw her. He called on his son first, the one he hadn't seen for twenty-odd years. Jake held out his hand and said, "I'm your Father," and his son put down his milking-bucket and fetched Jake a terrible blow to the jaw and Jake fell down and cracked his head on the cobbles.' Marthaann sighed. 'He lay at death's door in Bury St Edmunds Hospital for many a day.'

'But why?' I cried. 'Why did he *do* it?'

'What?'

'Leave you? Leave a good house, a good business with everything he wanted?'

Marthaann shook her head. 'I don't know. I'm not sure he did. Religion maybe.'

'He wasn't religious.'

'Yes he was, in his way.'

'Not him!' I couldn't see it.

'Anyway, that's all in the past. I've moved away from Newcastle, where everybody knew my business. I was afraid to look at people in the street. Nobody knows me here. They don't have a Chapel but I go to the Church of England, regularly. Never thought I'd do that.'

'Are you all right for money? The house?'

'It was in my name and I got Pickfords to move my furniture out of it the day he told me he was going.'

Whatever else she was, Marthaann was resourceful.

'Where is Jake now? Do you know?'

Marthaann shook her head. 'He came to this very door wanting to come back but I shut it in his face. Enough's enough.'
'Yes,' I said.
She never heard from Jake again.

Family Back on Its Feet

'He *could* hit a ball,' said George Elliott, looking across the Grand Hotel Billiard-room at my friend Jack. 'I say, he *could* hit a ball.' George was talking about cricket. 'When he hit 'em! I say, *when* he hit 'em!'

George Elliott, a small man with thick spectacles, was on just about every Cricket Committee in Blackpool.

We were watching Jack stumbling round the billiard-table. Jack stumbled sometimes because his brain moved faster than his feet. Sometimes, as now, he was stumbling because he had drink-taken to allay the pain in his wounded legs. The alcohol had become a habit with him. He never took any other medicine, having thrown away his pain-killers years before.

He and I were in a four-hand at snooker. We were playing the two restaurant Greeks, Andy and Tony. Tony had been arrested by the Greek Army for desertion years after the War's end but reinstated long ago with his young wife and baby. Even the Greeks had finally decided the War was over. Well, it had been for five years now. The Greeks were poor snooker-players but wild gamblers. The only Englishman they really liked was the Old Man, who was an even wilder gambler than they were.

As Jack said, carelessly missing an easy Red, 'They've elected him an honorary Greek.'

Andy missed the Red also, after taking extraordinary care not to. It hung over the pocket and I put it in and went safe, to an approving nod from the Old Man, who, for want of a better opportunity, had backed Jack and me to beat the two Greeks, to the tune of a pound a frame, a fair bet then.

Jack had five shillings on himself. I had half a crown.

I said to George Elliott, 'Jack and I are playing for South Shore Cricket Club again, you know!'

Said George, surprised, 'Never! Is he fit to do it?'

'No, he isn't.' Jack wasn't. 'But he wants to, and I've been playing for a couple of seasons now, so he's having a go on Saturday, first match of the Season, against St Anne's at Highbury Road.'

'He never is!' George was on the Committee at South Shore but this was obviously news to him. 'Can he move about on those legs?'

'He says he can. And he still has a great eye.'

'Not at snooker,' said George disbelievingly, as Jack ran In-Off, trying to pot a difficult Blue. 'I can't see him playing without a runner. If at all.'

I couldn't either but I knew Jack was determined to play one last season of cricket, no matter what. I said, 'The only trouble is that Owd Kenyon's come out of retirement and he's bowling for St Anne's Seconds nowadays.'

George Elliott was surprised. 'He's not! He must be seventy, must Owd Kenyon!'

'I saw him last night on the bus,' I said. 'I told him Jack was playing and Owd Kenyon said, "I'll hev him owt for nowt." '

George Elliott thought about that and then said, 'He can break 'em both ways, can Owd Kenyon. When didta say it was?'

'It's on Saturday afternoon, at Highbury Road.'

'I shall be theer,' said George Elliott, sipping his large gin, which he could afford, since he had two stalls on the Pleasure Beach. 'But my money's on Owd Kenyon to get Jack out int' first over.' He got to his feet, giving Jack a last pensive look. 'But he *could* hit a ball. When he hit 'em, I say when he hit 'em!' And he was gone.

Jack heard the remark. He said, 'I'll take Owd Kenyon to the cleaners. I'll get fifty off him, no messing. He's meat and drink to me, is Owd Kenyon. If he bowls those lobs of his at me I'll murder him!'

This was said with good-natured certainty but it was the Jack of ten years before talking, when he would have, as he said, taken anybody who bowled slow lobs at him to the cleaners. On the other hand, Owd Kenyon's lobs had a lot of spin on them. He belonged to a lost era of off-spinners and leg-break bowlers, long since superseded by fast chuckers, according to Jack's father, who now put in an appearance in the Billiard-room and bought himself a rum-and-hot-water, carefully avoiding everybody else's eye in case he owed them a drink. Jack called out jocularly, 'Mine's a pint, Stiffy,' but Mr Ashworth ignored him and, sipping his boiling-hot drink, sat down in the seat vacated by George Elliott. It was something of an event for Mr Ashworth to enter the Grand Billiard-room, which was, as they would say today, upmarket for him. In honour of the occasion he wore a bright-pink collar with a brass stud and a blue shirt but no tie. He soon revealed why he was there. 'I believe Jack's tekkin' on Owd Kenyon on Sat'day, is that reet?'

There always was a grapevine where cricket was concerned but this was ridiculous. 'How did you know that?' I asked Mr Ashworth.

Mr Ashworth grimaced over his rum-and-hot-water, as well

he might. It was a noxious mixture. 'I ran into Owd Kenyon at Club last neet. He told me as he'd told you he'd hev Jack owt for nowt.'

I said, dismayed, 'It was just a joke. It wasn't meant seriously, any of it.'

Mr Ashworth, who was covered in a fine sheen of flour from the Bakehouse and was getting towards his weekly shave (it being Thursday), said, 'Owd Kenyon tekks anything to do wi' cricket very, very seriously.' He lit a secretive Woodbine produced from the depths of one of his several waistcoats and inhaled deeply. 'He's got a lot of people owt for nowt as thought they could put him ower t' sightscreen, he has that.' He added, 'I'm talking about Lancashire League fellas an' all!'

I said, 'This is getting serious. I mean, Jack hasn't played for about seven years and he can't really run. He shouldn't be on the field at all, should he?'

Said Mr Ashworth, totally without sympathy, 'If he's playing cricket he's playing cricket, in't he?'

'Yes,' I said, unhappily. 'But I don't want it to develop into a blood match. I think Jack's wrong wanting to play cricket at all! But he's so keen, I've talked people at South Shore into letting him have a game. I've no idea if he can move about the crease at all.'

Said Mr Ashworth, 'Well, we shall find out on Saturday, won't we?'

I turned, sobered, back to the snooker. It was my turn to play safe again but we lost the frame on the Black and, before we could argue, the Old Man called, 'Double or quits, Andy?' to the older of the Greeks, and we were playing them again. Jack said, as the Old Man racked up the balls, 'I'm ten bob down if we lose this next frame. How much has the Old Man got on with the Greeks?'

'Too much,' I said.

The Old Man came round the table to greet Mr Ashworth and buy him a rum and hot water. As the Old Man had been an officer in the Army such behaviour was expected of him. They were by way of being casual acquaintances, Mr Ashworth having no friends or relatives he wished to know on a regular basis and the Old Man being on friendly terms with everybody, whoever they were, unless he owed them money – in which case not.

Returning from the bar, having bought me a Guinness, which he considered medicinal, he said, 'By the way, I don't want you to lose this match, but if you do I suppose you have the wherewithal?'

It was Friday and most people in the Grand had their wages in their pockets. In those days, a man paid his wife what was by osmosis agreed between them and kept the rest for himself.

'You mean I pay the lot?' I asked.

'It's only five quid all told,' said the Old Man, mildly.

'All right,' I said. It was fair enough. The Old Man had subbed me a lot over the year. I had already told him I'd had a couple of cheques that day, one from the BBC and the other from my publisher. Such information was, as Jack would say, meat and drink to the Old Man. Would I ever learn, I wondered, as I played a very careful safety-shot, Andy the Greek then putting a Red in front of the middle pocket, which was in turn promptly repudiated by Jack, who foozled (the Old Man's word) the easy Red with the whole table wide open for a decent break.

'What is the position here?' Onkel Frank had arrived and was sitting, drinkless, alongside Mr Ashworth and the Old Man.

Said the Old Man, rising to Do the Honours, not asking Onkel Frank what he wanted to drink since he knew, 'It's only a very small interest.'

Onkel Frank's dark eyes blazed with disbelief. 'You cannot wager monies on Dumps and Little Jackie.'

Nobody had called Jack that for years. Nobody had called me Dumps since I was six. These oddities of speech and memory were peculiar to Onkel Frank and were thought by all to be very peculiar indeed. He had only the previous week taken his daughters, aged eight, ten and twelve, to the Opera House to see *Rigoletto*. The Old Man had pronounced him, once again, certifiable.

'Just a small interest, no more,' reiterated the Old Man, putting a large whisky and a pint of brackish mild in front of Onkel Frank, who did not take off his hat or thank him, but motioned Jack across. Jack had little to do and neither had I, as the two Greeks had, as they say, suddenly found form and were potting a few balls.

'Yes, Onkel Frank, how are you? Okay?' asked Jack, making his way unsteadily to the table. 'Have you got a drink?'

'I'm all right,' said Onkel Frank. His dark, protuberant eyes found Jack's. 'The advice I have for you is *this*.'

Jack blew out his cheeks in despair. He'd had a lot of advice from Onkel Frank (everybody who knew him had) but he could have done without it at that moment.

However, there was no escape.

'Never,' said Onkel Frank, 'drink when you are playing billiards for money!'

'No, you're right, Frank, no danger,' said Jack gazing moodily at his cue, the tip of which desperately needed chalking, something Jack often neglected to do.

'*Never*!' repeated Onkel Frank.

'No, right, Frank, you're right. Every time.'

'Three or four pints,' said Onkel Frank, remorselessly. 'If you must. No more.' He paused. Jack waited, blearily. 'You can always have a drink afterwards!'

Onkel Frank's idea of a drink was a bottle of whisky. All to himself.

Jack snorted with delight; the Old Man remarked, 'I have said it before. The man is certifiable.' Then, to Jack, 'Attention to business, Jackie!' He lowered his voice and urged: 'Let's see you pot these fokkin Greeks off the table!'

Jack tried to do just that but failed gloriously, leaving the Reds and all the colours so open that, as the Old Man said, 'even those Greeks couldn't miss them', and we had lost the game.

I paid the Greeks personally and they accepted the money quickly but with an air of sadness. 'No more, Percy? We go again if you want?'

'No, thank you very much, Andy,' replied the Old Man. 'We'll leave it for now, if you don't mind!'

'Hokay, Percy, next time, hey?' The Greeks waved to him and disregarded me (whom they knew not to be a serious person, since I didn't gamble wildly) and departed to get back to their café in time for the supper trade. They were delighted at having won money. It happened rarely.

The Old Man brooded but a moment on the loss of my money, five pounds all told, since I paid Jack's losses as well. Everybody seemed to think I was rich all of a sudden because I was in the newspapers for my book reviews and sometimes had radio plays on the BBC. None of them read my books or listened to the plays except Jack and of course my young friends like Allan Coop. Jack it was who had pressed the proof copy of my first book into my hands and said, 'Best first novel since the War'; then he selected his favourite billiard-cue and a moment later was playing snooker for money.

I had called out to him, 'But *why*? Why do you say that?' and waited somewhat anxiously for his reply. 'Listen,' he said, 'with all that family material to hand and you growing up in a family where everyone has such a magnificent command of the English language, if you don't turn out to be a famous writer you should be taken out and bloody shot!'

'I'm not famous yet,' I protested, but Jack was engaged in missing an easy Red.

The Old Man's response to my local fame had been his usual absent 'I don't know how you do it', and Onkel Frank as yet had said nothing at all. My sole champion had been, unexpectedly, Mr Ashworth, who upon being questioned in the Highfield Road Working Men's Club about me had declared, back to the wall, 'He's best bloody writer in Blackpool, is the lad!'

Onkel Frank pronounced on the subject much later, when Jack pressed him in a private moment. 'What did you say?'

'Was he bright as a little lad?' repeated Jack.

'Who? Dumps?' A long pause. 'A Prodigy.' Jack waited. 'Don't know why he bothers with all those plays and novels. He could do better.'

Well, it was good to hear it, if only second-hand and very brief and possibly grudging. But that is how success is traditionally treated in the North of England. It comes with a health warning.

As I told Jack, my publisher, Michael Joseph, had said I'd be rich and famous inside six or eight books. It seemed a long time to wait. The reviews had been exceptional, although I did not really appreciate that. Most of the leading critics of the time had noticed the book. Richard Church, S. P. B. Mais, J. B. Priestley, John Betjeman, Julian Symons. I had met none of them. Nowadays, things are not done that way. Mostly, writers go to Oxford with each other. In those days the writing fraternity was spread wide, and after the War most professional authors had retreated to cottages and houses in the country, where living was cheap, to write about the things they had seen and done in the War years. I had written nothing about the War except my pieces that appeared in the Little Reviews and various hardback collections of short stories. I wasn't to write about the War for almost forty years. In the immediate post-war year I considered that a young novelist's duty was to write about what was happening before his eyes in England. So my early books had a background of broadcasting and journalism and (the first ever) of television itself. Some of that was to happen in the near future.

Meantime, the BBC had sent me on a course to learn how to write for this newfangled thing, television. It was highly instructive and I'd managed to take in, despite my resentment at having to learn anything remotely technical, how a television Studio worked, and the whole palaver of production, the understanding of which is essential to the television playwright. This was the beginning of the Golden Era of the Television Play. I had already written a play for the BBC (set, of course, in Blackpool), and for the Commercial company, ABC, I'd written my first Comedy to be produced in their new (but soon to become famous) *Armchair Theatre* series of original plays. I was well on the way to becoming some sort of a success, with all the attendant problems that brings, one of them being an approach from Pinewood Studios (the letter was in my pocket) offering me a contract to write a film script at a hundred pounds a week. I knew nobody who earned a hundred pounds a week. This information I had confided to Jack but not yet to the Old Man. Said Jack, 'When you tell him, it'll be like a new lease of life to him. Think of the betting credit he can get on the strength of that information!'

Jack was joking but I wasn't when I said, 'Not a word!'

Mr Ashworth's dual reason for calling in at the Grand Hotel was soon made plain. He had insurance money coming due and wanted to invest a little of it on Onkel Frank's fancies at the Dogs on Saturday night.

Onkel Frank rapidly sketched out from memory a synopsis for him, without thought of payment. To Onkel Frank it was enough to figure out his choices, based on times, mathematics, and inside knowledge, and to solve the puzzle set by the handicapper.

'I'll see you right, Frank,' protested Mr Ashworth, being properly moved to buy Onkel Frank a large whisky, which was accepted, of course, without thanks. 'If anything comes up, I'll see you get your reward.'

'Glad of it, if so,' said Onkel Frank briskly and despatched the whisky in two swallows.

Mr Ashworth then applied himself to Jack. 'I believe tha's tekkin' Owd Kenyon on tomorrow?'

'I shall have him for breakfast,' said Jack, enjoying a larger drink, as Onkel Frank had recommended, now that the game of snooker was over.

'Nivver in this world,' said Mr Ashworth. 'I've played cricket against Owd Kenyon in my time and I tell you he's favourite. He can break 'em both ways, can Owd Kenyon. He's won silver cups and all sorts in t' Lancashire League, Ribbledale League and everywheer else he's played. He's mustard, is Owd Kenyon.'

For Mr Ashworth, that was a very long speech indeed.

'He might be able to break 'em both ways,' said Jack equably, 'but it won't matter if he doesn't bounce, will it?'

I wondered how on earth Jack was going to dance out of the crease to hit Owd Kenyon on the first bounce or before, but I said nothing. I was afraid for Jack but, as he wasn't afraid for himself, that was, as the Old Man might have said, no contribution to the matter in hand.

A thought struck me. 'Have you got whites?'

'Somewhere,' said Jack, taking a swallow of best bitter that would have stunned a lot of serious drinkers.

'I can lend you a sweater.'

'I'll be all right, never bother.'

I said no more. Now that Jack was married, I expected he'd have arranged to have his whites cleaned.

I was wrong.

'Not a figure to inspire confidence,' said Ken Benson, Captain of South Shore Seconds and Chairman of the Blackpool Young Conservatives. I was Vice-captain, and no conservative. I still hadn't joined the Labour Party, reckoning a writer shouldn't do that. I was right about that, if not about much else.

Ken was talking about Jack, who was standing smoking a cigarette, preparatory to taking the field against St Anne's, a rather posh club by the standards of the local cricketing fraternity. I had played for them myself for a season or two before I went into the RAF. They had a very professional attitude to the game and boasted players from the local King Edward's School, who played in fancy caps and scarves and had striped ties knotted around the top of their white trousers.

Jack, by contrast, had on his father's old cream flannel shirt, three sizes too big and yellow with age (it had been made forty years before), plus a very old pair of badly creased whites that he'd had himself before the War and had now, it was clear, grown out of. He'd turned the turn-ups down. They were still far too short. On his feet, since he couldn't wear boots (they would irritate his wounded shins) he wore plimsolls, of a grey colour, retrieved from a dusty cupboard. His socks were black and boasted what used to be called a potato.

Repeated Ken Benson, immaculate in creams and minor-club colours, 'No, not a figure to inspire confidence.'

'Ken,' I said, 'Jack has more talent at this game than you and I and all the rest of the team put together.'

'Used to have,' replied Ken. He was, as Jack said, a bit of a tightarse. Well, the Tories are always realists, I thought.

Said Jack, throwing me a ball to catch, 'Have you seen who's here?'

'Who?'

Jack pointed. 'Over there, by the roller.'

Mr Ashworth (becapped and smoking) and the Old Man were sitting at the bowler's end of the ground. I was surprised. I had never seen the Old Man at a cricket match before, ever. He had once or twice turned up to see me play football as a schoolboy before the War, but cricket, he had declared, took longer than life. His father, Edward Prior the Music Hall owner, had experienced a gentleman's upbringing and had been a cricket bore. He had bored all the Brothers (Edwards the Bookie, Onkel Frank and the Old Man) by forcing them to take an interest in the game, with many stern Victorian warnings to show proper attention. There being no game more boring than cricket, unless you have an aptitude for it, they had all, with their father's untimely death, taken to Racing and, as they used to say, never looked back.

I hastened over to the Old Man and Mr Ashworth sitting by the roller. It was a typical Fylde Coast summer's day, bright and breezy. The Old Man looked bored already and the match hadn't started yet. They had been joined by George Elliott, who was not, for once, on the Committee at St Anne's. He knew the

Old Man (everybody knew the Old Man) and the Old Man was, to my surprise, engaged in striking a bet with him.

George Elliott, a connoisseur of cricketers, local and county, was fiddling with his watch-chain (which jangled with many medals), saying, 'Well, it's an even-money bet, Percy. I say young Jack won't get fifty and you say he will. It's for a pound.'

'Two,' said the Old Man automatically. He always raised bets, even when he couldn't really afford to pay. It usually unsettled his opponent and, often, when a later decision (such as an adjustment of the odds) needed to be taken quickly the Old Man's wits were still about him, whereas his opponent was probably still wondering if the Old Man knew something he didn't.

'Two pounds it is,' said George Elliott uncertainly. 'Harold to keep the money?'

'No need for that,' said the Old Man. 'We're all gentlemen here, aren't we?'

George Elliott, not being too sure about that, merely muttered, 'Well, whatever you say, Percy.' But he looked deflated.

The Old Man had that effect on everybody he ever gambled with, whether he won or lost. They were just having a bet but the Old Man was always thinking ahead. If he won, no problem, he pocketed the money. If he lost, well, maybe he owed it, or shifted the bet to something else, the next race, whatever, doubling the stakes as he went. It was a system that few gamblers cared to confront. They were likely to run out of nerve or options. But George Elliott plainly thought he was on a winner.

I said to the Old Man, 'We're fielding, but I haven't seen Owd Kenyon yet.'

Said Mr Ashworth, pointing a floury forefinger, 'There he is. He looks none different from what he were when I played against him fowerty year ago.'

I looked towards Owd Kenyon. He was indeed a strange old-fashioned figure. His cricket cap was an ancient model, barely covering the top of his head, and the sun of countless summers had faded it to a pale sky-blue. His sweater was large and of a cut more Queen Victoria than Attlee, and his shirt was of flannel and a deep yellow, not unlike Mr Ashworth's ancient garment, now worn by Jack.

'He cods 'em out, does Owd Kenyon,' said Mr Ashworth, respectfully flicking the ash off his Woodbine. 'But he can spin 'em both ways and has a Wrong 'Un as well.'

Owd Kenyon's secret weapon was none of these things, I thought. I felt it was a pair of pince-nez, welded to the bridge of his nose, over which he peered, when bowling, at his victims. I had battled against him a few times and it was the spectacles that worried me most. They seemed to read your intentions. Owd Kenyon had taken hundreds of wickets in his time, often through sheer effrontery. He pitched the ball up on all occasions and invited the batsman to hit it. Many generations of batsmen had been prompted to do just that. Few were afterwards inclined to boast of it.

Owd Kenyon's wicket-keeper always stood very close to the stumps. If any batsman was foolish enough to use his feet to Owd Kenyon, he took, as Mr Ashworth freely observed, a big risk. Of course, Mr Ashworth came from a time when batsman virtually 'read' the spinner's hand and fingers, the better to know, as the ball came fizzing through (in Owd Kenyon's case) the air, which way it would break once it landed.

'Owd Kenyon will hev him End and Side,' said Mr Ashworth, referring to Jack.

'Have you backed Jack?' I asked, carrying the fight to Mr Ashworth.

'Not wi' Bad Money,' said Mr Ashworth, stoutly.

'Nice to know everybody's behind you,' I said, 'when you haven't played for years and you've got the guts to have a go, despite your war wounds.'

Mr Ashworth did not reply except to utter a protesting 'Nay', which I could take any way I liked.

'I have to go now,' I said, trotting off to take my place on the field.

Ken Benson was waiting. 'Where shall I hide Jack?' he asked.

'Put him at first slip. He can't run about the outfield.'

'Bloody hell,' said Jack when I told him. 'I can't bloody slip-field.'

He soon demonstrated that he couldn't, so Ken Benson moved him to Square Leg, where he promptly dropped two catches. I saw Ken glaring at me. I avoided his eye.

Truth to tell, we were in a fix, as they used to say. St Anne's had a batsman, a bank clerk I recognised from my time at the club, who had his eye in and his head down: the runs came inexorably. He was fifty, then sixty, then seventy, and we couldn't get him out.

Said Ken Benson to me, 'If we don't shift this fellow, the game's gone.'

Some insanity possessed me to say, 'Put Jack on for an over.'

'Does he bowl?'

'He used to be a very good bowler.'

'But can he bowl *now*?'

'You've tried everybody else, Ken. Why not give him one over? He might unsettle this fellow, you never know.'

'What about you?'

I said, 'I wish I could. But the ankle's gone.'

It was true enough. I'd become a batsman now and it wasn't half as much fun. A bowler is almost always in the game. An average club-batsman has a lot of failures to his few successes. So he was often discontented. As I was.

Ken Benson said, 'It goes against the grain, but one over. You tell him.'

'Jack,' I said, 'you're on. This end.'

Jack looked astonished. 'Whose idea is this?'

'Can you do it?'

'Certainly I can do it.'

'Just pitch 'em up.'

Jack took the ball with total confidence. 'Right arm over,' he told the Umpire, who looked startled.

'Areta bowling, John?'

John was Jack's baptismal name. Jack was the ancient Norman-French diminutive, used by all who knew him well.

'Certainly I'm bowling,' said Jack.

The umpire asked, *sotto voce*, 'Canta run up?'

'As much as I need to do, aye.'

The umpire, who had been standing in local matches since before I was born, nodded briefly. 'New bowler! Right Arm Over,' he shouted to the dour bank clerk. 'Eight balls to come.' In the Northern Leagues, just to be different, they bowl eight balls to an over.

Jack's first ball was a wide.

The second was a full toss, well over the bank clerk's startled head.

The third was another wide.

The fourth bounced three times.

The fifth and sixth were full tosses that the bank clerk failed to hit, as they came, fast, from different angles.

The seventh was yet another wide.

I felt Ken Benson's eyes on me but refused to look at him.

Then Jack bowled the eighth and final ball. It was just short of a length on the leg side and it took the off-bail.

The bank-clerk was astonished. But he was out.

'What dosta think of that?' I asked the Umpire.

The Umpire pondered. 'He bowls Seven Bad 'Uns and One Good 'Un.' He had to say more. 'And it *is* a bloody good 'un!'

'Bowled Hutton, would that,' said Jack cheerfully, rubbing his sore legs.

The innings closed at two hundred and four, a decent score in a Saturday-afternoon match.

'Runs to play with,' said Mr Ashworth. 'Just right for Owd Kenyon. He can buy wickets wi' that many runs in hand.'

From the side Big Matt, Little Matt, Peggy and Ted applauded us as we trooped into the Pavilion for hot tea and tomato sandwiches. The family had come in two cars. Ted couldn't stay, he said: he had business. I was surprised to see him there, he was so busy these days.

'Got to get back to the shop,' he explained.

'You sound like Marthaann,' I said grinning.

'Yes, well, when it's your own business it's different.' He smiled back. 'I expect you're finding that yourself now?'

'Well, a bit.' I liked Ted, I always had. He'd had a hard time trying to make a living as a young man in the Depression. Now, he had a real chance to do a bit of good and he was taking it. I didn't tell him about the Pinewood letter in my pocket. I knew he'd wish me well but might have told the Old Man and I wasn't sure it was yet the time. Ted said goodbye and drove off in his Railton.

Why, I wondered as I sipped my tea, was the Old Man at the cricket match at all? I then asked myself the question the way the Old Man would ask it. What did he stand to gain by coming to a cricket match with Mr Ashworth? The answer came at once. Simple.

They would both be going to the Dogs after the match. And Mr Ashworth was holding folding.

Obvious really, once you thought about it, using the Old Man's theory, often tested in practice and rarely found wanting, that everybody acted always, but always, out of self-interest. All you had to do was work out what their interest was. That was, of course, the hard part, but not for the Old Man.

The second innings began. I opened the batting and was out early, having attempted to cut a concealed leg-break on the offside, bowled, of course, by Owd Kenyon, who nodded more in sorrow than anger at my rashness. Wickets were falling. When Jack went in at Number Seven we still needed sixty runs to win.

I went out as a Runner for Jack.

Owd Kenyon took the ball for his second spell, pince-nez glinting on nose.

As I took up position, he told me in a whisper, 'I shall get him for very few.'

Jack had said to me, as we walked out to bat, 'I'll have him out of the ground. No messing.'

Owd Kenyon wet his fingers, hid the ball in his flapping shirt sleeve, took two paces, and bowled. The ball fizzed through the air.

Jack stood his ground. Without moving a muscle, except those in his arms, he swung the bat.

Six runs!

There were cheers all round the ground. I saw the Old Man on his feet, waving his hat, a very Edwardian thing to do.

Mr Ashworth, still sitting by the roller, was impassive.

Jack twice hit Owd Kenyon for four in the next over and survived an appeal for Leg Before and a possible stumping.

Owd Kenyon bowled off-breaks, leg-breaks, Chinamen and straightforward lobs and Jack hit or survived them all (never moving back and always hitting with a straight bat) until he was on forty-six and needing a four to win the match. Everybody else was out. I could see Big Matt in the stand dancing on the spot with excitement. His son little Matt was aping his antics.

The Old Man and George Elliott stood by the roller, transfixed. Mr Ashworth sat, smoking. I knew somehow that he wanted Jack to hit a six more than anything in the world but would never say so.

The Old Man suddenly took off his Woodrow as he might at a race-meeting and called, as if to a rampaging favourite, 'Hit the bloody thing, Jackie!'

Owd Kenyon ignored all that. He wet his forefinger, took his two paces and bowled a fizzer, which looked like a leg-break but wasn't.

Jack hit it high, high towards the leg-boundary.

A fielder, far away, ran and ran and ran and plunged . . . and miraculously held the ball.

Jack was out, four short of his fifty, to thunderous applause from all two hundred spectators.

The team had lost by four runs.

The Old Man had lost money.

George Elliott had won money, there being no way for the Old Man to double the bet.

Mr Ashworth had neither lost nor won money.

Owd Kenyon said to me, 'I told thee I'd get him, didn't I?'

Said Jack, trudging off with a limp but grinning, 'I told you I'd get hold of the old bugger, didn't I?'

Everybody applauded them both off the field, where they shook hands without comment.

I saw the Old Man standing on the fringe of the crowd. I said, 'Well, Jack enjoyed himself.'

'Nice to see.' He liked Jack. They both believed life was for living. That is, living today, not tomorrow.

I was always a tomorrow man. Now I wonder if I was right.

I said, on impulse, to the Old Man, 'I've had a letter from Pinewood Studios. They're offering me a lot of money. I expect to be down South for a while.'

'Buying a house down there sooner or later, I suppose?' His voice was level but I knew it mattered to him.

'It might come to that. I don't know.'

'Buy something in the Home Counties, I would. Pleasant place to bring up the kids. Not London. It's all right if you're young.'

'Right,' I said, wanting to say more.

'The thing is,' said the Old Man, 'enjoy it. That's what it's all for, isn't it?' He nodded. 'You need to be down South. It has to come to that sooner or later.'

'Yes,' I said miserably, 'I suppose it does.' I added, 'But I'll be in Blackpool for a while yet, you know!'

Let go easily in life, he had once told me. Now he was showing me how to do it.

I would never learn how.

'Help yourself to life, that's the thing!' he said. 'It's there for the taking.'

'Yes, I suppose so,' I said.

'The thing is, you and Ted, and Matt with his excellent Fire Service job, well . . .' The Old Man paused, standing there in the sun, with his city suit and his starched white collar and the Northumberland Fusiliers tie.

'Yes?'